DARKNESS
RISING

Daughters of Light

Finding Jade
Solomon's Ring
Darkness Rising

MARY JENNIFER PAYNE

DARKNESS RISING

Daughters of Light

DUNDURN
TORONTO

Cover image: Model: 123RF.com/Karel Miragaya; London: istock.com/mammuth
Printer: Webcom, a division of Marquis Book Printing, Inc.

Library and Archives Canada Cataloguing in Publication

Payne, Mary Jennifer, author
    Darkness rising / Mary Jennifer Payne.
(Daughters of light)

Issued in print and electronic formats.
ISBN 978-1-4597-4103-4 (softcover).--ISBN 978-1-4597-4104-1 (PDF).--
ISBN 978-1-4597-4105-8 (EPUB)

    I. Title. II. Series: Payne, Mary Jennifer. Daughters of light.

PS8631.A9543D37 2019   jC813'.6   C2018-904813-1
                                                C2018-904814-X

1 2 3 4 5   23 22 21 20 19

  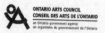

We acknowledge the support of the **Canada Council for the Arts**, which last year invested $153 million to bring the arts to Canadians throughout the country, and the Ontario Arts Council for our publishing program. We also acknowledge the financial support of the Government of Ontario, through the **Ontario Book Publishing Tax Credit** and **Ontario Creates**, and the **Government of Canada**.

Nous remercions le **Conseil des arts du Canada** de son soutien. L'an dernier, le Conseil a investi 153 millions de dollars pour mettre de l'art dans la vie des Canadiennes et des Canadiens de tout le pays.

Care has been taken to trace the ownership of copyright material used in this book. The author and the publisher welcome any information enabling them to rectify any references or credits in subsequent editions.

The publisher is not responsible for websites or their content unless they are owned by the publisher.

Printed and bound in Canada.

VISIT US AT

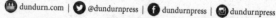 dundurn.com | @dundurnpress | dundurnpress | dundurnpress

Dundurn
3 Church Street, Suite 500
Toronto, Ontario, Canada
M5E 1M2

This book is dedicated to my friend, my auntie, and my mentor, Dianne Payne. You encouraged me to reach for the stars and I miss you greatly.

PROLOGUE

September 12, 2032

To Whom It May Concern,

My name is Jasmine Guzman. I'm sixteen years old (almost seventeen) and I live in Toronto, Canada. I have an identical twin sister named Jade. We live in Regent Park with our mom. And, if you find this in my watch, I'm likely dead. The thing is, I've been told if I die, you will die as well. If you're part of the human race, that is. Not exactly a win-win situation, is it? That's because, apparently, I've been deemed to be the Chosen One in some ancient Dead Sea Scroll, and my job is to save the world. Who's chosen me? I have no clue. I know what you're thinking: What a cliché. Plus, I'm all of about five foot two and weigh less than a hundred pounds soaking wet. Well, I agree with you. Believe me, I often wish this whole situation were fiction. But it isn't. And I need to tell the world the story of how my life has changed over the last two years, because it is pretty unbelievable. Everyone thinks I have a big mouth, anyway, so it will come as no surprise that I've decided to write this all down in a letter on my video watch. Let's just say keeping secrets isn't one of my strengths.

Our world is hugely at risk because of climate change. In fact, "at risk" is an understatement. Earth is dying, and humans are the cause. The pollution here in Toronto is so bad, it's impossible to go outside most days without wearing an anti-pollution mask at least part of the time. But, really, we've got it lucky, don't we? Countries like Australia, nearly the entire continent of Africa, and much of South Asia and South America, not to mention the Middle East, are barely habitable now. Oh, and I nearly forgot the state of California. Decades of drought, water and food shortages, and climate change–driven conflict have caused surges of desperate people to flee their homelands. All these climate change refugees were just trying to reach the areas of the world less impacted by environmental change and that still had an abundance of resources. They were trying to live. Literally. A case of stay where they were and die or leave (with a chance they might die trying). And when the politicians and a good amount of people in places like Canada, New Zealand, most of Europe, and the US saw the waves of desperate people racing toward their countries, what did they do? Well, rather than help their fellow human beings, they closed their borders and started campaigns of fear against the refugees.

Against the "other." And that caused terrorism to spike everywhere, including Toronto.

But that isn't the only thing going on in our world. There's also the little problem we've got with demons. Yep, you heard me right. Demons. I know, now I sound totally crazy. Believe me, I used to think I was. Crazy, that is. But don't stop reading. Because I'm not insane. Not in the least. I can explain everything, but I'll have to go back quite a few years to my sister's abduction in order to do so.

We were ten years old when it happened. When Jade was abducted. I tried to tell everyone that the person who took her was actually some sort of monster with dead, flat black eyes and teeth like sharpened bits of ivory, but no one listened. Not one adult listened when I repeatedly insisted that Jade wasn't taken by a human. Instead, I was sent to a long list of psychiatrists and psychologists who diagnosed me with PTSD and a host of other stress-related mental health issues. Eventually, I half believed the diagnoses myself and pushed the image of the teenaged boy with the demon eyes to the back of my consciousness.

Everything was relatively normal (if living with the loss of your twin sister can ever be called normal) until the day I was sent to Beaconsfield, a secondary school out of my district that is full of identical twin girls. That day was the beginning of my realization that I am a Seer, a Daughter of Light. We Seers, I was soon to discover, are identical twin girls descended from Lilith, Adam's first wife, from the Old Testament. We also each have a Protector.

Protectors are hard to describe. They're kind of like retired Seers who are now responsible for guiding and watching over young Seers of their own. Our powers develop around the time we hit puberty, and from what I've been told, they sort of dwindle away as we reach adulthood. My Protector is Mr. Khan. Though I hated him when we first met at Beaconsfield, I now can't imagine my life without him. He is kind of a father figure to me. Jade and I lost our dad to cancer when we were just little. Mom developed lupus shortly after that, and then Jade disappeared. So life was pretty tough, to say the least. Mr. Khan means a lot to me. Not only does he look out for me, he challenges me. I'm basically a better person now because of him. And, as crazy as it sounds, we Seers are tasked with saving the world from demons, climate change, and other nasties like corrupt politicians. We don't have powers in the superhero sense, but we can read minds and have the strength and speed of elite athletes. The bond Jade and I have as twins even allowed me to travel to the Place-in-Between nearly two years ago to bring her back. Oh, I forgot to mention the Place-in-Between. It's basically a reflection of London, England, that exists on a lower plane. Demons and lost souls populate the Place-in-Between, where they relive the most violent and bloody periods of the city's history. Apparently, all of this apocalyptic stuff, according to some obscure Dead Sea Scroll, is supposed to come to a head really soon in a Final Battle between good and evil, Light and Darkness. I guess saving humanity is sort of on our shoulders — no pressure.

On top of all of that, I'm kind of wheeling with an angel. Yeah, that's right. His name is Raphael and he's not just any angel, but an Archangel, and he can heal people. I've seen it with my own eyes. Things are kind of weird between us at times because he disappears when I feel like I really need him around. Totally annoying, obviously. I can't stay angry with him for long, though, and earlier today he healed Lily, my friend and fellow Seer, and then put himself at risk with London's terrorism squad so that we wouldn't be caught. Apparently, everyone in the UK is microchipped for identification, and since Lily, her sister Cassandra, and I are all from Toronto and don't have microchips, we'll be arrested if we're scanned. And that's not good, because we're currently wanted as terrorists. We're the prime suspects in a terrorist attack on Toronto's water supply. The thing is, we're innocent (you're just going to have to believe me on this one) and being framed by the city's mayor, Sandra Smith.

At the moment, Lily, Cassandra, and I are being hidden in a safe house in London (the real London, in 2032) by members of the group called the CCT and some Protectors. The official line is that CCT is a terrorist group — that's according to many of the world's governments. But the other side of the story is that they're not responsible for any of the atrocities being pinned on them; rather, they want to help support the world as it transitions during this time of extreme change and ensure social justice prevails. It's a tall order because I know some governments, most notably Toronto's, are pretty corrupt. I'm choosing to believe the latter explanation for the CCT at the moment, especially as they seem to be offering us sanctuary.

Which brings me back to right now. The three of us are in London because we got split up from the others — Amara and Jade — when we transitioned from the Place-in-Between. That's another one of our abilities: we're able to travel to the Place-in-Between. We can't stay there long, though, as being on that plane seems to drain us of our energy. I actually think it's draining our life force because we're travelling to a place inhabited by the dead. We had to go back to return Solomon's Ring, this ring that allows humans to control demons, to the Roman wall in London. It was Jade's first time back to the Place-in-Between since we rescued her from there, and things got really weird. First off, there was this guy down there who was about our age, and somehow Jade knew him. Not only did she know him, she lied to me about knowing him. I don't think he was a lost soul. And he definitely wasn't a Seer. Which means he would have to be a supernatural being of some kind. My gut tells me he's not one of the good kind. But I'm hoping I'm wrong about that.

I've got to go. The others will be wondering what I've been doing in the bathroom for this long. I guess the real reason I've written all of this down is not only to let people know what's happening in our world — I mean, what's *really* happening — but also to say that I feel scared. Really scared. It's not something I can really express to anyone, mainly because I'm the Chosen One.

And I'm not just scared for me. I'm scared for all of us. For the whole human race.

With love and in solidarity,

Jasmine Guzman

JADE

"If they catch you, the mayor will execute you, you know," the oversized woman says.

My heart is in my throat. The counter-terrorism squad is at the other end of the subway train, their semi-automatics ready, and they're moving fast. Everyone is being asked for identification, and no one is taking a second longer than necessary to show their credentials.

"Official government ID only!" one of the officers barks at an elderly man holding a cloth shopping bag filled to the limit in one arm and a tiny dog in the other. "Take off your mask. Now!"

The woman leans in closer to me and Amara. The stench of onions and sweet flowers emanating from her nearly overpowers me.

"Smith's gonna put you on the list to hang just like she's done with your friend Eva and that supposed subway bomber, Moore," she says, keeping her voice low.

Before I have a chance to reply, there's a crash and a high-pitched yelp as the elderly man's bag falls to the floor of the train, his tiny dog following closely behind. The officer grabs the man by the arm, wrenches him to his feet, and pulls off his anti-pollution mask.

"No ID? You're under arrest!" he barks into the man's pale face. The older man is trembling like a spider in a snowstorm — that's clear to me even from this far away. His tiny Chihuahua, having regained its composure after being dropped, begins snapping at the officer's pant leg in an effort to defend its owner.

"Please … please," the older man sputters, putting his free hand up in front of his face. His accent is thick.

"He's an illegal!" a woman sitting across from us shouts. Spittle flies from her lips. "Get 'im out of here!" she says, pumping her fist into the air. I can read her mind. Her thoughts are strong with emotion. She's excited by the drama unfolding and disgusted by the fact that the elderly man is an illegal — at least, that's what she's concluded, even though there's no proof of the man's status. She seems convinced he's a climate change refugee who's sneaked into the city and is possibly a terrorist as well.

With the fluidity of a panther, the officer brings his booted foot down onto the diminutive dog's midsection. A single canine screech cuts through the subway car.

We both look over. The dog twitches briefly before becoming absolutely motionless.

"Oh, my god," Amara whispers. She crams the palm of her left hand against her lips as tears stream down her cheeks, then begins to hum. Not any song or melody, just a low, steady hum. I know she's fragile, maybe even close to snapping after losing her twin, Vivienne, earlier today. Seeing this little dog killed in such a violent manner isn't helping her state of mind, that's for sure.

"I'm Mary, by the way," the woman sitting beside me says. She raises an eyebrow at Amara, who doesn't seem to notice. "Listen, youse need to get outta here before they recognize you." Her voice is raspy; it's the voice of a lifelong smoker. "In two, you'll know what to do. It'll be your only chance to escape." She smiles at me, revealing two very chipped front teeth, but her eyes are serious. "Good luck. It's easy to tell that something's not right with the leaders of our governments — for those of us that ain't brainwashed by 'em." She nods her head toward the woman sitting across from us.

The officer who killed the dog punches the button beside a set of subway doors. As the doors slide open, he roughly pushes the old man, who is now openly sobbing, out onto the platform.

"I can't breathe!" Mary cries out. She clutches at her large bosom, hoists herself up, and starts stumbling toward the officers still on the train, one arm stretched out toward them. "My heart! Oh, god! The pain!"

Her thoughts come to me. *They need to run. This is worth it. I've lived a long life.*

The officers point their guns at her. "Stay back!" one of them warns. "Don't take a step closer."

"Help me!" Mary cries again. "I can't breathe!"

I grab Amara's hand and yank her up off her seat. She stops humming.

"What the …". She glares at me as though I've just shaken her from a deep sleep.

"We need to get out of here. *Now*," I say, keeping my voice low.

We slide out the subway doors just before they close. Though he's in the process of cuffing the elderly man's hands, the officer on the platform turns to look at us.

"Freeze!" he yells. "Don't move!" He looks back at the elderly prisoner sitting on the bench in front of him and then at us, clearly unsure which situation to focus on.

The sudden sound of gunfire from inside the train takes his attention off all of us for a moment. Without even looking, I know it's Mary because I can't read her thoughts any longer. There's only dead air when I try. She's dead.

"I've got a bomb," the elderly man interjects. His voice is calm and the word *bomb* is spoken so softly, it's barely audible.

The officer snaps his head back toward the man, who is now slowly rising from the bench.

"What the hell did you just —"

Suddenly, with all the force he's able to muster, the elderly man drives the top of his head into one of the only unprotected areas on the officer: his crotch.

The officer doubles over in pain and shock.

Without a word, Amara and I begin to sprint toward the stairs at the far end of the station, knowing perfectly well that our exit might be blocked if an alert has been issued. If not, we've got a small window of time. Our speed is our advantage. We bound up the stairs and leap over the turnstiles just as two TTC workers, accompanied by a drone, emerge from the ticket booths and lunge at us.

"Stop right there!" yells the younger one, a wiry but muscular woman with a shock of spiky blue-and-black hair. She catches Amara by the wrist. "Sound the alarm!" she shouts at the other worker.

Amara glances at me, her eyes wild. The woman is strong. I know what Amara's thinking. We're supposed to be uber careful using force on anyone but the demons. But she doesn't have much of a choice but to be aggressive with this woman if we're going to get out of here.

The drone swoops in front of Amara, moving dangerously close to her face. It zooms back and forth like a mosquito on cocaine, trying to distract her. A high-pitched beeping fills the air. We don't have much time at all. There are likely extra patrols of counter-terrorism squads on every street corner right now.

"Get off me!" Amara shouts, swinging her arm forward and taking the stunned TTC worker with her. Making the most of the woman's shock, Amara donkey-kicks her in the stomach and then takes a swing at the drone. The TTC worker crumples to the floor, but Amara's not as successful with the drone. It swoops down and out of her range again, only to be back buzzing inches from her eyes within seconds.

Amara bats at it, but it's too quick. I glance toward the entrance of the subway station. There are sirens approaching, but I can't be sure if they are for us or another situation. Sirens are often the musical backdrop for large, urban centres like Toronto. Especially these days.

"I can't move forward," Amara says, frustration etching her voice. "It won't let me."

I glance at the TTC worker. She's lying completely motionless on the tiled floor. Her skin has become ghostly pale. There's no time to check, but I get the sinking feeling she's badly injured ... at best.

With a swift, high side kick, my shoe collides with the belly of the drone, sending it spinning off course. It rights itself and swoops back, toward me this time. I'm its new target. The lens at the front of the tiny aircraft swivels, directing itself at my face. My image is being recorded. More ammunition for Smith and everyone else who believes we're terrorists.

Amara suddenly grasps both sides of the drone. Its buzzing intensifies into a high-pitched squeal. With one swift motion, she tosses it to the ground where it crashes on the tiles.

"We need to get out of here," I say, seeing the other TTC worker on the phone in the booth, a look of sheer terror spreading across his face. I run my hand over the pocket of my jeans. My fingers trace the hard circular outline of the ring. I look at Amara, hoping she didn't notice. But I don't have to worry. She's still fully focused on the drone.

"One second," Amara says, before leaping into the air and jumping on top of the remains of the drone, smashing the lens and main body into pieces. The buzzing ceases completely. "I want to destroy its ability to capture any more of ... this." She glances uneasily at the worker on the floor.

"I don't think destroying it matters," I say. "Police and military drones send real-time data, you know? Smith and her cronies have exactly what they need. Which means we need to get somewhere safer. We've gotta dash."

Amara frowns. "Where do we go? If what Mary told us is true, we're not going to be safe anywhere. At least he" — she cocks her head toward the glassed-in booth to the right of us where the other TTC worker is standing, still on the phone and watching us intently — "is too terrified to even attempt to take us on."

I glance toward the main entrance of the station. It will lead us out onto a side street, but we're less than a block from the Danforth — a main road usually packed with people.

"We're going to have to try to just lie low somewhere in this neighbourhood, but far away from this station, until late tonight. Then I say we make our way to Beaconsfield and wait there until morning."

"*If* we make it to Beaconsfield," Amara says, throwing one last concerned look over her shoulder at the smashed drone and seemingly lifeless TTC worker before we slip out of the station and make our way toward the back laneway behind the nearest houses.

JASMINE

Raphael lifts his hands off my broken arm. The pain has completely disappeared.

"Good as new," he says, a smile tugging at the corners of his lips. "Actually, better. For some reason, bone tends to heal stronger than it was before a break."

I rotate my arm above my head, reaching out toward the sky, then down and behind my back. Nothing. It feels completely normal.

"So, what do we do now? I mean, are we stuck here in London while we wait for this 'Final Battle' or whatever to happen?" I glance around the platform at the commuters whose plans have been disrupted as I wait for Raphael's response. The atmosphere is as dense as an overcooked pudding.

"London is the epicentre. The place where time begins and the layers of existence come together. That's why the demonic activity is greater here as well. You know that. There's a reason you didn't get back to Toronto.

Remember, your part in all of this is different than the other Seers' ... but we really don't have time to get into it." He nods his head toward the officers making their way through the crowd.

Though Lily's still not 100 percent recovered, it's clear we need to get out of here. And fast. If what Raphael said about these officers and drones checking for microchips is true, we're about five minutes away from being arrested and detained on suspicion of terrorism.

A female hologram appears above the tracks. "Please be ready for an identification inspection. Officers will be scanning you momentarily." She smiles brightly, her snow-white teeth shining out at us. You'd think she just informed us that we've won the lottery.

Without prompting, many of the commuters start forming a line against the back wall of the platform.

"Do you think you're okay to walk on your own?" Raphael asks Lily.

She nods, tucking a stray piece of black hair behind her ear. "Yeah, I think so."

Cassandra's eyes darken with concern. She presses her full lips together. "Well, *I* don't think you are okay," she says, before turning her attention to Raphael. "How are we supposed to get out of here without the police noticing and gunning us down or something? According to you, if they recognize us, we'll be taken in as suspected terrorists. Sort of makes me think the last thing we should do is draw attention to ourselves."

"I'll distract them," Raphael answers, his voice as calm as an ocean sunset. "And when I do, you need to

slip down those stairs." He nods his head toward a staircase down the platform that leads away from the main
part of the station. One very serious-looking officer, his
gun drawn, is blocking the entrance to the stairwell.

"Great plan. Just one little hitch. What do we do with
that armed dude there?" I ask, my voice thick with sarcasm. I'm a bit surprised by Raphael's suggestion. As far as
I know, as an Archangel, he's allowed to guide us, but not
actually influence events. What he's about to do seems a
whole lot like changing events, and though nothing is ever
consistent with Raphael, I'm pretty sure this is not something his brothers and sister or whoever makes the rules for
angels would approve of. That being said, as far as I know,
he's not supposed to be around me, either. And yet ...

"Let me take care of that, okay, Jazz?" Raphael says,
interrupting my thoughts. "Once you're down the stairs,
you need to make your way to the river and then east
along it to the Trafalgar Tavern. It's low tide, so you'll be
able to walk along the edge of the Thames but try to be
as discreet as possible. Once you're there, ask for a bartender named Clarence. Tell him you're Seers."

I raise an eyebrow at Raphael. Is he serious? Just walk
up to the bar and tell some random bartender we've
never met before that we're Seers?

"What about you, though?" Cassandra asks. "We
can't just leave you here."

That familiar jealous twinge I sometimes have around
Cassandra rears its head. I don't know why, but there's
just something about her that gets to me sometimes. I
mean, it's an innocent enough question, but now I feel

like I look like an insensitive bitch next to her. Like I don't care about Raphael.

Raphael smiles. "I'll be fine. Remember that. No matter what, I'm going to be fine, and regardless, you can't turn back. Be ready. There will likely be only a small window of time for you to get away."

He gets up, brushes his ebony hair off his forehead, and gives us a wide smile before turning to jog toward the main group of officers.

Lily, Cassandra, and I slowly move toward the back wall of the platform and try to look like we're simply waiting for our turn to be scanned. A light drizzle begins to fall. I look over at Lily. Her skin has a greyish hue similar to the colour of the sky. She definitely doesn't look fine to me, either.

"Hey!" Raphael shouts out in the direction of the police, throwing his hands up into the air.

The officer by the stairs looks concerned and grips his gun tighter but doesn't budge from his post.

"Hey, coppers!" Raphael yells again. "What's happening? Why aren't you telling us exactly what's going on that we need this random identification scan? A bomb? Suicide? Or did you just feel like wasting our time?"

The officers turn their attention from a couple of drunk guys they were in the process of cuffing and scanning.

"You need to stand back," one of the officers says through gritted teeth.

Raphael keeps walking. "Come on," he says, his voice nonchalant, "give these blokes a break. They were only having a tipple whilst on the train. Oy! Are we not allowed to have any fun in London town anymore?" He shoots them a wide grin.

The officer by the stairwell moves a few steps away from his post to follow Raphael.

Cassandra, Lily, and I look at each other. Without speaking we share our thoughts: *Not yet. He needs to be farther away.* The last thing we want is to have to battle this officer. We could bring him down easily with our strength, but bullets are just as deadly for Seers as they are for any "normal" human. And for sure that would not be a discreet way to exit.

All the officers' attention is now firmly on Raphael. They begin to surround him in a half-circle. It looks like they're going to try to corral him.

What he's doing is suicide.

"Stand back! Don't come closer," another officer says, lifting his gun ever so slightly. The officer by the stairwell has joined them now, too. His back is to us as we slowly move along the wall, inching closer to our exit.

"Seriously, mate," Raphael is saying, keeping his voice loud enough for us to hear. "How do we know this isn't just a way for you lot to puff out your chests and feel more powerful?"

We reach the top of the stairs. From my limited vantage point, the area around the bottom of the staircase looks clear. No people and no police. Cassandra leads the way, with Lily sandwiched between us.

Halfway down the stairs, the sound of tasers followed by shouting erupts from the platform above. My heart freezes. I turn toward the sound of the commotion.

Cassandra looks at me. Her eyes are hard. "No, Jasmine. You heard what Raphael said. We need to keep moving."

She's read my thoughts. I feel naked. My feelings for Raphael have just been on display for her to view. She's possibly the last person I wanted knowing what he means to me ... or how muddled my feelings for him are.

We continue down the stairs, taking two at a time. Just as we swing around the concrete post at the bottom of the stairwell, two gunshots thunder from above us. Though every cell in my body screams at me to run back up to the platform, I know Cassandra's right. We need to keep going.

"More police!" Lily whispers, pointing toward the tunnel to our left. A group of at least five officers, all of them decked out in military gear, is emerging from it.

We quickly duck around the corner of the stairwell and press ourselves up against the concrete wall. I hold my breath as the sound of their boots gets closer, hoping they didn't see us.

"Male. Late teens to early twenties. He's down. Profile not found and not coming up on any terrorism data-bases. A 999 call has been put in."

Raphael. Those gunshots were most certainly meant for him. A tight fist closes around my heart. He's an angel. Surely normal bullets can't harm an angel. Can they?

We hear the officers race up the stairs. "Everyone against the wall! Hands where we can see them!" There are a few muffled cries, but no more tasers or gunshots.

"How do we find the river?" Lily asks as soon as they're out of earshot. "We really need to get away from here in case more officers arrive." Panic is rising in her voice like hot lava.

I nod. There's a path lined with rock gardens and a variety of tall grasses and catnip blooms just to the right of us. The sound of seagulls echoes faintly from somewhere farther along it. "If you listen closely and take in the smell, the sea — or at least the river leading to it — seems to be down there," I say, pointing. "Besides, I think the tunnel is an obvious no go for us."

"No kidding," Cassandra says. "Who knows how many more of those goons are on their way." She glances at the path. "Trafalgar Tavern. That's what it's called, right? But do you really think it's safe for us to be telling some guy we've never met before that we're Seers?"

"I don't know. I guess we have to trust Raphael," I say, trying to push down the memory of the many times he's shown up in my life only to disappear again. "At this point, unless either of you can think of an alternate plan, I really don't see that we have any other choice."

JADE

"When do you think it'll be safe to leave here?" Amara whispers to me. "Because I swear, girl, I feel like I'm going to boil to death like a lobster."

Her breath is hot on the back of my head. My own hair is sticking to my neck like sweat-drenched spaghetti and I'm beginning to feel faint from dehydration. Not only is the midday sun making the temperature in this back garden shed unbearably hot, we're also hiding under a tarp for extra protection in case anyone comes in. At least Amara's stopped the humming for a bit.

"I suspect we'll need to wait until at least after midnight. Even then there will likely be night patrols out. The drones are what we need to worry about. They'll be able to pick us up on infrared cameras in the dark. I bet there are a lot more patrols tonight because of what happened in the subway today."

Amara nods, brushing back her braids to wipe away a wall of perspiration on her forehead. "You mean we need to worry about drones and demons. Now that

Smith and her lot don't control the demons, I guess they'll be terrorizing the city, munching on anyone out after curfew … and hunting Seers."

I pause for a moment, uncertain whether to tell Amara that I've got the ring. And not just any ring — Solomon's Ring. After all, the reason we went back to the Place-in-Between was to return it. And going back is the reason Amara's twin sister, Vivienne, is now dead. But it's not like I'm going to be able to hide the fact that I've got it if we're confronted by demons tonight. The ring controls demons, so I'll use it if I have to.

I take a deep breath. "I have to tell you something," I say, trying to steady my voice.

"Okay," Amara says, nodding. The lightness in her voice tells me she has no idea how serious what I'm about to say is.

"You know how we were supposed to place the ring in the wall, the old Roman wall around London?"

"Yeah, Jasmine put it in before …" Amara's bottom lip quivers. "Before the demons came … and Vivienne …" She sucks in a deep breath and stops talking as two giant tears spill over her lower lids and race down her cheeks. "Damn," she says.

I reach over and hug her. "I'm so sorry about Vivienne.… But Amara, I still have the ring. We don't need to worry about the demons tonight."

Amara's eyes widen as the gravity of what I'm telling her sinks in. "What?" she says incredulously. "How?"

I try to keep my eyes steady on her. Try to remind myself that it was the right thing to do.

"I took it out of the wall. Just after Jasmine put it there," I whisper.

Anger darkens Amara's eyes like thunderclouds. "Why did we even go to the Place-in-Between, then? What the hell, Jade?" Her voice is rising.

"We have to keep quiet," I whisper. "There could be patrols nearby."

Amara clamps her lips shut and glares at me.

I hold my hands out to her, palms forward in a gesture of surrender. "Look, I screwed up, okay? Well, sort of."

"Sort of? You *think* so?" Amara says with a sarcastic laugh.

"Let me explain. The ring, if we left it there, in the Place-in-Between — well, we'd be in more danger now. Think about it, how would we have gotten the demons here in Toronto under control? They're already feeding on civilians again because no one is controlling them. You saw the news just before we transitioned to the Place-in-Between."

Amara opens her mouth to speak and then closes it again. She narrows her eyes at me.

"Because when we behead them, we're not actually destroying them, are we?" I continue. "I mean, we're killing the vessel the demon was in, but —"

"The vessel?" Amara interrupts, her voice shaking. "You mean when we kill people like my sister? Real human beings?"

I pause. "Vivienne lost too much blood in the battle, Amara. You know that. She wasn't going to live even if we could've driven out the demon possessing her ... and we don't know how to do that."

"But there's a difference, right?" Amara says. "A huge difference between the other possessions and when a Seer is possessed and her body dies. Because — and this is what you don't understand, Jade — the other half of me, the other half of my soul is now in a very dark place. A place so dark, so full of pain and screaming, you can't imagine. I can feel it. Not the full extent of it, but I can feel her pain and suffering. And if I'm feeling even a fraction of what she is, it's unbearable for her. That's why I've been humming. I'm sure you've noticed me doing it. I'm not going crazy. It's to block out the pain ... to block out my sister. When a demon takes over one of us, they don't just use the body as a 'vessel,' like a hermit crab or something, and then leave us seamlessly like they do the others. They take the Seer's soul with them. Our souls get hijacked. Vivienne is trapped inside that demon. She's *intertwined* with it. Her existence is now perpetual pain. They keep us for our power — imprisoned with them. *Forever.*"

I have no reply. Though I have no idea what it's like to be possessed by a demon, I was abducted by one and spent nearly half a decade living in the Place-in-Between, where negative energy pervades everything. Not pleasant, but clearly nowhere near what's happened to Vivienne. Plus, the memories of my time there are nothing more than faint whispers in my consciousness, so I don't even suffer from any sort of post-traumatic stuff. I often wonder why the demon that took me didn't

kill me and take my soul for itself. It makes no sense …
it would've been dead easy for it to have had my soul.

"Remember, we don't destroy the demon when we
behead it," Amara says, breaking into my thoughts.
"When the demon isn't in a 'vessel,' it's not gone, it's not
dead. It's simply searching for a new place to inhabit."

I stare at her. The air is so thick, so humid under our
tarp, I feel like I might pass out. Sweat trickles down my
forehead and into my eyes, stinging them.

"We're always being warned by Ms. Samson and all
the Protectors about demons and Seer souls. But I guess
I never really thought about what would actually happen. I imagined the demons would kind of just suck
away our powers … and our lives," I say.

"Well, now you know," Amara says flatly. I can feel
the anger emanating from her in waves.

Heavy silence fills the air between us. "I am sorry," I
say, though the words sound hollow even to me.

Amara narrows her eyes at me again. "The thing I
want to know is, *why* did you take it? I mean, I'll admit
part of me is glad we'll be better protected tonight, but
we were supposed to return the ring to the wall for a
reason. So what made you think it was okay to do this?
Does Jasmine know you have the ring?"

"Yeah, she knows," I say with a nod. "And she's furi-
ous with me." I pause. Really? This whole thing with
Jasmine again. It's like whatever Jasmine knows or
doesn't know, feels or doesn't feel, is of critical importance to everyone. I take a deep breath, trying to ignore
the nauseous feeling rising in my stomach. I want to tell

Amara everything, to make her realize I'm not the villain here. I'm pretty certain she would've done exactly what I did, given the same information. But there's no way I can fully explain why I took the ring without mentioning Seth. And yet, if I don't give a decent explanation, Amara is going to hate me. She might even hate me if I do tell her the real reason I took the ring back.

"I can't tell you everything. Yet," I say. Amara's already trying to pry into my thoughts. "And what I do tell you needs to be confidential, okay? Just for now."

Amara regards me carefully, as if I'm some new species of creature she's never come across before. Something to be wary of.

"Um, okay," she says, enunciating each syllable slowly.

I've got to be careful what I reveal to her; I'm pretty sure she's not too concerned about doing anything I ask of her now.

"There are some … people that don't trust the Archangels. They don't think we, the Seers, should be putting so much trust in them, either. In fact, I've been told that it's dangerous for us, that the angels aren't necessarily looking out for our best interests."

"Okay," Amara says. "So … who are these people, exactly? And why are they any more trustworthy than the angels? Why are you choosing to believe them?"

"That I can't tell you," I say. "Not yet, anyway."

"Seriously, Jade?" Amara says, throwing her hands up. "You're supposed to be a second-born. The way you're behaving and talking, you're acting very much like a first-born, and not a very bright one at that. Plus, not only is it pretty effed up for one Seer to keep secrets from the rest of us, but you're also …"

A sudden noise stops Amara midsentence.

We both freeze. I'm afraid to breathe. Maybe it's just an animal.

Footsteps. And the sound of keys jingling.

Someone is outside the door.

We both lie down flat, hoping to make the tarp look more natural, as if it's just covering some garden tools or has been thrown in the corner haphazardly. I hold my breath. My heartbeat seems unnaturally loud. I can't imagine whoever is out there won't be able to hear it as soon as they enter the shed.

"Goshdarned thing. Always jamming." The voice is female and elderly. She sounds slightly confused and shaky with nervousness.

"Open it!" a male voice snaps. His voice is laced with impatience. "And you'd better not be stalling because you've got something in there to hide. Something that might show you're part of the resistance, part of the CCT."

"No, no, not at all," the woman replies. "There's nothing of the sort. I'm a proud supporter of Mayor Smith. I came here decades and decades ago as a much younger woman, when the economy in Greece collapsed. And I came here *legally*. I'm in full support of our government keeping those illegals out." Her voice cracks. She sounds like she's on the verge of tears now.

"Step aside. We'll take care of it for you," a younger woman says. "And by the way, Billy," she adds, "you can tone it down." I'm guessing she's an officer or military personnel of some sort, if she can talk to him that way without any consequences.

There's a moment of silence. Then a loud bang like a gunshot, followed by a splintering sound at the door. Amara begins to softly hum again. I nudge her with my elbow.

Another bang. And another, all in rapid succession. I hold my breath, knowing they're about to enter the shed in the next few seconds. I glance over at Amara. Tears are streaming from her closed eyes and down the sides of her face. I wonder if she's in pain, if she's feeling Vivienne's pain right now. My heart tightens with guilt.

After one last thunderous crack, there's another moment of silence. The wood frame has surrendered.

"And just who is going to pay for this?" the elderly woman asks. "Thieves are going to have a field day if there's no door."

"We'll send somebody from the city to fix it later today," the female officer assures her. She's in the shed now. Her voice is so close, I feel like I could reach out and touch her. If they have any drones with them, we're done. But it's a good sign that the officers are inside the shed already; their body heat would confuse any drones' heat sensors, so we're likely safe from that threat.

"Check the cupboard over there," the female officer says. A door bangs open.

"Nothing but pottery and art stuff," Billy says. There's disappointment in his voice. It's almost like he's hoping to find something that will mess up this elderly woman's life. So much for "To Serve and Protect." Unless, of course, you apply that policing slogan to Mayor Smith; our police and military seem to be serving and protecting her over everything and everyone else these days.

"All right, all clear in here," the female says. "Ma'am, I'll personally make sure that someone is here for your door within the next few hours."

"I hope you find the murderers, including the ones that poisoned all those innocent people. Barbarians," the elderly woman says. "Hard to believe that even our beautiful young women are being recruited by the CCT now. Just shocking. The more terrorists we execute, the better. Might put some fear into anyone thinking about committing such evil acts." She pauses. "What's the death toll at from the water being poisoned? How many millions have passed as of now?"

"We can't release that information, ma'am," the female officer says. "But official news reports estimate at least a million dead, and many more still in critical condition. I've lost family members and friends myself due to that attack, so I have to agree with you. Those girls responsible — if they're responsible — should hang. That's part of the reason I'll be pulling a double shift today."

We're not guilty! I want to scream. *We're being blackmailed by Smith and her crooked government!*

"God bless you," the elderly woman says. "I look forward to seeing those terrorists in cuffs on the news broadcasts tonight or in the very near future."

Over my dead body will you see us in cuffs tonight or at any point in the future, I think. I just hope my thoughts aren't prophetic.

JASMINE

"Careful, it's slippery," Cassandra says, as she edges her way onto the first moss- and algae-covered stone step of the staircase that leads down to the riverbank. The steps look like they're blanketed by an emerald carpet, the vegetation is so thick. "We'll be lucky if we don't break our necks," she adds grimly, as she tightens her grip on the rusty metal handrail and descends.

I glance at Lily. Her face is covered with beads of perspiration even though it's cooler here than in Toronto. A pale-grey hue still lingers under her skin, and dark, bruise-like smudges frame her eyes. Usually Raphael is able to heal us completely, so Lily's ongoing weakness is super concerning.

"Low tide," Cassandra declares as she steps onto the wet sand beside the river's edge. "I guess that's why we're able to walk down here." There's barely anyone in sight along the riverbank. Other than a couple of guys around our age goofing around throwing chunks of wet sand at each other, and a man with his head down, likely examining the ground beneath his feet for washed-up treasures, this stretch of the bank is mostly empty.

"London is one of the only cities that was somewhat prepared to prevent the flooding from rising sea levels that would've destroyed it," Lily murmurs. She points downriver, away from the city proper. "They built these barriers to keep the rising ocean from flooding large parts of the city. And then they had to keep building them higher and higher and reinforcing them as the ocean levels rose further. That's why London hasn't sunk like Mumbai or Miami or even Toronto Island. I mean, it's not even half-gone, like New York. And the population is much more dense here. Imagine if they ever had to evacuate millions of people to higher ground, like New York City did after that storm."

"I have no idea how you know all of that stuff, but maybe it would've been good if the city did sink, considering how it's the epicentre of all of this demonic and Place-in-Between junk," I say, kicking absently at an empty shell with the toe of my boot, flipping it over to reveal a shimmering pearl-coloured belly. "Maybe if London here in our world had been completely destroyed by water, then the Place-in-Between and all the demons would've disappeared as well."

"Sure," Lily replies. "Maybe you're right, and maybe it would've destroyed the Place-in-Between or something. But if that had happened before this year, chances are Jade wouldn't be back with us now." Her voice is tinged with sarcasm. "Honestly, Jasmine, I love you, but sometimes you need to *think* before you say things." She wipes away the perspiration on her forehead.

Heat rises from my chest up to my face. I keep my lips clamped shut tightly because Lily's right — even if I do think she's overreacting to my comment, which was only meant to be kind of a joke. I've heard the same message enough times from enough people to realize that plenty of individuals get tired of my smartass comments. I might be impulsive, but I'm not super thick. I just need to remember to think before I let words spew from my mouth.

I watch as a solitary seagull glides overhead, emitting a sad cry. Looking at the murky, winding trail of the river, I wonder just how much life is still left in there, what with the warming of the water. No wonder this is the first gull I've spotted; its food sources are probably pretty scarce.

"Raphael was smart to send us this way," I murmur. "Much less chance of getting seen and recognized."

Lily and Cassandra both nod. "I just looked up the Trafalgar Tavern in my video watch," Cassandra says. "The guide is telling me we only need to walk about three or four more minutes at this pace."

As we trudge along, the heavy, wet sand and silt sucking at our feet, I look out at the buildings lining the other side of the Thames. There are a variety of modern-looking apartment buildings, many of them in various states of disrepair, though nearly all boast solar panels and green roofs.

I bring my gaze back to Cassandra's back. Like her, I'm nervous about revealing our identity to this Clarence guy, but what other choice do we have? It's not like we can wander endlessly around London, especially when we're wanted for terrorism, and I'm pretty sure we don't have the power to flip between locations in the here and now, and commercial air travel is totally suspended … so it looks like we're not getting back to Toronto anytime soon. I wonder how Mom is doing, especially with the current attacks. My throat tightens and tears blur my vision. Hopefully Jade made it back and is with her right now.

Cassandra stops at a short flight of grey stone steps nearly identical to the ones we took to get down to the river's edge. I notice the waves are now licking at her shoes. It seems that the tide is coming back in.

"This is it," she says. "We need to go back up to street level and into that building right there." She points toward an imposing ivory-coloured building towering above us. The words *Trafalgar Tavern* appear along the upper edge of the building in black lettering.

None of us move toward the steps. And that's because we're all wondering the same thing: are our faces and identities as wanted criminals being shown constantly during every news presentation, live-streamed 24-7 onto video watches and plastered on the side of every form of public transit? Will we emerge at ground level only to be spotted straight away and reported to the authorities? Or has ours been just an intermittent story, one of the many about the CCT, refugee "invasions," and the need for nations to be vigilant against outsiders that threaten to overburden their fragile economies, ecosystems, and resources? Regardless, there're bound to be drones patrolling London's streets, and they'll be able to pull up our profiles in no time if we're in databases as suspected terrorists.

The odds are not on our side at all.

I take a deep breath. The grey clouds above me suddenly feel ominous and suffocating. "We need to make sure we're reading the minds of the people around us, especially this Clarence guy," I say.

"If he knows we're Seers, he might just block us, though," Lily says.

"That's true," I admit. "But if he's on our side like Raphael says he is, there should be no reason for him to do that." I pause, glancing along the riverbank. "In fact, if he does block us, that's a clear sign that we need to get out of there. And fast. If that happens, we should have a meeting place."

"The only place we know is that train station," Lily murmurs.

"And going back to that station would be nothing less than suicide," Cassandra says. She glances down at her video watch and presses the screen. "Meeting places in Greenwich," she says. Looking up, she gives both Lily and me a wry smile. "Either we meet at a secluded place, where we completely stand out to anyone who happens by and one or more of us might get lost trying to find it, or we chance going to a more crowded area and hope that people don't recognize us."

"But let's try not to get split up, okay?" Lily says, her eyes widening with worry. Her voice is breathless, weak. It's easy to read her thoughts: she knows something's not right with her health-wise and is afraid of being left alone without me and Cassandra's protection.

"Of course," Cassandra says, taking her sister's hand and giving it a squeeze. She's obviously read Lily's thoughts as well. "But we need to be ready for any situation, and Jasmine's plan is a good one."

I raise an eyebrow in her direction. Did she just compliment me twice in the last few minutes?

Cassandra looks back down at her watch. "Apparently there's an observatory at the top of the hill over there." She points beyond the Trafalgar Tavern. "Across that road. We can meet there. It's in a park, so if one of us begins to feel nervous about being spotted or anything, there should be bushes and stuff like that to hide in. I say we meet around the back of it if anything bad happens. Of the observatory, that is."

"Sounds good," I say. "Looks like it's time for us to go and have a little chat with Clarence." Stepping forward, I reach out and grasp the black wrought-iron bannister beside the staircase.

I really hope Raphael's guiding us in the right direction.

The three of us step onto a grey cobbled street beside the Trafalgar. The small pedestrianized area directly in front of us is dotted with several long wooden picnic tables that are likely from the turn of the century; the wood is frayed and peeling from the passage of time and what little rain England still gets. And there's a metal statue of this skinny, serious-looking dude wearing what looks like a pirate's hat punctuated by a feather. I'm guessing he was once someone important.

A smattering of people are sitting at the tables, chatting, reading, and intently watching their video watches and tablets. They don't give us so much as a glance. Nearly all of them are clutching what look like pints of cider. It's pretty much the only alcoholic beverage available in most parts of the world now. A memory of Smith drinking her blood-red wine floats into my mind, and I push away the worry about Eva, Jade, Mom, Mr. Khan, and the others that rears its head as soon as I think about home. I've got to focus on the here and now.

"Heads down, and move toward a wall once we're inside, so we're not as obvious," I whisper as we weave our way around the outdoor tables toward the thickly lacquered black doors at the entrance to the pub.

We step inside the building.

"Woah," Lily says, keeping her voice low as she looks around. "It's like stepping back in time. Like, centuries." She wrinkles her nose. "It even smells old."

She's right. It's almost creepy how antique and musty this place is. It reminds me of being inside the church in the Place-in-Between. The light is low, as the windows along the river don't offer much, especially with the day outside being as grey as dirty dishwater.

My eyes slowly adjust, and I take a moment to assess everything. Nearly every centimeter of the powder-blue walls is covered with framed illustrations of maritime scenes and portraits of naval officers from centuries ago. A massive gold-framed mirror hangs over a black wrought-iron fireplace just to the left of us. We're definitely the youngest people in here. There's an elderly couple at the table just in front of us eating mounds of mashed peas and fries, and a couple of older men, deep in conversation, nursing ciders at another table. It's quiet, but not the type of quiet that seems threatening.

I move toward the bar. A middle-aged black man with a shock of silver hair is wiping the counter with a wet cloth. The glossy wood already gleams like a mirror. He must be doing it just to look busy, more than anything else.

"Do you think that's Clarence?" Cassandra asks, leaning in close to me. "I don't see any other bartenders, but you never know if someone is in the back or something."

I nod. I know what she means. We certainly don't want to be caught out by going up to the wrong person, especially as we don't exactly fit the regular pub-going types.

"I'll go up and find out," I say. "The two of you can take a seat at that table close to the door. If anything seems off or goes wrong, I'll raise my right hand and snap my fingers. That will be the signal for you to leave — and fast."

Lily's eyebrows draw together in a frown. "This seems risky. And it doesn't feel right, letting you approach him alone."

"It's better than all three of us going up. The chance of someone recognizing one of us is a lot higher if the three of us are standing together," I say, trying sound as reassuring as possible. "Here goes nothing."

With reluctant nods, Cassandra and Lily slip away toward one of the tables nearer to the door. I can feel Cassandra's eyes on the back of my head as I turn on my heel and walk as casually as possible to the bar.

I'm fully aware that Cassandra and Lily won't actually

follow the plan and leave if there's trouble. Though I have to admit, I would defend my fellow Seers to the death before taking off, too.

The bartender glances up when I'm about ten feet away, even though I'm being as discreet and quiet as possible. I'm struck by a sudden feeling of déjà vu. There's something intensely familiar about him. As I get closer, a smile spreads across his face, reaching up to his deep-set chocolate eyes. He stops wiping the counter and stands back.

"Yes, young lady?" he says, his voice full of warmth. "Can I help you?" His eyes wander over to Lily and Cassandra as he finishes the question. But I've already reached into his thoughts. This is Clarence. He knows exactly who we are. And what we are. Not only that — he's a member of the CCT and just happens to be the brother of Frederick, Mayor Smith's driver. Well, that's a surprise. I always got a good vibe from Frederick.

I smile at him. "You know exactly who I am."

He lets out a howl of delight. "Indeed! My brother has told me a great deal about you, young Jasmine. He said you've got a quick tongue and an even quicker ability to hit a target."

"Yeah, well, I'm working on the big-mouth bit," I say.

He bellows with laughter again. I think about telling him I'm totally serious about my smartass mouth but decide against it. It's probably better if he thinks his brother was exaggerating about that.

"Vashti?" Clarence shouts over his shoulder at the open door behind the bar. "You need to come out. They're here. The girls are finally here."

JADE

Amara and I stay in the shed for about an hour after the police and the owner depart. If the female officer was telling the truth, someone will be back to repair the door before the end of the afternoon. And the only reason we were able to get in in the first place was that the door to the shed had been mistakenly left unlocked. That was likely why the older woman was having so much trouble opening it. She'd put the key in and likely locked it without realizing her mistake. If we stay in the shed, we chance getting locked in, and there's no telling when the owner might be back to open the shed. We very well might be two piles of Seer dust by that time.

"I really don't love having to go back out there," Amara murmurs as we peek around the corner of the shed. The afternoon sun is still high in the sky overhead.

"Yeah, I hear you. We have about three hours before the sun sets," I say, "so either we try to get as close as we can to the school now and hope that we can stay incognito while doing so, or we find a place to hunker down until it's dark." My stomach is rumbling uncomfortably. With the time difference, I can't tell how long it's been since I've eaten. For sure, breakfast before heading to the Place-in-Between was my last meal. I'm so famished, I feel ill.

Amara bites nervously at her bottom lip. "I know we're protected from the demons, but I'm worried about search drones if we wait until late evening. Their night vision will make it so easy to find us, especially with fewer people out after dark because of the curfew. I say we try to get to Beaconsfield now and hide there." She swallows hard. "Plus, we're going to need water. I can't stay out here another four hours without any. I'm already feeling hugely dehydrated. And if we wait, we might be too weak to even make it to the school later."

I nod. She's right. My throat and mouth are desert dry and my head is pounding. At least Amara's anger seems to have abated. Or maybe she's just in survival mode at the moment. Either way, I'm relieved.

"Should we should try to contact Mr. Khan or the others before heading there? In case we arrive after classes are over?" Amara asks as we duck behind a line of scrubby bushes a few streets away from the shed. It's nearly impossible to remain completely hidden because of the lack of green foliage.

I flatten my body up against the backyard fence behind us and squat down on my haunches. The bushes give us some protection at least, and there doesn't seem to be much activity happening in the houses around here. I'm guessing most people are probably still at work.

"I'll try to reach Mr. Khan," I say. "I'm pretty sure he doesn't have classes on Thursday afternoons, other than combat and cross-training, so he should be able to answer." I punch in urgent mode so Mr. Khan will be alerted to the critical nature of the call.

One ring, two, three … Amara squats down beside me but continues scanning the area around us. Aside from a scraggly orange-and-white cat that looks like it hasn't eaten in about a decade, the area appears empty, but we can't be too cautious at this point. The last thing we need is to have someone pass by and overhear me speaking to Mr. Khan.

Mr. Khan's face pops up on the screen. His cheeks are flushed and his dark eyes are wild with worry.

"I hope I didn't disturb your instruct—"

"I can't speak to you," he interjects breathlessly. "And as soon as I end this call, you need to get rid of this video watch. ASAP."

"But Amara and I —"

"No buts. I need to go. And so do you. They mustn't find me, especially not speaking to you or any other Seer, so I'll make this quick. The two of you need to try to transition, to go back to London. The membrane between the worlds is so thin, it's nearly non-existent, so it is my hope that you can just flip straight to contemporary London. Think of modern landmarks. Look at images on Amara's video watch if you need to just before you try to transition. And, for the love of the world and all its inhabitants, put the ring back as soon as you get there, Jade." The anger in his voice is palpable.

My heart stops for a moment. How does he know I have the ring?

"But …" I begin.

"No buts. And, whatever you do, *do not* contact me again." He glances over his shoulder at something behind him, then turns back, his face flickering for a moment on the screen before being swallowed by blackness.

"What the eff is up with him?" Amara asks, wiping at her forehead. "That was a really messed-up conversation. Though I'm with him about the ring and being pissed at you." She leans back against the wall. "What do we do now?"

I pause. My head is still spinning from the conversation with Mr. Khan, and my body is shaky. Pretty ironic that my Protector has apparently ditched me. Totally contradictory to the job description, if you ask me. And how did he know about the ring? Who could've told him?

"I don't know, but he was pretty adamant about getting rid of this," I say, slipping my video watch off my wrist and throwing it into the middle of the overgrown lawn that stretches out in front of us. Since electric and gas-powered mowers have been prohibited, most lawns are now just a tangle of long yellowed grass. "Something's definitely up. Who would be telling Mr. Khan he can't speak with us?"

"Maybe Ms. Samson did, because you took the ring," Amara says, her voice flat.

"I say we still need to check out Beaconsfield, maybe even more so now, before we try to get to London.

Something's definitely not right." I purposely ignore Amara's quip about the ring, because it would be useless for us to get into things right now. Down deep, though, I worry that she might be right.

Amara looks doubtful. "If we're not supposed to contact Mr. Khan, and he's telling us to try to transition to London as soon as we can, then I think we should do that." She looks me in the eye. "I'm not one to ignore what our Protectors tell us to do."

The ring pulsates in my pocket as if reminding me of what I've done.

"Listen," I say, "there are two sides to everything. I mean, how do we know that the people we've been listening to really have our best interests at heart? Raphael just came into our lives, *boom*, like that, and we followed what he said without question. Same with his sister. Do you not find that odd?"

Amara glares at me. "Are you talking about our Protectors, as well? Are you implying the same thing about them? My father has studied the texts about us, the Seers, for decades. He doesn't …" She pauses, tears welling up in her eyes. "He *didn't* tell Vivienne and me everything, but one thing for certain is that our Protectors can be trusted. No, they *need* to be trusted. They were Seers themselves, don't forget. And Raphael is the reason you're back here at all. He guided your sister, Lily, and Cassandra to you. Or did you conveniently forget that in the year since you've been back? Do you think they would have been able to find you or navigate the Place-in-Between without —"

Amara's rant is cut short by the sound of fast-moving wheels crunching along the gravel of the alleyway behind us. The vehicles screech to a stop. Multiple doors slam, followed by heavy footsteps.

"The signal is over there. Behind the house," says a voice directly behind us on the other side of the fence. "They might still be in the vicinity."

I stare into the garden at the grassy patch ahead of us where I threw my video watch. Mr. Khan was right. We're being tracked like foxes in a hunt. We should've left this area immediately after I tossed it. I honestly thought we'd have more time than this.

Amara's eyes are wild with panic. "What are we going to do?" she whispers. "They're going to find us for sure as soon as they get over the fence."

I open my mouth to reply, but no words emerge because I have no solution. Amara's right. The house is going to be surrounded in a few seconds, and we'll probably be apprehended under the Anti-Terrorism Act shortly after that. Or we'll simply be shot dead, with the police claiming self-defence and coming up with a tidy story to justify our murders.

JASMINE

A tiny woman emerges from the doorway. She's so slim that from a distance she could almost be mistaken for a child if it weren't for her deeply lined face. Long, glossy black hair streams down her back like water.

"Jasmine," she says as she steps forward. Her walk is slow, a careful shuffle, as though she's in some pain. Stacks of golden and jewelled bangles cover her slender wrists and jingle like wind chimes in the breeze as she moves toward me.

I reach into her thoughts. She's riddled with bone cancer that had been kept at bay since she was a young woman, but in the last year or so, the drugs have stopped working. Her time is short. Our planet's time is also short, unless something changes soon. The Seer and Protector communities are counting on me to help change that.

"What can I possibly do?" I ask, realizing a moment too late that I've actually said the words out loud.

Vashti smiles at me. Her smile is wide and bright, despite her immense pain. "Call your friends over. We'll go upstairs for tea. Clarence will stay down here and keep an eye on the house. Right, Clarence?" she says, covering her mouth as she lets out an almost girlish giggle.

Clarence smiles warmly back at her and winks. "Yes, Mum," he answers with a nod of his head. "I'll give you the warning signal if anything seems amiss."

I wave at Cassandra and Lily to come join me. They've both had their eyes glued to me the entire time and immediately jump up to cross the room.

"This is Vashti, and this is Clarence." I nod toward both of them. Vashti smiles at Lily and Cassandra while Clarence extends a strong hand toward each of them in turn.

"We're so glad you've made it this far," he says, keeping his voice low. "Vashti will tell you more upstairs, but we were very worried we'd never actually lay eyes on the three of you."

We follow Vashti down into the cellar of the pub, a damp, dungeon-like cavern where the smell of the ocean nearly overwhelms me. It's so strong that it wouldn't surprise me to find out the walls are lined with dead fish, with a few medieval pirates thrown in. The cellar is also incredibly dark, and so we walk single file behind Vashti, who leads the way with a high-powered flashlight. Once we reach the other side of the cellar, she unlocks a modern sliding door with fingerprint identification to reveal a flight of incredibly narrow and winding wooden stairs that have been polished to a high gloss.

Lily sucks in her breath in awe as the staircase becomes brightly lit with a solitary wave of Vashti's hand. I'll admit to being both surprised and impressed as well.

At the top of the stairs, there's another sliding door activated by fingerprint recognition. As Vashti presses the four fingers of her right hand against the touchpad, she glances over her shoulder at us.

"Anything said past this point must stay between us and the walls of this flat. Do you understand?" she asks, her voice solemn.

I nod. I should be feeling apprehensive about being taken to a place with a single escape route that can be activated only by this woman — a woman we met less than ten minutes ago — but something tells me we're safe with Vashti. I hope my Seer intuition is right.

The stainless steel doors slide open, revealing a light-filled, spacious apartment. Enormous skylights take up at least half of the ceiling. There's a bed in one corner, and a full wall of 3-D plasma screens. They appear to be playing different international news stations; the one closest to us is playing the BBC World News headlines on a loop.

Vashti steers us toward a sitting area with deep leather chairs and a crimson-red couch before heading into the kitchenette area to put a kettle on the stovetop. "Have a seat. Make yourselves comfortable. Would you like some tea?"

"Yes, please," I murmur. Lily and Cassandra also make sounds of agreement. My stomach is rumbling uncomfortably. I hope that some food will be offered along with the tea, and I'm pretty sure they're wishing the same.

Between the slight shift in time when travelling back from the Place-in-Between and how long it's been since we ate breakfast in Toronto before we even went there, I'm starved.

Taking a seat on one of the leather chairs, I lean back and look around. The apartment is open and airy, completely different from the darkness of the pub below us.

Vashti brings over a tray containing a plate piled high with cookies, a pot of tea, and four mismatched cups. "Cassava biscuits," she says with a smile. Her hand shakes ever so slightly as she attempts to place the tray on the low, glass-topped coffee table in front of us.

Cassandra leans forward. "Let me do that for you," she says, gently taking the tray from Vashti and putting it down. "The cookies look really great," she adds. Her eyes reflect the same raw hunger that I suspect mine do.

"Thank you," Vashti says, easing herself into the other leather chair with a sigh. She leans over, picks up the teapot, and begins to pour the tea. "Please, help yourself to some biscuits," she says, with a nod toward the tray.

The three of us reach for the tray at once like a flock of lunging seagulls. If I weren't so hungry, I'd be embarrassed. But as it is, I stuff nearly all of the first cookie into my mouth, barely giving myself time to chew.

Vashti watches us eat and gulp down the hot tea. Her enormous brown eyes radiate a motherly gentleness from under their canopy of slightly sagging skin. My tongue initially burns from the heat of the tea, but the warmth feels good as it hits my stomach.

After allowing us three or four minutes to stuff our faces in silence, Vashti clears her throat with purpose.

Lily and I stop and place our partially eaten cookies and teacups back on the table. Cassandra continues to chomp on her third cookie, a fourth one clutched in her right hand, until Vashti clears her throat again, this time much more loudly.

Cassandra stops chewing and looks up at the three of us. With a sheepish grin, she chases the last of the cookie down with some tea before placing the other one onto the edge of the plate.

"Now we must talk," Vashti says.

Lily and Cassandra are sitting on the couch directly across from me. We quickly glance at each other. This is unknown territory. We need to be ready for anything. After all, we're in a foreign country without proper identification and wanted as terrorists.

"What your sister has done puts all of us in grave danger. A danger with far greater implications for our survival — for all of humanity's survival — than I can even begin to explain," Vashti says, turning to me.

Surprise crosses both Cassandra and Lily's faces. They're not just curious about what Jade did, but also wondering why it's been kept secret from them. I avert my gaze from them and turn it back on Vashti.

"I told her she shouldn't have done it … that the ring was supposed to stay in the wall," I say before Vashti can speak. I don't want to be blamed for my sister's stupidity.

Vashti slowly nods. "Yes, I thought as much. But that doesn't matter. What matters is that it needed to be returned; the ring should've been placed back into the Roman wall. The final prophecy is upon us, and if the ring were where it is meant to be, there would be a safe space for us here. The churches designed by Hawksmoor were carefully placed around the city to form a pentagram, an area of magical protection from the dark forces. However, as it stands, Jade's insolence has rendered Hawksmoor's protection impotent …"

A loud giggle erupts from Cassandra. She places a hand over her mouth in an attempt to stifle it.

Vashti's dark eyes flash with anger. "All of you must leave your juvenile thoughts and behaviours behind immediately," she says, her voice shaking with emotion. "We are soon to enter the Final Battle. You Seers are our only hope. And if we don't have Hawksmoor's protection, absolutely nowhere in all of London that is safe, nowhere to take a moment's reprieve." She pauses and looks at Cassandra. "Thus, the Seers and all of your allies will surely be slaughtered."

"But who exactly are we battling?" Lily asks, her voice quivering like violin strings. "I mean, will it be the demons? Or is it someone, or something new? And who is this Hawksmoor guy?"

Vashti regards Lily silently for a moment as if deciding how much to reveal. "The world is dividing in anticipation of the Final Battle. What we don't know is who and, indeed, what entities will be joining the forces of Light and who will be siding with the Darkness." She pauses. "You are not well."

Lily's eyes widen. "I'm fine," she says. "Just recovering from an old injury." However, her voice betrays the fact that she's anything but fine. Her skin is a greyish hue and has this strange sheen to it that makes me wonder exactly what is happening to her. Usually, when Raphael heals someone, the effect is immediate. Lily knows this as well.

"Let me try to get this right," Cassandra says, diverting the conversation, though concern registers in her face when she looks at Lily. She flicks her dark hair behind her shoulder in a way that I think is a little overdramatic. "The ring isn't in the wall? We went to the Place-in-Between, watched our friend die, my sister get injured badly, and Jasmine have her arm snapped by a demon ... and you're telling us that the ring isn't there? How can that be?"

Vashti looks over at me. A heavy silence descends over the room like a lead blanket.

"I don't really know when she did it, or how, or even why," I say, meeting Cassandra's gaze. "But Jade definitely has the ring. I put it back in the wall, so she must've taken it out when we were battling the demons afterward."

"Are you kidding me?" Cassandra says, practically spitting each word at me. "Your sister took the ring? Whose side is she on?"

The words hit me like a slap. "I'm not sure why she did it," I say. Though her actions are indefensible, I still feel the need to stick up for her. "But she must've had good reason."

"Oh, yeah?" Cassandra says, leaning forward with her arms on her knees. "Did she tell you what that 'good reason' was?"

My face burns. *I'm not my sister's keeper*, I think. And yet, I kind of feel like I am, at the same time. After all, as

Seers, we hold immense power. "I don't know why she did it," I finally say.

"Your own sister didn't tell you she was doing this? Or why she did it?" Cassandra says with a sarcastic laugh.

"It doesn't matter why she did it," Lily interjects softly. "She betrayed us. And she got Vivienne killed. She's a Judas."

I feel as if I've just had the wind knocked out of me. There's nothing I can say, and I'd feel exactly the same way Cassandra and Lily do if I were in their shoes.

"How did you know my sister took the ring?" I ask Vashti, trying to avoid Cassandra's laser-like gaze.

"Raphael told us," Vashti says. "And that was relayed to your Protector. We're concerned that Jade is under the influence of some dark forces."

"Jade?" I say with a laugh. "Really? She's the good one of the two of us, believe me."

JADE

Amara grabs my wrist and hauls me to my feet. She's shockingly strong. I suppose we're all pretty strong from more than a year and a half of intense training.

"We need to get up this," she hisses in my ear as she drags me toward a towering tree in the corner of the garden.

She releases my wrist as we reach the enormous trunk, and we begin to scramble up it, with her slightly ahead of me. The bark is dry and practically crumbles under my fingers. So many trees have died due to years of drought; I hope this one still has enough life in its limbs to support our weight. I glance up. The leaves are thick enough to offer us some coverage, but we'll have to climb fairly high, and it still may not be enough. At a glance, I'd estimate the tree is about thirty feet high, with limbs that are worryingly anorexic toward the top.

We're halfway up it when the first heavily armed officer enters the yard. He crouches low with his semi-automatic drawn and ready to fire. There's no way we can climb any higher now without being heard.

There are at least eight officers, all with guns drawn. They've really sent in the heavyweights. These are members of the elite anti-terrorism squads that are deployed after CCT attacks. I guess we're considered part of all that now.

Amara is just above me, clinging to the trunk. I've found a foothold in the crotch of a branch and have managed to wedge both feet there, giving me a steady place to stand. I'm not sure Amara's found a stable position, as I can hear her attempting to maintain her grip on the trunk by shifting her feet ever so slightly, which sends bits of dried bark down onto the top of my head. The combination of heat and adrenaline has made my hands slick with sweat, and I imagine Amara's are the same.

One of the officers is pushing apart the brush we were just in with the butt of his rifle. "Nothing here," he shouts at his colleagues.

Two other officers climb the back steps of the house and begin to hammer at the door with their fists. "Anyone in? Police! Open up!" one yells.

There's a scrabbling sound above me, and what feels like a tsunami of bark falls onto my arms and head. The sound isn't loud compared to the banging on the door, which I'm glad we've got to cover the noise, but it gets my heart racing violently all the same. If Amara can't maintain her hold on the tree, they'll find us for sure. She might be trying to climb higher, for all I know. I'm not about to look up to find out.

A series of bangs loud as gunshots fills the air as the officers begin to break in the door to the house. More bark lands on me. What is Amara doing? I try to reach into her thoughts. She's having trouble maintaining her hold on the tree, just as I suspected, and is trying to climb to a higher and more secure place while the officers break down the door.

The officer that was searching the bushes is coming closer to us. Amara can't move now — he'll notice the bark falling for sure. My heart is pounding so loudly against my rib cage, I swear it can be heard for miles.

"Have a look at this," a female officer says from the middle of the yard. I glance over toward the voice. There's a sliver of an opening between the leaves to my left, but it's not wide enough for me to see what she's talking about.

The officer that was near us walks away, over to her. I breathe a quiet sigh of relief.

"Is that where the signal's been coming from?" he asks. My video watch.

"Yep. They probably got rid of this here in an effort to throw us off their trail. Even the youngest CCT terrorists are clever, apparently," the female officer says, her voice thick with sarcasm.

"All clear in here," another one of officers shouts from the vicinity of the back door to the house. "We'll have to send someone around this evening to explain the state of the house. The residents are likely at work."

"We've found one of their video watches," the female officer yells back. "Let's get it back and into forensics.

Smith really wants us to apprehend these two by nightfall. If they're behind the water massacre, there's no telling what evil they'll get up to."

One of the male officers laughs. "I figure Smith wants to get her hands on these young ones to break them. To find out who's actually heading the CCT. There's no way those Barbie dolls can be the masterminds behind the water contamination. For god's sake, they're just teenagers. Probably more interested in the latest lip gloss than in terrorism. Likely doing all of this for some boy — or girl — they're interested in."

"Did you even watch the subway video, Ronnie?" the female officer snaps. "Not only is your rant the biggest pile of sexist shit I've heard in a long time, but one of those little bitches snapped an officer's neck like it was nothing more than a dried turkey wishbone. It's right there for you to watch. Then the rest of them *disappeared*. I don't know if the CCT has new technology, if these girls are some sort of AI, or …"

"Or what?" one of the male officers laughs. "C'mon, Sarge, you're letting your imagination run a bit wild, don't you think? That video of the girls disappearing had to be doctored. I mean, we know it wouldn't be a first for Smith and this administration to be making up dodgy news stories."

"That's Sergeant Puri to you," the female snaps. "And I think what you're saying is very dangerous. I'd reconsider it immediately, if I were you."

The male officer laughs. "Or what? We all know this is the most crooked Toronto administration in the last half century. Maybe in all of the city's history. She's got an agenda, and we're just puppets in all of this. Have you seen the *Real News* holographic broadcasts she's begun splashing all over every street corner? Just because I'm a police officer doesn't mean I'm going to bend over and let her shovel her lies up my ass. And she's in bed with other crooked mayors around the world, too, including the one in New York. Just look at that poor bugger, Moore. He's no more a terrorist than my grandmother —"

A sudden rapid-fire volley of semi-automatic shots rings out, cutting off the officer's words and sending sharp spears of pain through my ears. A soft thud follows. Bits of bark fall onto me as Amara shifts her footing. Likely she's just as shocked by the sudden noise as I am. I hold my breath, willing her to stop moving before we're discovered.

"If either of you breathes a word of this, you'll find yourself at the centre of a terrorist investigation yourself," Sergeant Puri says, her voice as hard as ice. "Regardless of your personal views of our mayor, you're employed by her, and you need to keep your wits about you. Smith is extremely powerful, and I'm not risking my life, my family, or my career because an officer under my authority has a mouth ten sizes bigger than his brain. Is that clear?"

Amara and I wait around for about ten minutes after the officers pull away before making our way back down the tree, but it seems like hours.

"What the hell was that all about?" she whispers, her eyes wide with shock as our feet hit the dried grass of the yard. She rubs her hands up and down her thighs. "My muscles would have given out if we'd stayed up there a minute longer."

I glance over at the corpse that is face down about five feet away from us. A crimson halo of blood has spread out around his head.

"I don't really know," I say. "But it worries me that Jasmine was so involved with Smith's government."

"If you really wanted Jasmine to be safe, if you wanted all of us to be safe, you would've followed Mr. Khan and Ms. Samson's instructions," Amara says with a smirk. "Suddenly you're all worried about your sister, but you're willing to completely mess up what we're meant to do to keep safe? A good example would be Mr. Khan's instructions to get rid of the video watch and get as far away from it as possible."

"I get it," I say, "and I agree that we messed up by not getting away from here sooner. But you need to trust me on the other things. We'll transition just like Mr. Khan asked, but we have to go to Beaconsfield first. We can't just leave when something's obviously really wrong there."

Amara glares at me. "Why the *hell* would I trust you? You realize that you made our whole trip to the Place-in-Between useless? And I don't mean just a waste of time. Because if we hadn't gone there …" she stops, her voice cracking with emotion.

"But what makes you think we can trust *anyone*?" I ask. "Who told Mr. Khan and Ms. Samson that we had to return this ring, anyhow? The very act of going there put us in harm's way. The demons were on us like dogs."

"The CCT told them. The CCT, which my father be-longs to. The CCT, which is trying to ensure some justice in this world for climate change refugees and which has also been researching us Seers, our Protectors, and the Lost Scrolls for decades."

It's obvious I won't be able to change Amara's mind unless I tell her everything, but at this point, I simply can't do that.

"Okay, I understand. Honestly, I do. But can we just go to Beaconsfield before we try to transition? I know you owe me nothing, and I promise you that we'll try to transition right after. I just really need to see Mr. Khan before going back. I mean, don't you find it strange that he just hung up and told me not to contact him again, even though he's my Protector?"

Amara pushes her braids back from her face and stares off into the distance for a moment. "Yeah, it's weird. I'll give you that. Maybe he's really pissed that you took the ring." She looks at me, obviously wanting a reaction.

Not about to give her the satisfaction, I remain stone-faced. This is practically the millionth time she's said it.

"Okay, we'll go to Beaconsfield, but then everything — and I mean *everything* — is by the book. Got it?"

"Deal," I say. "Now we just need to stay safe until we get to the school."

Amara stares out into the distance again. "We definitely need to get a move on. The way Smith is gunning for our heads is pretty intense."

I nod in agreement, swallowing back the hot vomit that's risen in my throat. My stomach is doing cartwheels like an acrobat in the circus again.

JASMINE

"Do you know what my mom, what our parents, think is happening?" I ask Vashti. I know it's a long shot, but if she and Clarence are CCT, they'll at least be in contact with Mr. Jakande and Noni, who might be in touch with Mr. Khan and, hopefully, my mom. At least Mom knows that Jade and I are Seers, so she'll hopefully understand some of the craziness that's been happening because of that. I'm not sure what Lily and Cassandra's parents might have been told to explain their absence. Maybe Frederick will be able to give Clarence some information about our families.

Vashti presses her lips together. "Again, nothing we speak of within these four walls is to be talked about outside. A great deal has happened in and around Toronto since you left. Of course, you know about the water contamination. Luckily, your families were not impacted by that. Clarence's brother confirmed that. However …" She looks at each of us, her eyes dark with sadness. "Eva was taken into custody in the subway after you transitioned. She killed two officers, but likely saved your lives in doing so. In the days following, she was coerced into confessing that all of you were responsible for poisoning the water and that you're all members of the CCT."

There's a sharp intake of breath from Lily. I look over. She's clutching the cushioning of the sofa on either side of her as though her life depends on it.

"You okay?" I ask.

She nods, eyes wide. "We knew she was arrested and that she confessed. She was tortured, though, right? Is she okay?" The question is directed at Vashti.

"Eva is missing at least three fingers and has been burned multiple times," Vashti says, her voice quiet. "Even seasoned members of the CCT would break under those conditions. In fact, we give members something to take in case they are going to be subjected to that sort of interrogation."

"You mean to kill themselves, right?" Cassandra asks. "Instead of giving away CCT secrets?"

"Yes," Vashti answers grimly. She takes a sip from her tea with a shaking hand.

"Then how come that guy Moore, the one who was caught after the last subway bombing in Toronto, didn't take it?" Cassandra asks. "He's now waiting to be executed. That's torture in itself, just sitting on death row. And you can bet Smith is going to make a huge deal out of it. It's going to be live-streamed in holographic vision in Dundas Square, right outside City Hall, and in every other prominent place in the city that she can manage. I wouldn't put it past her to make the execution mandatory viewing in high schools. She wants as many Torontonians to view it live as possible. It's gross. Feels like we're back in the time of gladiators."

"Moore's not CCT," I say.

"Jade's right. He's not one of us," Vashti says. "But you're absolutely correct that Smith's treating him like some trophy animal she's personally hunted down is barbaric, all the more so because Frederick believes Moore was an addict that Smith grabbed off the streets just months before the bombing. On top of the drugs they plied him with while keeping him in some camp, he was promised boatloads of money and drugs to place some packages in the subway that night. They burned his fingertips down to the fat to help conceal his identity, knowing he would be caught if he followed their instructions. All his memories prior to the bombing and arrest were wiped away, and he was implanted with a new story — a story that has him believing he's a member of the CCT. An elite member in charge of highlevel terrorism. Thus, he would fail any detector test in which he tried to claim otherwise." She rolls her eyes. "Ironically, no one in the real CCT is allowed anything more mind-altering than a glass of cider with dinner, let alone hard drugs."

"There's technology that can wipe out actual memories and replace them with fictional ones?" I ask.

"Yes," Vashti nods. "Corrupt governments are privy to many technologies, including life-saving ones, but keep them from the general public."

"And our parents?" Lily interjects. "Can we contact them from here? Will our video watches work?"

Vashti shakes her head. "They work, but you mustn't use them. Your signal will be immediately identified."

"I already used mine," Cassandra says. "On our way here. Just before we got here, actually."

Vashti's eyes widen. "Turn if off immediately and give it to me," she says, holding out a shaky hand. "You are wanted internationally. Furthermore, your parents, and your mother, Jasmine, are now also at grave risk. Eva's being captured and interrogated resulted in Beaconsfield being revealed. Anyone associated with the school in any way is now being treated as a terror suspect. The school is currently on lockdown, with no one allowed to enter or leave. Basically, it's been turned into a holding cell, a prisoner-of-war camp of sorts. And, unfortunately, that is all we can glean for now. Neither we, nor any member of the CCT, can risk making contact with Mr. Khan or anyone else at Beaconsfield now."

My stomach plummets. "I've been to one of Smith's 'camps.' It was for climate change refugees who'd tried to enter Canada. It was a nightmare. I actually wouldn't have believed it if I hadn't seen it with my own eyes." The image of Penelope, a young girl I'd met in the camp who was later executed by Smith's demonic guards, flashes through my mind. I think about Mr. Khan, Ms. Samson, and the others and wonder what conditions they're having to exist under at the moment. One thing I know for sure is that Smith will stop at nothing to protect her power and her ego.

"What's going to happen to Eva?" Lily asks. "I mean, it can't be good that they've got her on camera killing police officers. And, by the way, are there demons here?"

"To answer your second question, yes, there are demons here. After all, London is the epicentre, the beginning of time and the place where all the layers of being converge. As for Eva … she's scheduled to be executed alongside Moore. It's now a two-for-one," Vashti says grimly. She glances at a clock on the wall. "We'll need to leave sooner than anticipated. Clarence will have the video watch taken far from here and destroyed, but we've likely been tracked already. Now that there is no safe place for us in London, we're going to have to keep moving all of you — as well as all of our Seers — nearly every night."

"How many Seers are there here? Are they all in London?" Cassandra asks.

Vashti slowly gets to her feet. "There are eight Seers with us at the moment. We tried to gather as many as possible between here and in Toronto. It seemed safest to do so in large, diverse cities. A few perished in Northern Africa and South Asia due to the rapid closing of so many borders, including ours. The political and economic sanctions resulting from climate warming came about much more quickly than anyone could've anticipated — as did the acceleration of planetary changes. That also meant that some of the last Seers we tried to gather ended up in government-run climate change refugee camps where they are treated as chattel. Eva was one of them. We have them here as well — the camps.

Nothing new, really. Except now, there is no deportation and also no chance of admittance to the UK. These poor souls languish without hope until their death. Many end up taking their own lives, including children."

I shudder, thinking it sounds a bit like the Place-in-Between. Our own version of lost souls.

"Smith's climate change refugee camps were completely evil," I say. It's obvious that Vashti knows about the demons because she didn't bat an eye when Lily asked about them being in the Final Battle. "The guards were demonic. I guess she was using the ring to control them. Giving them orders ahead of time, so there wasn't a mass slaughter of the prisoners …" Penelope comes slamming back into my memory again, her tiny white wrist extended to me, the tan-coloured Band-Aid making her pale skin all the more dramatic. "She also made the prisoners, including children, give blood every few days. I guess it was another way to ensure the demons stayed fed and happy." I grimace and stop talking, feeling the cookies I've just eaten turn uneasily in my stomach.

Vashti grips the side of her chair so tightly, her knuckles pale. "You will discover, Jasmine, that there is no such thing as pure evil, nor pure good. Those states are fluid. Never fall into the trap of believing otherwise. It is a gravely dangerous fiction. Evil deeds can be done by people you'd never expect. Desperation can breed extreme behaviours. By the same token, very ordinary folk can be supremely heroic under duress." She looks around at us. "Now we must go."

JADE

"What the hell?" Amara whispers as we crouch down behind a row of recycling bins off to the side at the very back of the school's athletics ground.

We've made it to Beaconsfield in pretty good time, considering we mainly used alleyways and quieter streets to get here. We also tried to keep to backyards as much as possible to avoid being seen. Not the easiest way to get to the school, but definitely the safest.

I stare in disbelief at the spectacle in front of us. Multiple police cars, including RCMP and one armoured tank, surround the building. Dozens of heavily armed men and women can be seen. Some appear to be standing guard while others move in and out of the school carrying various computers and boxes. News reporters swarm like bees, and about a dozen drones buzz around the scene. We need to be careful — they might be equipped with heat-sensing detectors. Luckily, no human or drone is patrolling too close to where we are. Yet.

"So this is why Mr. Khan didn't want us to contact him," I say, sitting back on my haunches. "This is terrible. Do you think they're holding everyone in there?"

Amara shrugs. "They probably took over the place during school hours. That only makes sense. So, yeah. I'll bet no one's going to be allowed in or out until they're cleared of being suspected terrorists. Maybe some of the regular students were let out. But school staff and Seers? No way."

I nod. "No wonder my watch was tracked so fast."

"Yep. We're definitely public enemy number one," Amara murmurs, her dark eyes fixed on the armed guards. "Those are pretty massive semi-automatics they've got."

"Do you think there's any way we could get in there?" I ask. My mind is racing with loads of scenarios of what might be happening to Mr. Khan, Ms. Samson, Jennifer, and everyone else.

"Seriously?" Amara says with a derisive snort. "I know you can't get hurt by demons with that ring on you, but unless you're bulletproof as well, there's no way you can safely get anywhere near there. And I'm sure as hell not —"

"She's right," a voice says from directly behind us. I nearly jump out of my skin as Amara swivels around, fists raised and ready in front of her face.

It's Mr. Khan. He's crouched down behind the line of scrubby brush about ten feet behind us and motioning us over to him. We move toward him, hunched over and crab-like. Every move feels like such a risk.

My first instinct is to throw my arms around him, but the stormy look he gives me as we scuttle up beside him makes me pause.

"What in god's name are you doing here?" he asks. Dark circles ring his eyes. He looks nearly a decade older than the last time I saw him. "I specifically told you to transition to London, reunite with Jasmine and the others, and put Solomon's Ring back in the bloody Roman wall." He regards me as if I'm a wriggling specimen in a science lab. Ever so gently, I try to reach into his thoughts. It's always a strange feeling, a bit like peeling back the skin of an orange to get to the juicy bits inside.

"Don't even try it, Jade," he snaps.

I look up and raise an eyebrow at him, but say nothing. My stomach begins to cramp uneasily again.

"What's going on?" Amara breaks in, leaning forward with the palms of her hands on the ground to take some pressure off the balls of her feet as she crouches beside us. "How come you're not in the school? How did you escape what's going down over there?"

"The raid began just after first period this morning," he says, his voice heavy with sadness. "I just happened to have a spare from teaching and stepped out to get a cup of chicory from the cafe down the street. They didn't use their sirens on the approach, and I was only about half a block away when the armed police began spilling out of unmarked vans. It was easy at that point to figure out what was happening. We'd only learned about the video of Eva and the news of her arrest a few minutes before, from Frederick." He stops speaking and

grimaces. "I assume he didn't know about the impend-
ing raid because he told us he didn't think there was
any reason for us to go into emergency mode. After all,
Eva was new. We hadn't formally registered her at the
school, as her identification profile would have linked
her with the refugee camp. Unfortunately, as we discovered, Frederick is not always privy to Smith's oper-
ational plans beforehand."

"Yeah, we heard about everything that happened with
Eva from a woman on the subway when we first transitioned back," I say. An image of Mary walking toward
the officers, knowing it was suicide, flashes through my
mind. I swallow hard to prevent tears from forming in
my eyes. "And that's how we found out that we're wanted
in connection with the water poisoning."

Mr. Khan nods. "The video of her killing two officers in the subway is all over the news. It was playing at
the cafe when I was getting my chicory. It seems Smith's
invoked the new Anti-Terrorism Act to decline Eva a
trial due to it all being caught on video." He shakes his
head. "They're planning to execute her at the same time
as Moore … tomorrow evening."

There's a sharp intake of breath from Amara. "That's
terrible. Eva totally sacrificed herself for us. We'd all be
dead if she hadn't stayed behind and dealt with those officers when we transitioned." She pauses. "By the way, isn't
it dangerous for you to be around the school? Shouldn't
you be getting as far away from here as possible?"

"I figure that's exactly what Smith's little army will be
expecting me to do — to try to get away from here. My

apartment has likely already been torn apart for clues as to my whereabouts, and my little dog, Reggie, shot or worse ..." Mr. Khan stops speaking, his eyes clouding over with tears. "I'm not sure when our governments changed from at least pretending to protect our rights and liberties and our lives from terrorists to terrorizing their own people as a means of social control. I suppose the two of you are too young to remember anything but this."

"So Ms. Samson and everyone else are still in there?" I ask.

Mr. Khan nods. "I assume so. I'd imagine everyone is being taken into custody. There's no way I can contact them now, but I've been out here for the better part of the day, and I haven't seen anyone — neither students nor staff — be released."

Amara grimaces. "What are you going to do for tonight? I mean, if you can't go back to your place ..."

Mr. Khan shrugs. "I guess just see how things unfold here. To tell you the truth, I haven't thought that far in advance. I mean, we obviously had an emergency plan and protocol in place in case something like this ever happened at Beaconsfield. Despite Jasmine being on Smith's advisory committee, we knew we were walking a tightrope as far as security was concerned. I just wish ..." His voice trails off, his gaze wandering back to the scene outside the school. "But perhaps there isn't a way to protect oneself from a government like this," he says with a heavy sigh.

"We've got to get them out," I say. "They haven't done anything, and neither have we. I mean, Eva did, but that was in self-defence …" I stop, my stomach rumbling again as I remember the TTC guard from this morning.

Mr. Khan shakes his head emphatically. "Absolutely not. You're beginning to sound like your sister, which is worrying. Actually, there's a lot about you that is worrying me, but I'll leave that for now. Both of you must get to London. Ideally, you'll end up in contemporary London to reunite with the others and get the ring back to its proper place. But if not, you must at least get to the Place-in-Between to return it. And then we'll need to figure out how to get you to the others. You and Jasmine must be together for the Final Battle."

"Then you need to come with us," I say. "You're our Protector after all, and it's not going to be safe for you anywhere in Toronto. With the way the city's borders are patrolled, there's no way you'd get out, even if you had somewhere to go."

Mr. Khan wipes at the sweat on his forehead as he stares at the school. "No regular human has ever ventured to the Place-in-Between," he finally says. "All of you've been there and survived, but …"

"But you *were* a Seer. Once a Seer, always a Seer, right?" I say, hopefully.

"Our abilities seem to end once we become young women … or men, as the case may be," Mr. Khan says with a rueful smile. "That is why it is important for us Protectors to train the next generation of Seers, and to keep an eye on them as they approach puberty. Sadly, you may be the last group of Seers, and thus, may never become Protectors."

You will not likely survive to become Protectors, is what Mr. Khan's really thinking. I smile at him. He's let his guard down. He frowns back at me.

"But you'll be a dead man walking if you don't come with us," Amara says through gritted teeth as she watches the school. "So you might as well try. Plus, I've got a plan that might buy us some time. We'll also be able to get some food and water in us, if it works."

Mr. Khan sits back on the dried grass, his black hair glistening as the sun hits it. "You're quite right. I'm likely just as wanted as you two are, considering my ties to Smith's government, Jasmine, and Beaconsfield," he says with a nod toward the school. "And as Jasmine's Protector, it is my duty to see her as far as I can into the Final Battle." He pauses. "It will also allow me to ensure the ring is put back in the Roman wall once and for all."

"Are you in?" Amara says, a wide smile spreading across her cheeks.

"I'm in," Mr. Khan replies.

JASMINE

Vashti pulls her shawl over her head so that it acts like a hood and motions us to follow her out the door of the Trafalgar. The sun is just slipping from the sky, making our shadows stretch out in front of us like dark, faceless giants.

"We must hurry," she says, leading us down an alleyway directly behind the pub. The cobblestoned ground is slightly uneven, and I worry about Vashti losing her footing.

There's another pub just ahead with several patrons sitting at a table and on the low windowsills out front. Panic rises in me at the thought of being recognized, and I take deep breaths as we walk by to try to push down the feeling. We're not even given a second look. It seems Londoners are still enjoying life, despite the terrorism and madness happening around them and in the rest of the world.

"There's a car waiting for us on the Old Woolwich Road," Vashti whispers. "It's driverless, so we're safe. And it will take us to the current location of our Seers."

"Is it still in Greenwich?" Lily asks, somewhat breath-lessly.

Vashti shakes her head. "No, in a different borough. But at this point in time, I feel it's prudent not to tell you the location yet. Give the other girls a chance to get to know you and trust you first."

We turn a corner onto another side street, and Vashti motions for us to stay standing in front of one of the brown-brick row houses that line the street. The sky is now a dusky ink colour, and the streetlamps flicker on. It's strange. Though it's 2032, I've been to this city before and can still see the remnants of the past. It's as though there are layers upon layers to London, shadows upon shadows. Which makes sense. Maybe the Place-in-Between is sort of like that. Maybe it truly is the shadow, the dark side, of the real London. If that's the case, what does it mean if the membrane, the dividing line between contemporary London and the Place-in-Between has thinned so much that it's practically no longer there?

"Do you hear that?" Cassandra whispers as Vashti disappears around a corner at the top of the street. The street that runs perpendicular to the one we're on is busy with cars and buses whizzing past, their head-lights briefly illuminating the road ahead. The rumble of traffic makes it hard to hear anything.

I shake my head. "No, what?"

We wait a few moments. All I hear is the whoosh of cars and electric buses.

"There is it again," Cassandra says.

This time I hear it. A slow dragging sound. As if someone is shuffling along pavement or dragging something heavy. It seems to be coming from somewhere to the left of us and near the side of the house we're standing in front of. It's impossible to see anything, as a high stone wall with an equally high wooden gate in the middle of it separates us from the sound.

"What do you think it is?" Lily asks, moving closer to her sister.

"No idea. It sounds like it's coming from the side of the house, though," Cassandra replies.

I laugh nervously. "It's probably just an injured raccoon or fox or something."

We hear it again, and the sound cuts my laughter short. That's because it's a lot closer now. Close enough that I find myself glancing around for something that can be used as a pole. Because whatever it is, it sounds considerably bigger than a raccoon or fox.

I scan the road ahead where Vashti went, hoping to spot her. What's she doing? Has she abandoned us? *Don't be stupid*, I think. Protectors don't abandon Seers. But then, I never thought my sister would take Solomon's Ring right after I put it back in the Roman wall, so maybe I'm not the best predictor of people's behaviour.

A sudden low moaning sound emanates from behind us. I freeze.

"What the hell?" Cassandra whispers. The fear in her voice is so strong, I can almost taste it.

And that's not good, because fear feeds them.

The next moment, there's a flurry of movement, and something drops seemingly out of the sky and down onto us, causing me to lose my balance and fall back against the wall. Lily's sent sprawling into the street on her hands and knees with a sharp yelp. She leaps up and swivels around, fists raised in front of her face in the defensive posture we've been taught to take if we're ever caught without a pole or any sort of weapon ... the kind of situation we're now in.

I backflip away from whatever has jumped onto us, landing beside Lily. Looking up, I see that the scene unfolding in front of us is bad.

At first glance, it looks like a demon is feeding on Cassandra. Its head is bowed over the fleshy part at the top of her arm. But, unlike our familiar demon friends, this creature is gnawing on her flesh, ripping at it, and Cassandra is screaming, her voice filled with such pain and fear, it's almost unbearable.

Lily sprints forward and fly-kicks the creature in the back. "Get off my sister!" she screams.

I move to help her. Whatever this thing is, it's not your typical demon. And that's because it's still chewing away on Cassandra's arm like she's a juicy Thanksgiving turkey.

The thing stumbles off Cassandra and looks up at Lily, head cocked sideways, with a deep moan. There's blood running down its lower face and little bits of flesh are stuck to the corners of its lips. The creature's face is as pale as a full moon and sickly grey. The eyes are sunken and ringed with skin so dark, it looks almost bruised. A milky, translucent film covers one of its eyes like a curtain. The creature takes a few moments to find its balance, its feet landing on the sidewalk unsteadily.

Lily kicks at the thing again, her foot connecting with its abdomen. A demon would've grabbed her leg with lightning speed, but instead, this creature stumbles backward for a brief moment, another long, low moan escaping its lips. There's a gaping hole where Lily's foot entered its midsection.

Cassandra falls to the ground, clutching at her arm. She's still screaming. That's when I notice Vashti is beside me. I didn't even notice her approach. That scares me. It means I'm not being as careful as I need to be.

"The prophecy is upon us," Vashti says as she places what looks like a cotton scarf into Cassandra's mouth to bite down on. The trepidation in Vashti's voice is strong. "It's a zombie, Jasmine. The lost souls are walking amongst us now and taking the bodies of the dead in order to do so. Go and help Lily. I will tend to Cassandra."

"How do I kill it?" I ask, panic scrabbling at my throat. The creature lunges at Lily as I speak, and though it's moving faster than it was, it continues to be unstable on its feet.

"The skull. Crush the skull. The temples are best. You have no weapons, but as Seers, you are extremely strong," she says. "Now go."

I run at the creature and bring my fist down onto the side of its head like a hammer, just as Lily kicks at it again. Her leg connects with the side of its hip at the same time that my fist hits the zombie's head on the opposite side of its body. I'm thrown off balance momentarily by both the movement of the zombie's body toward me and the stench of rotting flesh mixed with garbage that's coming off of it in waves.

The zombie moans loudly as I remove my fist from the side of its head. A distinctive, fist-sized area of the creature's skull is now caved in like a month-old jack-o'-lantern. It stumbles for what feels like a lifetime in a half-circle like an intoxicated sailor, grey bits of brain spilling from the hole in its temple, before collapsing onto the sidewalk.

Lily stares at the corpse for a moment, her eyes wide with disbelief. "What the hell is that thing?" she says, her voice barely a whisper.

"Vashti called it a zombie," I reply.

"Seriously?" Lily says. "Like, walking dead, Halloween costume zombie?" She gives it a little kick with the toe of her shoe.

The stench of the rotting corpse hits us at the same time. My already compromised stomach can't take any more of the smell, and I double over, vomiting up half-digested biscuits and tea onto the sidewalk.

Lily covers her mouth, and runs over to where Cassandra is lying. Vashti is crouched over her, applying pressure to Cassandra's badly mangled arm as I approach.

Vashti looks up at both of us, her eyes dark with concern. I try not to stare at her hands; they're so slick with blood, it looks like she's wearing crimson gloves.

"The car is here. Just around the corner. You'll see it: a white Tesla. Both of you must leave this place immediately."

"I'm not going without my sister," Lily protests, kneeling down beside Vashti.

"She's dying, and you will as well, if you don't make it out of here and to a safer space as soon as possible. What is happening now is bigger than the two of you, and there will be sacrifices, so get used to swallowing your emotions," Vashti says. "I will get Cassandra to a doctor we can trust. She has no hope unless I do that. Perhaps she won't be recognized. Perhaps she will be. However, the three of you staying together guarantees detection."

"But she's not microchipped. We don't have the proper identification for here," I say.

Vashti looks at me. "I've got ways of dealing with challenges such as that. Now, both of you must *go*," she says. Her voice is hard as rock. "If you don't, I will snap your necks in half myself."

JADE

We've been walking for about half an hour, staying as hidden as possible as Amara leads us north, parallel to Yonge Street.

"It's the place where my dad always told us to go to if we ever got into any sort of trouble," Amara says breathlessly. "Being a part of the CCT, I guess he was always thinking one step ahead. It's the secret place he created to keep our entire family safe, if there were ever an emergency. This seems like the right time to use it." She stops talking and scans the ravine. "I hope he's okay."

Mr. Khan nods as rivulets of sweat run from his drenched hair down the nape of his neck. "Your father strikes me as a very astute man. I'm not surprised he'd be so forward-thinking."

I notice he doesn't answer Amara's question about her father's safety. Maybe Mr. Khan doesn't know, or he doesn't want to give her false assurances — either would be so much better than the third option: that he does know something but doesn't want to upset Amara with terrible news.

"Have you talked to my mom?" I ask. "Like in the last twenty-four hours or so? Since we left for the Place-in-Between?"

Mr. Khan purses his lips together, squinting as sweat drips into his eyes. "The police have been at the apartment to question your mother. That's to be expected. You're wanted on suspicion of terrorism. I don't believe she's been taken into custody."

My heart plummets. Of course they've questioned my mom. The police will be questioning anyone, everyone, who has anything to do with us. I think about Mom being interrogated by the police after all she's been through with my disappearance. She's resilient but fiery, and rarely holds back from speaking her mind, which worries me. The police don't always take well to people of colour trying to defend their civil rights and freedoms.

We're climbing down into the ravine now, and though I should feel better down here under the cover of dense foliage, below the hustle of the city above, the thought of drone patrols still makes me anxious. Cicadas sing loudly from the trees. I don't want to be out in the dark, but I wish the sun would set faster as the heat, combined with our lack of food or water, is making me increasingly faint.

"Where are we going?" I ask.

"Just up here," Amara says, pointing to a rectangular grey-stone building up the hillside on the opposite side of the ravine.

"Interesting building," Mr. Khan says, leaning against a tree in an attempt to regain his breath. "It looks quite old. It's residential?"

Amara nods. "Dad says it's a carriage house. It used to house horses centuries ago, but was changed into a home about sixty years ago."

It takes us another ten minutes or so to reach the building. It's situated behind what can only be called a mansion, and it's far enough back from the street to feel quite secure. Tendrils of overgrown, tear-shaped ivy crawl along the exterior brick, stretching toward the sky like fingers.

"The main house belongs to Noni. That makes it safe for us to stay a while, if we need to," Amara says as she rummages around underneath a series of potted plants. "I know we need to transition," she says, glancing at Mr. Khan. "I'm just saying, if we need to."

"Just having a place to compose our thoughts, what with all that's going on, is a blessing," Mr. Khan says. "Even if it is for just a few hours. I'm exhausted, and I'm sure the two of you are, as well." He places a gentle hand on her shoulder. "You need to rest after the trauma you've been through."

Amara fishes a fob out from under one of the pots. She holds it up triumphantly. "We're in!"

I frown. I get what Mr. Khan is saying. Amara needs to process what's happened to Vivienne. But selfishly, a part of me doesn't want her thinking about it too much, as her anger toward me will probably flood back with a vengeance if she does.

Amara opens the door. "It might be a bit musty," she says apologetically.

Mr. Khan and I follow her in. The carriage house is surprisingly roomy inside, with a full kitchen and living area. There's a narrow, steep staircase toward the back that leads to a loft area where, I imagine, there is a bedroom or two.

Amara walks over to a desk, opens it, and pulls out a video watch. "Holographic," she says with a grin. "Direct line to my dad's emergency phone. I need to let him know I'm okay."

Mr. Khan watches her, his eyes darkening with concern. She's doing the humming thing again. "If you are able to connect with your father, it would be prudent for him and for us to get rid of the devices directly afterward. Perhaps it would be best to contact him when we're ready to leave. Then we could throw the device down into the ravine." He pauses. "And … Amara?"

"Yeah?" she says with a wide smile. She pours three glasses of water, puts them on the counter, then reaches up to take several silver packets out of a cupboard. Her T-shirt rides up, exposing the muscles of her brown abdomen. "There's a dew harvesting system," she says, handing us each a glass of water. "Collects the water in the morning and stores it indefinitely, for both houses."

"You should tell your father about Vivienne, if we do connect with him. Gently, though," Mr. Khan interjects.

A shadow flits over Amara's face like a cloud blowing across the sun. It's brief, though. "Oh, yes. Definitely. First, let me make us some food. Dad's got a pretty amazing selection here. Butter chicken and jasmine rice sound good?" She's acting more like the host of a dinner party than a wanted fugitive.

My stomach growls uneasily, despite my nausea. I'm starving. It's been at least twenty-four hours since I've eaten anything. Even the cold water, which feels amazing as it flows over my parched lips, hits my belly like a ton of bricks.

Mr. Khan continues watching Amara closely as she puts on a kettle. His face is a mask of concern.

"The food is freeze-dried. Like what the astronauts and passengers to space eat," she says, tearing open one of the shiny packets with her front teeth. As soon as she stops talking, she begins the flat, bee-like humming again.

"Why don't you two lie down and rest for a moment while I prepare this?" Mr. Khan says, walking over to Amara. He reaches out and gently takes the packet of dried butter chicken from her hands.

Amara crumples as though she's about to break down and cry, but she regains her composure. Plastering a bright smile across her face, she nods. "That sounds good. I'd like to just kick back for a minute and chill," she says, walking toward the sofa. "News. Toronto and international," she says, and one of the flat monitors attached to the wall opposite flickers on. It's a 3-D holographic display model, so everything jumps out at us as though it's in the room.

Amara flops onto the deep-purple faux-suede sofa, drawing her feet up and under her. She pats the cushion beside her. "Come on, Jade. You heard what the man said. Take a load off. I wasn't sure if voice recognition would work for me here. My dad was really thinking when he set this place up. He programmed my voice into everything and probably ..." She stops speaking as the news headlines come on.

Mr. Khan catches my eye. I know he no longer trusts me. That's pretty clear. However, the look on his face tells me that he's concerned Amara is losing her mind.

I fully share his concern.

I sit down beside Amara to watch the news. I'm a bit afraid how she'll react if I don't. She's still humming with that strange smile on her face.

"A lot of very bad things are happening today," she says as our pictures, along with those of Vivienne, Lily, Cassandra, and Jasmine flash up.

"That's an understatement," I murmur back.

Each holographic image slowly spins a full 360 degrees. It's really jarring to watch my own profile. I turn away until the segment is done.

Amara seems to show no recognition of the fact that that's us on the screen and that we're being shown to help the public identify and report us as soon as we're spotted. The journalist is warning people not to approach us, especially if we are in pairs or a group, and that we're *extremely dangerous* members of the CCT responsible for the murders of millions of people in the water poisoning.

Images flash up of bodies covered by sheets and of families crying, some of them holding dead or dying children. The children convulse in their parents' arms, white and pink foam spilling from their lips. A weeping first responder clings to his colleague.

We're dead women walking, I think. With this kind of reporting, Smith won't have a chance to get her claws into us. Members of the public will do the job for her. And I suspect their ferocity when doing so will be off the charts.

Then we see Mayor Smith on camera, her jaw muscles clenched tightly, a deadly serious look on her face. Her cropped hair is now a deep blue-black colour. The contrast with her porcelain-white skin makes her look even more severe than ever. I suspect she wants it that way.

"We are facing an unprecedented threat to our city and beyond. The CCT has, in the past, been ruthless, but the training and manipulation of girls to become cold-blooded mass murderers is a new and dangerous low. These girls are barely into their teens and may appear innocent; however, they are trained killers and *must not* be approached under any circumstances. This is particularly true of Jasmine Guzman, who we suspect is the ringleader of the group. This young woman deceived me and infiltrated my government in order to further her terrorist aims." Smith raises a fist in the air, the muscles in her neck straining against her skin. "I will, on behalf of the Torontonians in my care, impose the death penalty without mercy."

As if on cue, two heavily armed anti-terrorism officers enter the broadcast as Smith punches the air. They're leading two hooded and handcuffed figures.

One struggles defiantly. Even before the hood covering her head is torn off, I recognize that it is Eva. Her eyes are wild, and the scars along the side of her head won't help the public's perception of her — and of us. But if she's scared, she's not showing it. Taylor Moore's face is revealed seconds later. He looks as terrified as a deer in headlights.

"Tomorrow night, these two CCT terrorists will pay the ultimate price for their murderous ways, and thus, will serve as an example of what happens when you commit treason in Toronto, or anywhere else in Canada, for that matter," Smith says, her eyes narrowing into tiny slits while the camera pans in for a close-up. "Their executions will take place in Dundas Square tomorrow at seven p.m. sharp, and they will be live-streamed internationally."

JASMINE

The white car sits by the curb, quietly idling. It's easy to spot, just as Vashti said it would be. Lily and I move into the back seat. Cool air bathes my face as we enter the car. It's a great surprise. Even in electric cars, air conditioning is a rare occurrence these days.

"Welcome," a very calm-sounding female voice says. "Please press your fingertips against the display in front of you, and then we will be on our way to your destination."

Lily raises an eyebrow at me. "I hope we can trust Vashti," she says nervously.

I understand her anxiety. If we follow the AI's instructions, we'll be totally leaving our details here to be easily traced. Thing is, we don't really have a choice. And Clarence and Vashti have kept us safe this far. Not only that, Cassandra's survival depends on that trust, as well as some really good medical help.

"We don't have a choice," I say, pressing the fleshy pads of my fingertips against the monitor.

"Fingerprint identification registered," the voice says as the engine jumps to life. The car slides out, silent as a cat, into the darkness of the early evening.

"How do you think the car recognized your fingerprints?" Lily asks. "Wouldn't that information have to have been programmed in?"

"Yeah, I'd think so," I say. It's not like I know a ton about the technology. My mind races back through the last few hours. "The only time we'd have left any fingerprints behind was on the mugs, when we were having tea. Our fingerprints could've been scanned from those, I suppose."

"Then we're already traceable, I guess," she sighs. "It seems risky."

We ride in silence for the next few minutes. I stare out the tinted windows at London. We pass roads riddled with people, pubs, and corner shops. It all looks about the same until we move toward a bridge, and suddenly the river, Big Ben, and the parliament buildings around it appear. The buildings are illuminated, making them sparkle like jewels.

"Do you think they'll be able to save Cassandra?" Lily finally asks. Her voice is barely a whisper.

I turn to answer her and see that her cheeks are streaked with tears.

"I don't know," I answer. There's no use being dishonest. "There was a lot of blood."

Lily nods. "Yeah, I know. She's still alive, but there's crazy pain. Pain that feels like acid. I think her wound has an infection that's spreading." She gulps at the cool air in the car like a goldfish tossed from its bowl. "And she's scared. Really scared. Of dying."

I reach out and touch Lily's arm. "You're feeling it too, right?"

She pulls away as though burned and nods, fresh tears spilling from her eyes. "It hurts so much, I can barely think. And I'm scared, Jasmine. I wish we weren't Seers. I wish we were just normal. Why us?"

"Why not us?" I reply.

"But I don't want this. I don't want to fight demons or any of it."

"If you weren't a Seer, you might not be a twin, either. And personally, I kind of like having both you and Cassandra in my life," I say, immediately regretting my words, since we can't be 100 percent sure that Cassandra will still be with us after tonight. Silence spreads between us for a few moments. "You want to hear something strange?" I ask, hoping to take Lily's mind off Cassandra's injuries, even if only for a few brief moments.

Lily nods again and sniffles wetly. She wipes at her nose with the back of her right hand.

"I don't have that with Jade anymore ... that connection." It's something I haven't told anyone, because I don't really understand it myself.

"What do you mean?" she asks. "You really didn't know she was taking the ring?"

"Of course not," I say. I'm shocked and more than a bit hurt that Lily thought I was lying about that. And I'm sure she can hear that in my voice.

"Sorry," Lily says. "It's just that, you know, reading and feeling your twin's emotions doesn't seem like something that could change. When did it happen?"

I pause to think about it. "It's hard to know for sure, but I definitely noticed it just before we went to the Place-in-Between to return the ring. I guess sometime around then. Something shifted. But I don't think it was with me."

"What do you mean?" Lily asks, her eyebrows drawing together into a frown.

I chew on my bottom lip and look out the window for a moment. We're in a residential area now, with houses looming above us like ghostly white giants.

"Something strange happened to Jade." I pause. "When we were down in the Place-in-Between, there was this guy. About our age. Really skinny."

Lily shrugs. "I didn't see him. One of the lost souls?"

"That's just it. I don't think he was. And do you want to hear something even crazier?"

Lily smiles, but it's a sad smile that doesn't reach her eyes. "Isn't everything in our lives crazy? Sure. Shoot."

"Jade knew him. Seriously. I could tell by the way he looked at her and vice versa. And she was looking at him like she was in love or something."

"Was he hot?" Lily asks.

"Gross! Um, he was so not at all," I answer. "Skinny and freckled with wiry red hair and a nose that looked like his mom pinched it all the time when he was a baby."

The car seems to be slowing down.

"Our destination will be on the right in five hundred metres. Please gather all your belongings. Mind the step between the car and the path whilst disembarking," the AI says.

"And you think this guy has something to do with you and Jade losing your connection? And what Vashti said about Jade being under the influence of someone or something?" Lily asks. "How did he do that? Do you think she knows him from her time there, in the Place-in-Between?"

"I have no idea," I reply. "It's just a gut feeling. He's definitely not a lost soul, but if he was down in the Place-in-Between, he's not a regular human being, either."

"Maybe another angel?" Lily asks as the car rolls to a stop outside one of the houses. "And where is Raphael when you need him, anyway? He could've helped Cassandra tonight."

"Yeah, I know. He seems to leave me … I mean, us … whenever he's needed," I say, my face reddening. I'm glad for the darkness of the car's interior and its air-conditioning. "I dunno what his deal is. But, no, I don't think that guy Jade knows is an angel. I think he's something else."

"Something else? Like what?" Lily asks.

I open my mouth to answer, but the words catch in my throat as the car door beside me swings open.

"Get out. And make it quick," a voice snaps.

Despite having been previously freeze-dried, the butter chicken and rice taste like heaven. I'm so hungry, I want to gobble all the food on my plate down without stopping to breathe between bites, but the roller coaster ride in my stomach warns me against that.

"I've been thinking, Amara," Mr. Khan says, pushing his half-finished plate away. "Your father must also be under surveillance. I'm not sure getting ahold of him is the best idea. However, I do feel you should tell him about Vivienne. I'd hate for him to discover it via the media or some other means." He pauses, clearly torn about what to do. "I assume that, to ensure safety, the video watch here is not registered to your father, but regardless, all of his incoming communications are sure to be ruthlessly and immediately scrutinized." He turns to me. "Do you still have the ring?"

I nod and instinctively feel the right front pocket of my jeans, though I know it's still there.

Mr. Khan rubs his chin as he thinks. The beginnings of a small goatee are sprouting from the skin under his fingers.

"If we do make contact with your father, we must be prepared to transition from here directly afterward, as I estimate we'll have less than half an hour before the authorities storm this place — if we're lucky."

"Okay," Amara replies, her voice bright. "And then throw away the video watch, right?"

Mr. Khan's eyes darken with concern again. "Yes, then we throw away the video watch," he says, sounding somewhat defeated. It must seem like the Seers currently under his protection are coming apart like a badly sewn pair of pants.

The rest of our dinner is finished in silence, aside from the news broadcast that we've left on. We're all thinking about the transition. Will it work? Can we flip into contemporary London? And, if we can, will we be able to connect with Jasmine and the rest of the Seers? Will Mr. Khan be okay in the Place-in-Between? He could end up reacting just like us, feeling sicker and weaker the longer he's down there, or he could become very ill right away … or worse. There are so many unknowns. One thing I do know: staying here is not a choice.

"An update from Toronto public health official Rodney White on the death toll from the water poisoning. Currently, the official number of dead stands at one million, eight hundred and fifty-eight thousand. An estimated two hundred thousand further casualties are currently hospitalized in critical care, so it is expected that the number of fatalities will increase."

"Whoa," I say, my fork clattering to my plate. My hands are shaking. "That's insane."

Mr. Khan nods. "Mass murder on a scale not often seen in human history. The African slave trade, the Holocaust, Syria … Humans have done this kind of thing before. But not usually in just a few days. Perhaps the Rwandan genocide is the closest equivalent."

Seconds later, images of us flash up again. The broadcaster's voice is urgent.

"These young women are the prime suspects in the water poisoning. Eva Gonzales, the only terrorist — I mean, suspected terrorist — to be apprehended thus far, has not only confessed to aiding in the poisoning of the water, but also pleaded no contest to the first-degree murder of Constable Jeffrey Brick of the Toronto Police. Constable Brick, a thirty-five-year-old father of three …"

"Turn it off," I say, clenching my teeth so tight they nearly crack. I can't listen any longer to the horrible things they're saying we've done, and I can't bear to see my face, my sister's face, the faces of our friends — one of whom is now dead — shown over and over while we're attacked verbally like this. *Terrorists. Murderers. Criminals. Teen sociopaths.*

Standing up, I shove the chair back, and, clutching my stomach, dash to the bathroom. There's not even time to close the door behind me before I'm kneeling over the cool porcelain rim of the toilet, throwing up every last morsel of the rice and chicken. My stomach spins like a washing machine on overdrive.

After about five minutes, Mr. Khan comes to the door.

"Jade?" he asks, his voice soft and caring for the first time since I took the ring.

"I'm fine," I answer weakly, though I can't even stand up at the moment. I feel like a whirling dervish, the room is spinning so much.

"Can I come in?" he asks.

"Sure." It's not like I can stop him. If I didn't have this ring in my pocket and some crazy demon came into the house right now, I'd be dead meat. In fact, judging by the way Amara's acting, we'd all be killed.

Mr. Khan kneels beside me and holds back my damp hair. "Here," he says, holding out a wad of toilet paper with his free hand. "Give your mouth and chin a wipe."

I take the paper gratefully and wipe my lower face. "Sorry," I manage to say. "My stomach has been off for a while."

Mr. Khan frowns. "What's going on, Jade? Why did you take the ring?" He pauses. "You must've realized doing so could put you and the rest of the Seers, not to mention many others, in enormous danger."

I stare at the puke-splattered toilet bowl. What defence do I have? I'm not about to tell him what Seth said about not trusting the Archangels or others close to me — like Mr. Khan. And I'm for sure not telling him how Seth warned me that putting the ring in the wall would mean certain death for many Seers. I mean, it makes sense — why put such a powerful weapon, something that can protect us from the demons that are actively hunting us, in a place where it can't be used? It's not that I don't trust Mr. Khan, but …

"Just an impulsive thing, I guess," I say. "When the demons began to attack, I ran back and got it. To keep us safe."

Mr. Khan regards me silently. He's staring at me so intently, I swear he can see my inner organs. For a moment, I get a bit nervous, wondering if all Seers lose their powers as they get older, or if Mr. Khan might be an anomaly. I don't feel him reading my thoughts, but I am a bit paranoid that he might slide in at any second. When a Seer is reading your mind, like when Jasmine does it to me, it's this definite feeling. Sort of like someone is prying your head open with their fingers and walking around inside your brain. It tickles and feels like a mild electric shock all at the same time. Not an entirely unpleasant sensation, really.

"For a second-born, that is really unusual behaviour," he says, drawing out each word slowly like he's savouring its taste. His guard is really up with me. "May I ask where you were when Vivienne was attacked?"

My heart stops. I was with Seth. He'd called me over. And I just went to him. It felt sort of like my body was on automatic. After that, things get hazy. My memory always gets kind of broken when it comes to Seth. The memories are there, but they're jumbled, like the pieces of a jigsaw puzzle when they're first tossed from the box. There was thick fog, and Seth leaning against a wall waving to me … then the demons came down from the wall, it seemed … and he told me things, things that scared me, things that I'm supposed to keep secret for now … then I was at a different part of the wall and reaching in and the stones were as wet as fish … and the ring was there. For the taking.

By the time I got back to the others, the demons were gone, Vivienne was dying, and Jasmine was injured.

"But did it help you save her?" Mr. Khan asks quietly, interrupting my thoughts. "Not such a great safety net if we're losing Seers while you have it in your possession, is it?"

"I was retrieving it when Vivienne was attacked," I answer indignantly. "If I'd been faster, I could've stopped the demon from hurting her, but I did save us after that. Jasmine and me. When we beheaded the demon inhabiting Vivienne's body."

"Do you really believe that, Jade?" Mr. Khan asks. "Because according to all the prophecies and writings in the Dead Sea Scrolls about the last battle, that church is a safe haven from demons … when the ring is in its proper place. And while you fought that demon, the others were in danger in the church. It's lucky we didn't lose more of you that day."

"How do we know all of that is even true? All of the stuff about certain places being safe when the ring is in the wall?" I ask him. It's a totally sincere question. "How do we know these scrolls written thousands of years ago aren't fictional? It's kind of like religion. How can some people believe in one god while other religions have a multitude of gods? Is it simply a matter of *I'm right, so you've gotta be wrong*?"

"A fair and wise question," Mr. Khan says, sitting down beside me and leaning his back against the wall.

He lets out a heavy sigh. "All I can say is that everything in those Lost Scrolls has thus far proven to be true. It's wise to question and analyze things, Jade, rather than swallowing information whole. That's true. Many corrupt governments ensure that their people stay uneducated and unmotivated to learn, and thus, are unable to truly understand, analyze, or question whether what they're being told is truth. This, as well as turning different groups of people on each other, causing constant division, is always done to maintain social control and create fear. Smith is just one example of such a leader. That is why throughout history, dictators turned on the intellectuals first: the media, the writers, the educators, the artists. Unfortunately, this ploy generally works very well." He stops speaking for a moment, and a look of immense sadness crosses his face; I'm afraid he may begin to cry. "All I can tell you, again, is that, rationally speaking, the scrolls have proven to be true. Thus far, anyhow."

I nod. "I guess we need to get ready to transition," I say. I'm feeling confused about everything, but at least I feel well enough now to try to stand up. "Do you think Amara is okay to do this? Like, in the head okay?"

Mr. Khan shrugs. "Yes, I understood what you meant. I honestly don't know, but we need to try. There is no other choice."

He gets to his feet and holds out a hand to support me. I feel a little like Bambi on ice, but I'm steadier after a few seconds of standing.

"Let's do this thing," I say with a forced smile.

What I don't tell Mr. Khan is that my stomach is doing its crazy dance again, and that that has made distrust flare up like a bad rash. Luckily, I don't have anything left to vomit out. And, for some reason, on top of it all, I miss Seth. I mean, I really miss him. So much it's like a physical hurt in the core of my being.

Maybe he'll be in London again when we get there. This time a genuine smile slides its way across my face at the thought.

"What's made your worries suddenly disappear?" Mr. Khan asks, reflecting my smile back at me.

"I was just thinking how great it'll be to reunite with Jasmine," I lie as we walk back into the living area of the carriage house.

JASMINE

The beam of a flashlight shines directly into my eyes, making me squint from the sudden brightness. I'm unable to see the person barking commands at us. The only thing I know is that the voice is female and sounds around our age.

"Aren't you special?" I say, as I lift my hand to shield my eyes and slide out the door, with Lily close behind me.

The girl with the flashlight grabs my arm. "C'mon. A bit bloody faster, will ya?"

I tear my arm from her grasp. "Two things," I say through clenched teeth. "Who the hell are you? And get your damn hands off me."

"Oy, we've got a live one here," the girl laughs. It's a nasty laugh that makes me think of worms crawling through garbage. Lily's beside me now. I can see just from the faint reflected light of the flashlight beam off the ground that the girl is white and her face is very round and a bit doughy-looking, though that could just be the shadows. "Follow me. And try to make it quick, yeah?"

We don't have much choice, so Lily and I somewhat reluctantly follow this girl up the sidewalk two or three houses beyond where the car stopped.

"They don't even trust technology no more," the girl says as she swings open a black wrought-iron gate and leads us to one of the towering white houses. "That's why they're giving the car a bit of the wrong address and stuff."

"Who are *they*?" I ask as we walk into a large foyer. There are numbered doors to the left and to the right, so I guess the house is divided into apartments.

The girl raises an eyebrow at me. She's tall, a lot taller than me, anyway, which isn't hard because I'm pretty short for my age, but I'm okay with it — most of the time. Her cheeks and forehead are covered in tiny inflamed whiteheads.

"Our Protectors and the CCT," the girl says, as though I'm stupid not to already know the answer.

"We're kind of new here, so if you could go easy with the attitude, it would be appreciated," Lily says.

"Okay, Snow White," the girl shoots back.

"What exactly did we do to you to make you so pissed off at us?" Lily asks.

The girl smirks as she begins to walk up the stairs. "On second thought, maybe you ain't Snow White, because she wasn't Oriental, was she?"

There's a sharp intake of breath from Lily, and her eyes widen.

"You know what?" I say. "We're not going a step farther with you. We don't even know who you are, other than the fact that you're a complete bigot." My fists are so tightly clenched, I swear my knuckles are going to pop through the skin. At the moment, it's all I can do to keep from punching this girl in her pimply face. What the hell is her problem?

"Sara, stop being bloody obnoxious," a voice calls from just above us. A face that looks very similar to that of the girl we're with leans over the bannister and smiles at us. "Ignore my sister. She's being a right cow. As usual."

Lily and I look at each other.

"Shut yer piehole, Susie," shouts the girl with us who I now assume is Sara. "I'm Sara," she says to us. "I'm a Millwall supporter like my daddy, and I'm just taking the piss." She sees the confusion — and in my case, the anger — on our faces and smiles. "Just trying to make sure what's what with you lot."

I guess this is supposed to be her very screwed-up, whitewashed version of an apology. She may look like she's our age, but she speaks like she's about eight. Being greeted by a sociopathic Seer was not a great way to instill trust in Vashti and Clarence having our best interests at heart.

Susie comes down to meet us. Though they are twins, there are significant differences between them. For one, Susie smiles a lot more than her sister. And her skin is clearer. She just looks altogether healthier — both mentally and physically — than her sister.

"Vashti and Clarence told us you were coming. We've been here for two nights, so I expect we'll be moved on tomorrow. The flat is just up there," she says, pointing in the direction she came from. She looks at us. "You look hungry and you need poles ... in case of demons and stuff because you never know. Come with me."

We follow Susie and Sara up to the next landing. Susie opens a red door with a silver 4 on it. A long wooden-floored hall stretches out in front of us with a ceiling higher than that of any apartment I've ever seen in Toronto.

"Sara, can you get —" Susie pauses and looks at us.

"I'm Jasmine and this is Lily," I say.

"— get Jasmine and Lily some food. I think there are crisps left. See if there's anything to make sandwiches with, too."

My stomach rumbles like the thunder before a massive storm at the thought of sandwiches. Not sure what crisps are, but as long as they're edible, I'm game.

Sara mumbles something incoherent and disappears into the first door we pass on the right. I assume that's the kitchen.

"Apologies for my sister. She's okay once you get to know her. Well, most of the time. She's just a lot like my dad. And he's a wanker," Susie says. "I'm more like my mum."

We reach another doorway that opens onto a living area, where three other girls are sitting around, playing cards. They look up in unison when we enter.

A pretty, almost elfin girl gives us a friendly wave. She's really slim with long, incredibly straight, and shiny black hair that flows down her back. Her nose is pierced through the septum. I've always wanted a piercing like that. However, I value living more than having a nose ring, and knowing that Mom would kill me if I ever showed up with a hoop hanging from the middle of my nose, I've never gotten it done. This girl's twin, who is equally pretty, gives us a welcoming smile from the other side of the coffee table.

"All right?" she asks.

I pause. Do we look that bad? It's a definite possibility, considering how long it's been since we've showered or slept.

"I'm okay," I answer, a bit more defensively than intended.

"Me, too," Lily says.

The girl stares at us, confusion filling her eyes. "Oh, you're American!" she says after a moment. "'All right' is just a greeting. We don't actually expect an answer."

"Oh," I say as the other girls laugh. My face burns with embarrassment.

"We're Canadian, actually," Lily says, "not American. But it's hard to hear the difference, I guess."

"Nah, it's not hard," one of the other girls says. She reminds me a bit of Vivienne with her halo of dark curls and wide, bright smile. "Americans are an obnoxious bunch. Big mouths and even bigger egos." She pats the cushion beside her enthusiastically. "Come join us."

Everyone sits on overstuffed cushions on the floor around the coffee table. Some of the cushions have been taken from the clearly well-loved brown corduroy sofa that fills at least a third of the room. The girls place their cards down on the table, pausing their game for us.

The girl that reminds me of Vivienne pats an empty sofa cushion beside her again. "We don't bite … at least not much," she says with a laugh. "I'm Kiki. My sister, Dani, is sleeping. Cramps." She scrunches up her face into a mask of mock pain. "That time of the month. And this is Fahima and her sister Atika."

I take a seat, cross-legged, on the cushion. Every muscle in my body is sore, and I need sleep. It takes all my concentration stay upright and to follow the conversation around me.

"So," says Fahima, the twin with the pierced nose, "you're both Seers? How did you get here with the borders closed? Especially since you two are —" she pauses and clears her throat uncomfortably "— you know … wanted for those poisonings."

"But we didn't do that," Lily says quickly. "Just so you know. We're being framed by Sandra Smith, the mayor."

"Don't worry, Vashti told us," Kiki says. "But how did you get to us, to London, in the first place? All the borders into the UK are sealed tight."

I glance over at Lily. They're all Seers, so we should be able to trust them. I mean, they're in the same situation as us … kind of.

"We transitioned here from the Place-in-Between. We were trying to get back to Toronto," I say, just as Sara kicks open the door and enters the room, balancing a tray unsteadily on her thick arms.

All eyes are on me. Atika's mouth has dropped half-open in surprise.

"The Place-in-Between?" Kiki parrots. Her disbelief is apparent. "You mean London Below?"

I shrug. "It's definitely London, and I guess it's below us. I mean, I don't know for sure. We often transition there from places that are below ground level, like subways and stuff, so maybe." I stop speaking because I'm confusing even myself. My exhaustion is overwhelming.

Sara plunks the tray down in the middle of the table. Water spills over the rims of the two glasses in the middle onto the plate of sandwiches and into the bowl of potato chips also on the tray.

"Bollocks!" she says, red splotches blooming across her cheeks. "Demons and lost souls dwell in that place. Seers can't possibly go to London Below. You're liars."

Just looking at the sandwiches, soggy with water or not, is making me salivate. I don't dare make a grab for them, though, because Sara is practically foaming at the mouth like a rabid dog now.

"I've been there twice," I say as calmly as possible. Really, this girl is practically begging for a punch in the face, but I realize we're the new kids on the block and we need to appear sane. Even if Sara isn't.

"We do get more and more sick the longer we're down there. I still feel kind of unwell, in fact," Lily says. She glances sideways at Sara as she finishes speaking. "It definitely feels like it's below here. Don't ask me how. Just a feeling. And it's Victorian times — Jack the Ripper and stuff."

Susie raises an eyebrow at us. "We've learned about London Below, or the Place-in-Between, as you call it, during training," she says.

"Yeah," Kiki chimes in. "But we've always been told that it's a death realm. A place where only souls that are trapped between here and the final place exist. Oh, and where demons that have moved from the Darkness dwell. The migrating kind. Same ones that make it here when they're able to."

The Darkness.

Just the word sends shivers through the core of my being. Though I know Kiki is talking about a place and not that thing that's supposedly going to reveal itself in the Final Battle, I still feel as though every last drop of blood in my body has suddenly turned ice cold.

"But Jasmine's twin was taken there for five years," Lily says. "She's still alive, and I've been there before, like I said, so I guess it's not just demons and lost souls down there all the time."

I flash her a warning look. We don't need to share this information about Jade. Especially not with Sara in the room. I'd trust a cockroach before trusting that girl.

Lily presses her lips together; a pink hue spreads across her cheeks. *Sorry*, she mouths silently at me, looking mortified.

Sara snorts. "Then where's your sister at right now? Why aren't we meeting her rather than you, if she's so bleeding special? Or is she still on holiday in your Place-in-Between?"

"She's in Toronto," I reply, my voice clipped. I'm not willing to tell them any more than I have to. It's none of their business, and I'm not 100 percent sure where my sister is. Grabbing a sandwich, I stuff a huge bite of bread and salty brown spread into my mouth so that I can't answer any further questions — for now, anyway.

JADE

A wide smile spreads across Amara's face as soon as her father's face appears on the jumbo-sized monitor hanging above the gas fireplace.

"Hello, my bokkie," Mr. Jakande says, his white teeth gleaming out at us. "Hello, Jamil. And you must be Jade." He nods warmly in my direction.

"Daddy, we're at the safe house," Amara says, sweeping an arm around excitedly in a half-circle as though she's at an amusement park or some equally leisurely place. I notice Mr. Khan's concerned frown return to his face.

Mr. Jakande nods, his dark eyes mirroring Mr. Khan's worry. "We must be quick, because this call will be investigated. I am so glad to see you, my angel. Where is your sister? And why have you sought refuge there?"

"Vivienne is with the others," Amara says brightly. "We got split up in the Place-in-Between. We're going to transition soon to join them."

Mr. Jakande doesn't reply right away. Instead, he glances at Mr. Khan, who firmly shakes his head.

Confusion clouds Mr. Jakande's eyes, but he doesn't miss a beat with Amara. "I love you, my beautiful, brilliant girl. And your mother loves you more than anything as well. Whatever happens from this time forward, you need to remember that you are eternally loved, and therefore, be brave and carry on. Be like Madiba in the face of challenges and hate."

"Yes, Daddy," Amara says, nodding enthusiastically.

"We need to go, Craig," Mr. Khan says, cutting into the conversation. "If you're being monitored, which I agree you must be, the authorities will be kicking down the door here shortly. You're putting yourself in grave danger, as well. I'll take care of Amara as best I can, I promise you that."

Mr. Jakande nods. His eyes are full of sorrow. It's clear he's realized that something very serious has happened to Vivienne. "Thank you, Jamil," he says solemnly. "No matter what happens to me, please know that I am eternally grateful."

"I love you, Dad," Amara says. Her voice sounds more normal now, less like that of a lost little girl.

There's a loud bang from behind Mr. Jakande, and his image flickers for a moment like the rippling of a pond's surface after a rock has skipped across it. He looks away from the camera at something or someone just out of view that we can't see. His face then disappears into blackness as the communication suddenly ends. This seems to be Mr. Khan's cue to act.

"The video watch," he says, nodding to Amara. "We have to dispose of it now. As soon as I'm back inside, we need to try to transition." Taking the video watch from her, he walks to the sliding glass doors that face the ravine. He slides open the translucent door, then turns back to us. "If anything happens, if anyone shows up here before I'm back, transition. Don't hesitate. And don't wait for me."

I open my mouth to protest but then close it again; he's already out the door and heading down the brush-entangled side of the ravine to dispose of the watch.

"Okay," I say to Amara. "Let's prepare. Can you put some images from present-day London on the monitor? That might help us." I don't say anything about how the call to her father just ended. Maybe I don't want to think about what the loud noise was, either.

She nods. "Images of the city of London in 2032, please. Three-dimensional."

I grab her hand. "Don't start to visualize until Mr. Khan is back," I say.

Images float out of the monitor and begin to move around the room. It's a pretty cool app, and one I haven't seen before. But that's not totally unusual. I missed a lot in the five years I was away. Each individual image does a slow, circular dance around us before evaporating. A voice — that of the computer, I assume — starts to speak:

"Tower of London; Millennium Bridge; Royal Observatory, Greenwich; Jeremy Corbyn Park ..."

I stare at the park with its trees and patches of green grass. Though England, like all countries, suffers droughts, it still gets more rainfall than most of the world. The grass in Toronto is yellow and brown so much of the time that I'd almost forgotten its ideal colour is an emerald green.

"I'm getting weird sensations," Amara whispers.

I'm getting that tingling, odd feeling as well. We're starting to transition. The best way to describe it is sort of the way it feels when you're just about to fall asleep. Your body feels heavy and relaxed, but you're still pretty aware of your surroundings.

"Did you already start visualizing?" I ask.

"No," Amara says. "At least, I don't think so. The pull seems more powerful this time, though."

"The Tate Modern; Dalston's Cloud Railway; Borough Market …"

I look out the windows of the carriage house. The sun is going down, and twilight is descending on the ravine. There's no sign of Mr. Khan, though I doubt he went far. Lights flicker on in the room around us, and now all I see is my own reflection. At least we don't need to worry about demons.

"It's happening," Amara says. Fear dominates her voice. I'm not sure if this is better or worse than the happy-go-lucky, kind-of-crazy Amara who's been around most of today.

"We can't go yet," I say, focusing on the windows and trying to maintain our physical link here, hoping to slow down the process of transitioning. "We need to wait for Mr. Khan."

"I can't stop," Amara says, her voice rising. Her panic is palpable. "It's pulling me. And it's so much stronger than before."

She's right. I feel like I'm not fully in the Jakandes' safe house any longer. A floating sensation overtakes me — it's like I'm swimming in a pool of salt water.

Someone grabs my hand and places it in their own.

"The London Eye; the Globe Theatre; Camden Market ..."

The sound of breaking glass fills my ears. Then shouting.

I'm falling ...

JASMINE

The promise of sleep never felt so good. There are three bedrooms in the flat, each with two single beds — the smallest has a set of bunk beds.

Kiki and Susie lead me and Lily to one of the bedrooms with two separate beds. They give us each a bag of essentials: pads, a toothbrush and toothpaste, hemp oil for washing and moisturizing our faces, and a small bar of soap.

"Let us know if you need anything," Susie says. "And sorry again about my sister. She hasn't been right since our dad left. It shattered her. He was her hero."

"That's sad," Lily says, sitting down at the edge of the bed. I hope I don't look as exhausted as her, because she looks terrible. "Where did he go?"

"Was in prison. Assault with intent to do grievous bodily harm," Susie says. She watches Lily's eyes widen with surprise. "Bound to happen," she says with a shrug. "Mum was always having to go and pull him out of the pub at the bottom of our estate to keep him from fighting. One time she was too sick to go, and he didn't come home. The police were his escort that night … straight to the clink."

"Is he still there?" Lily asks.

Susie shakes her head. "We were only nine when he went in. Mum took us every month to see him. When he was paroled, he came home for about two nights, then disappeared. Meant loads of hassle for Mum for about half a year. I think the police suspected she'd helped him do a runner, and they hovered around her like flies on honey. But she didn't have anything to do with it. Cried at least once a day for nearly a year straight, she did. Then he was dead to her. Sara blames Mum for him leaving. But the truth of it is he was just a right twat who drank too much and didn't give a toss about his family."

"That's rough," I say, feeling like I need to respond in some way, though I still have absolutely zero empathy for Sara. No matter what, I won't be developing warm fuzzies toward that girl. I mean, we've all had it tough and lost people. My dad died when I was really young, and then my sister was abducted by a demon, and my mom was deathly ill with lupus for years until Raphael cured her. Just thinking about him makes my chest hurt. And, yes, it's the left side of the chest kind of hurt.

All of us sit in an awkward silence for a few moments.

"I'll be back in a minute," Lily says, grabbing her toiletries. "Where's the washroom again?"

Kiki smiles. "The toilet's down the hall. Second door to your left."

I take off my shoes and jeans. I'm not bothering with my teeth and face tonight. Just pulling back the comforter on the bed exhausts me to the point of collapse.

"Thanks for welcoming us and everything," I say to Susie and Kiki as I lay my head on the pillow. My eyelids feel like they're lined with lead. It takes all my effort just to keep them open.

"We're all Seers. You're one of us. Of course you're welcome. After all, we're all in danger right now. If we don't have each other's backs, we're toast," Kiki says.

I nod. I'm slowly slipping into sleep, images from my subconscious mind mingling with those in my conscious mind.

There's a loud buzzing noise. My eyes fly open.

"That's me," Susie says apologetically as she glances down at her video watch. "It's Vashti." She hits a button, and a small holographic version of Vashti springs from the watch to hover in the air above Susie's wrist.

"Did Jasmine and Lily make it safely?" she asks.

"Yes," Susie says with a wave in my direction. "Jasmine's right over there, in bed. They're hungry and tired, but okay."

The holographic Vashti swivels to look at me. A smile breaks out across her face, but it's fleeting. "Good, good," she says. "Where is Lily?"

"In the loo," Susie replies. "Should be back any minute."

"I can't stay on here long," Vashti replies. "You need to pack up just before dawn tomorrow. Cars will come and meet you out front just before five thirty a.m. You must be ready. And be alert tonight. We have good reason to believe that your location is no longer secure."

Lily walks back into the room. "Vashti!" she says breathlessly. "Where is Cassandra? How is she? Can I see her?"

Vashti holds up her hand, palm forward. "Settle, child," she says. "Second-borns are supposed to have patience. Find yours." Her voice is gentle, though. "Your sister is stable. But she's lost a lot of blood and is in immense pain. We've managed to get her a blood transfusion, and she's on morphine. Tonight will be critical, but I expect her to pull through. She's a fighter. A true first-born."

"And her arm?" Lily asks. "Will it be okay?"

Vashti's face is grim. "It's bad and will require a long recovery. She will stay with a private nurse at one of my family member's homes for the next while. Worst-case scenario, she will lose her arm above the elbow."

"Can I please see her?" Lily asks again.

Vashti shakes her head. "Not at this time. It's not safe. You must all stay together as things progress toward the Final Battle. Cassandra may be well enough to participate, but if not, we'll keep her as safe as possible during that time. Lily, this means that you may not be as powerful as you would've been together, if you are one of the seven Seers in the battle."

"Seven Seers?" Lily asks.

"Seven Seers. Seven Angels. Seven Archons," Vashti says. "We don't know who the Seers involved will be, but seven of you will be directly participating in the battle.

Perhaps seven is the number of Seers that will survive. We're only beginning to learn everything as we collaborate more fully with the CCT."

"Well, that's a cheery way to end the night, isn't it?" I say, propping myself up on the pillow with my right elbow. "Should I do 'Eeny, meeny, miny, moe' to decide which Seers might live to experience another day and which won't?"

"You know, we've been told about your cheek, Jasmine," Vashti says, a wry smile spreading across her face. "And, as such, you're not going to get any reaction from me. Girls, I've got to go. Please be on time and keep a low profile whilst moving. Your very lives may depend on it."

JADE

I'm somewhere dark and damp. The sound of trickling water reaches my ears. It's running close to where I'm lying. The surface I'm on is as hard as rock, and my right arm, which is twisted under my rib cage at an odd angle, hurts. The air around me is damp and slightly chilly. As I gain consciousness, I hear voices around me.

"Who's this lot? And how did they find their way down 'ere?" growls a male voice as rough as sandpaper from somewhere above and to the left of me. "Who's on bloody guard tonight? David? Jermaine? Eh? Who's the wanker that let 'em in 'ere?"

Groaning, I open one eye and then the other. It's shadowy, dark. Large candles burn in rows just a few feet in front of me, black fingers of smoke curling above their flames. I place my palm on the ground. It seems like I'm on a concrete platform of sorts.

Mr. Khan slowly sits up beside me. "Where are we?" he asks.

So he's the one who grabbed my hand during our transitioning. Thank god.

I pry my right arm free and sit up beside him.

"You're in our space, that's where you're at," the man says, spittle flying from his lips. "Lord's Tube station, to be precise. Uninhabited and unused for years — nearly a century, to be precise — until we took it over," he adds, his voice swelling with pride.

I look up at him, my eyes adjusting to the dim light. Though he's thin and wiry, he looks strong. At first glance, I'd say he's somewhere in his late fifties to early sixties, judging from the deep creases in the leathery skin beside his eyes and the folds that run from his nose to his mouth. A hand-rolled cigarette dangles from the corner of his mouth, its ashy tip ready to fall to the ground. His salt-and-pepper hair is shoulder-length and unruly, and it makes me think of a windblown bird's nest. I suspect DIY haircuts and a dearth of shampoo and combs to be the main culprits.

"Ow!" Amara says. "What did you do that for?"

I glance over. She's landed a few feet away from me and Mr. Khan, close to a graffiti-covered wall at the other end of the platform. A group of about five people stand around, peering down at her.

"To see if you was alive," a tall, broad-shouldered man says. His back is to me, so I can't see what he looks like.

"Maybe just talk to me, instead of kicking me like a soccer ball. Or, here's a revolutionary thought. You think I'm dead? Check for a pulse," Amara says with eyes narrowed as she gets to her feet, brushes off her jeans, and starts over toward me and Mr. Khan.

"We don't know if you're armed. If you're one of them," one of the girls snaps. "Mick, you want them just moving around here?"

The older man tosses the remainder of his cigarette to the floor and grinds it under the toe of his boot. "You answer this question fer me, then. How did you get in here?" he says to Mr. Khan.

"To be honest, we're really not sure how we got here," Mr. Khan says to Mick, who's clearly the leader of the group. "And we didn't mean to land here ... in your station."

The group of young men and women that were standing around Amara walk over to where we're standing. Like Mick, it appears to have been a very long time since they've seen the inside of a shower stall or bathtub. Or even a facecloth.

"How do we know you lot are telling us the truth?" asks a girl maybe three or four years older than Amara and me, her eyes narrowing as she regards us with obvious suspicion. She looks at the older man. "Mick, how do we know they ain't lying to us? How do we know *they* haven't sent 'em?"

A grumble of agreement rolls through the group like thunder.

"There's no way this posh lot are going to put a microchip in me," the guy that kicked Amara says. His eyes are wide, and I can hear fear in his voice, even though he's built like a professional football player.

"Are you from MI5?" Mick growls at us. "'Cause if you are, we'll tear you apart, limb by limb, before you get microchips in us."

Mr. Khan puts up both his hands, palms forward. "No, no, no. We're not from MI5. We're not even British. In fact, we're from Toronto … Canada."

"They're taking the piss! They're spies!" the pale girl that spoke before shouts. Her hair hangs to her shoulders, dirty brown and dreadlocked. Leaping forward, she shoves Mr. Khan firmly in the middle of his chest, sending him sprawling backward onto the crumbling cement.

Mr. Khan sits for a moment in shock, then slowly rubs his hands along the upper part of his pants. Bright spots of blood seep onto the surface of the skin of his palms. I hold back the urge to run to him and see if he's okay.

Mick steps forward, his boots crunching bits of gravel and decayed cement. He holds a leathery hand toward Mr. Khan in a gesture of support. An oversized silver skull ring sits on his index finger.

"C'mon, mate," he says, clenching his teeth as he speaks. "Up you get. Let's have a wee bit of an honest chinwag, shall we?" He hoists Mr. Khan to his feet, a bit more roughly than necessary. "You three, keep yer hands where we can see them whilst we talk. Understand?"

The three of us nod in unison. This Mick guy smells rancid — I detect stale cigarette smoke and dirty armpits in the odour wafting off him.

"I'll ask you this once, and once only," he says, his eyes narrowing. The skin beside them crinkles as his face contorts into a sneer. I guess this is his way of trying to look tough.

Mr. Khan and Amara nod again. I stare Mick straight in the eye, my gaze and facial expression unwavering. He might have control over us right now, but I want him to know I'm not happy about it. I notice Amara doing the same. And she's humming again.

"Are you lot sent from MI5 to take us in? To microchip us?"

"Absolutely not," Mr. Khan says. "Like I said, we're from Toronto."

"Microchip you?" Amara laughs. "Why would we microchip you? Are you a dog?"

The girl with the dreads lunges at Amara, holding her curled fist centimeters away from Amara's face. "Give me one reason I shouldn't beat the shite right out of you for disrespecting Mick," she snarls. "And stop your bloody humming whilst you're at it."

Her breath stinks. I can smell it from where I'm standing. Mr. Khan's giving us a death stare. Amara needs to be quiet. And fast.

"Leave the little girl alone, Martha," Mick says, taking a deep drag off his cigarette. "Bring me the reader. Let's see what the identity of this lot is. Enough with the games."

Martha scampers down the subway tunnel into the darkness.

"Our identity?" Mr. Khan repeats. "I don't think a UK reader will be able to do that. We're Canadian. Unless it's an iris scan. Is it an iris scan? I've got identification on my video watch, if you'll just let me —"

Mick raises a finger to his lips. "Shut it," he snaps. "Let's just do this. Enough procrastinating."

Martha re-emerges from the shadows. She holds out a small metallic object about fifteen centimeters long toward Mick. From my vantage point, it looks like a wand.

Mick takes it with a nod and tosses the remains of his cigarette onto the pavement, crushing it with the toe of his boot.

"Hands out," he says to me, spitting each word into my face with such violence, they might as well be daggers laced with poison.

I stick my hands out so quickly toward him that Mick jumps back. That makes me smile — more inwardly than outwardly, of course. Jasmine's not the only one who can be defiant. Second-borns might be patient, but this guy would push even the patience of a saint.

He takes the silver wand, which, at the push of a button, comes to life with a low purr. "Keep still, lassie," he says, his voice deadly serious. He moves the wand up and down the inside of my forearm, just above the skin, so close I can feel pulsing heat emanating from it, but at no point does it actually touch me.

Mick turns off the wand and frowns at me. I raise an eyebrow at him but say nothing.

"You next," he barks at Amara.

She sticks out her arms in compliance, but she's shaking with anger. Her anger is slight, but definitely there. Hopefully I'm the only who notices. I want to tell her not to let this guy get to her, to remind her that we could

take him and his whole crew down in a matter of minutes, even seconds, if we wanted to.

She begins to hum again.

C'mon, Amara, I think. *We're Seers. Don't let this old
piece of gristle get to you.*

The wand does its thing up and down her arm. Same
frown from Mick.

"Everything okay?" I ask, making sure to plaster a
bright smile on my face.

Mick frowns at me, but says nothing. His posse
stands around, watching intently. The air is so thick with
tension, I can almost taste it.

Mr. Khan is next. Same thing. Same annoyed look
on Mick's face. Same feeling of smug satisfaction in me.

"I need to talk to the three of you privately," Mick
barks. "The rest of you, secure all the entrances and
exits. *Now.*"

JASMINE

The alarm on my video watch slices through my dream like a knife. I bolt awake and stare into the darkness, trying to get my bearings. My tongue sticks to the roof of my mouth as though cemented there with peanut butter. I'm dehydrated. Badly.

"Turn it off, Jazz," Lily moans from the other bed. "Please. I can't possibly get up right now."

Everything comes tumbling back to me. I sit up, swing my legs over the side of the bed, and reach around on the floor for my jeans.

"We need to get ready," I say, putting on my jeans and standing up. Using the flashlight function on my video watch, I find the sensor for the bedside light. It flickers on, causing Lily to moan again.

"C'mon, just five more minutes."

I shake my head and lick my dry lips. It's a futile gesture. There's not a spare bit of moisture left in my body.

"Vashti was clear that we can't miss the time for our pickup. This is important," I say, grabbing my toiletries bag and opening the bedroom door. "Judging from what she said, we're likely in danger. I'm going to be back in two, and you need to be up and dressed. Seriously."

The hall is quiet, though I can hear some movement from the other bedrooms. Hearing footsteps behind me, I swing around. It's Atika coming from the living room.

"Sorry, I didn't mean to startle you," she says as she secures a red elastic around the single black braid she's woven her hair into. "My favourite colour," she says, pointing to the elastic with a smile. "It's my warrior colour. To give me bravery when we go into battle as Seers." She tosses the braid behind her shoulder.

I smile back. "I like that idea." I pause. "So, you've had to battle demons here in London?"

Atika nods. "Yeah. I mean, we've only been together as Seers for the last two and a half years or so. Most of us, anyhow. We all ended up at the same comprehensive, despite not being in the proper postcode or even applying to go there."

"Comprehensive?" I ask. I'm not sure if it's fatigue or lack of sleep that's causing me to be so confused, but I almost feel like she's speaking a foreign language.

"I think you call it high school in North America," she says with a wry smile. "Anyhow, it was all very strange at first, and then we found out what was going on. Honestly, I thought I was going absolutely mad, until my sister and I were attacked on our way home one night. Thank goodness Vashti's my Protector. Mine and Fahima's. She's so kind to all of us. I have no prob-lem trusting that she's looking out for our best interests. Initially, though, I suspected she was a complete nutter," Atika says with a sad smile. She pauses, looking down at her feet. "But she's the only reason Fahima and I even had our poles on us when we were first attacked. She saved my life."

"I guess that's why they're called Protectors," I say with a smile. "I get what you're saying. I actually thought I was the one going nuts at first. Same thing happened to me — I was sent to a school that I wasn't supposed to go to — but unlike you, I hated my Protector at first." I'm not about to tell Vashti that Mr. Khan is not my original Protector.

"That's tough. We have to put so much trust in them. Do you like her now?" Atika asks.

"Yep," I say. "In fact, I'm totally sick to death not knowing what's happening to him and my mom and everyone in Toronto."

"I thought you said I had to hurry," Lily interrupts, coming out of the bedroom. She rubs the crusty sleep from her eyes as she shuffles over to where we're stand-ing. "We need to be outside in less than twenty minutes, FYI. I hope that Vashti comes to see us, or at least lets me know how Cassandra is doing."

I notice the dark circles framing Lily's eyes and the way she can barely stifle her yawns long enough to speak to us.

Atika reaches over and places her hand gently on Lily's arm. "Vashti is brilliant. She's my Protector, and I trust her with my life. Cassandra is in good hands, I swear to you."

The door to the third bedroom flies open.

"There are people outside," Susie says, her voice breathless as she and Sara race into the hall.

"What do you mean?" I ask. I want to add that of course there are people outside, we're in London, a city of millions, and people are always out on the street, but decide that I'm better off keeping my mouth shut at this point.

"It's hard to tell, but it looks like four or five blokes. They're standing on the pavement and seem to be looking straight up here. At this flat. At our windows," Susie says. Sara nods.

"That's mad," Atika says, her eyebrows drawing together in a frown. "It's five in the morning. And it's not like anyone ordered a curry."

"Are you saying we're lying?" Sara asks, puffing out her chest like a bulldog.

"For god's sake," Susie says, placing a hand on her hip with exasperation, "pick your battles, Sara."

It's nice to see that Sara pisses off even her twin sister. I can't help but smile.

"It's definitely not good if people see us leaving," Atika says. "I'm going to go and make sure Fahima is up and getting ready. She's in the living room."

"Yeah, we should make sure Kiki and Dani are awake, too," Sara says. She's definitely more subdued since being told off by her sister.

There's a rapid banging on the door to the flat. All five of us stop speaking immediately. A heavy silence descends on the hallway like a fog. After a few moments, I realize I've been holding my breath since the knocking.

"It's *them*," Susie mouths at us.

I shrug my shoulders. After all, *they* could just be a random bunch of drunk guys … but my instincts tell me that we're in danger.

The knocking starts again. It's as sudden and loud as gunshots. Lily visibly jumps at the noise. This time a loud bang follows.

"I think they're breaking the door down," Atika whispers. Her chestnut eyes are wide with fear, and her hand shakes as she tosses her braid behind her right shoulder. "It has to be demons. No human has that strength. Not with that door."

"Red," I whisper back to her. "Remember your elastic. They grow stronger if we're afraid. They feed on fear and anger."

"Well, sod this," Sara says, drawing her thick lips together. "I'm not mucking about, waiting for that lot to break in and kill us. I'm getting my pole and going out there. We have a ride to catch. Jasmine and Lily, you can back us up and grab curtain rods from the bedroom."

The rest of us nod in agreement. As we turn to get our weapons, there's a final, thunderous boom as the door to the apartment finally surrenders and slams open against the wall.

JADE

We follow Mick down the station platform. He motions at us with a sharp wave of his hand as he turns to the right, toward a low archway. There's already another lit cigarette clamped between the index and middle fingers of his right hand. I watch the little red beacon at its tip disappear along with Mick.

I glance up and down the shadowy platform as Mr. Khan and Amara enter the archway. Is it safe for us to just follow this guy? After all, we're in a subway station. That could definitely mean demons, and we don't have a clue where Mick is taking us. By following him into a place with a single entrance/exit, we may be willingly and stupidly getting ourselves into a very dangerous situation.

"Come on, Jade," Amara says, impatiently waving her hand at me. "Hello?"

I realize I've stopped walking. "Two seconds," I say. Looking up and down the platform, I try to scout any alternate exits, in case we need to make a quick getaway.

"Girl, don't make me carry you in here," Amara says. I can tell by her voice that she's only half-joking.

There's no other way out. As I jog back to Amara, I can't help but be more than a bit surprised that Mr. Khan is so casually following this guy. Amara's a first-born, so it's understandable that she's a little less cautious. Yet, it's undeniable that we're safer if we're together — even if we're not as strong as we would be with our sisters.

Amara raises an eyebrow at me as I approach her.

"Sorry," I say, though I'm not at all. As I step under the tiled archway behind her, something flashes in my peripheral vision. It's only for a second, but I could swear a shadowy figure just ran across the tracks toward the side we're on. And, though it sounds crazy, I'm sure it's Seth. My stomach turns uneasily. That nauseous feeling is back. Big time.

"Take a seat," Mick says as we step inside. He points at two empty chairs. We're in a small alcove that's furnished with a couple of lamps and a card table with four chairs. Mick and Mr. Khan are already seated at the table, an opened bottle of Irish whiskey and two glasses between them.

"I really don't drink," Mr. Khan says, as Mick pushes one of the glasses toward him.

"I don't trust a man that doesn't drink or a woman that doesn't wear makeup!" Mick proclaims, picking up his glass and throwing the whiskey back in one gulp. He slams the glass back down on the plastic tabletop with a hammer-like bang. "You're up," he says, wiping the back of his hand across his mouth.

"I don't drink," Mr. Khan repeats, his voice calm. "I'm Muslim. It's haram."

"One of London's best mayors — if not the very best — was Mooslim," Mick says with a wide smile. "Back about ten years ago he finished up. Sadiq Khan. Maybe one of your relatives? Son of a bus driver and cared about us, the regular people. The working class and the poor. Not many of us left in the city any longer, though. Despite his best efforts, London's just the filthy rich and the begging classes now. So at least drink to him, to Khan, because everything went to shite directly after his mayoralty ended." Mick pours himself another as he speaks. "C'mon, mate. Allah won't know. And I won't tell, neither," he says with a wink.

Mr. Khan's eyes widen at Mick's suggestion.

"Give it here," Amara says, reaching across the table with lightning speed to pick up the shot glass. She throws it back in one go like Mick did.

"Looks like the girl has more balls than you," Mick says with a laugh, as Amara clamps her hand across her mouth, eyes bulging.

"You don't know the half of it," Mr. Khan says. I nearly laugh at that. After all, what would Mick say if he knew Amara and I could snap him in half like a twig faster than he could do up the fly on his pants?

"All right, ladies, have a seat, then," Mick says, pulling one the chairs out with the toe of his boot. "You've bloody well earned it."

Mick leans forward on his elbows as we sit down. The stench of the whiskey is now rolled into all the other offensive smells wafting off him. I lean as far back in my chair as possible while still being somewhat discreet.

"Let me get straight to the crux of the matter. None of you has a chip," he says, his eyes dark with concern. "Just like us. How is that possible, if you've been up there for any length of time?"

"Up there?" Amara says. "What do you mean?"

"In London. Above ground. What did you think I meant?" Mick says with a sandpapery laugh. "No more whiskey for you."

"What Mr. Khan said is true. We haven't been in London at all," I say. *At least not in 2032 CE.* But I'm not about to say that to Mick. "We've somehow ended up here from Toronto. I think it might've had something to do with that virtual reality gaming technology we were using. The developer said it was pretty new, didn't he?" I say, staring hard at Amara and Mr. Khan.

"Yeah, yeah, he did," Amara says, nodding a little more enthusiastically than I'd like. "And I pressed London. I wanted to see where Jack the Ripper lived."

We had an brief encounter with the Ripper's lost soul the last time we went to the Place-in-Between.

"The Ripper?" Mick laughs. "Well, you can tell the developer that his game is rubbish. You're sitting under one of the poshest areas of West London — St John's Wood. The Ripper lived in the East End of the city, in Whitechapel." He leans forward again, looking thoughtful. "So you're telling me this game somehow teleported all of you from Canada to here?"

"It's the only explanation that seems feasible," Mr. Khan says, flashing me a look of gratitude. I've got to admit, my story is pretty good, considering I made it up on the fly. At least it seems to have convinced Mick that we're not MI5 agents or whatever crazy idea was floating around inside his unwashed head.

"Where's this game gear now, then? How come you ain't got it on yer 'eads?" he snaps.

Damn.

"I honestly haven't a clue," Mr. Khan says, his voice calm. "May I ask why you and your crew down here aren't microchipped either? I mean, judging by your accents, you're all local."

Mick smiles proudly. "I am. Born and bred in Lewisham and a proud Charlton supporter. Even with the borders closed, we still have the Premier League, we do. The entire lot of us down 'ere aren't chipped. Some of the younger ones were going to be taken to the camps for breaking their ASBOs. And I'm no friend of the police, so I brought them here. One or two were in the UK illegally, as well. We came together and decided that we weren't going to let the filth get a hold of us only to deport us, book us, or worst of all, send us to them camps."

"What camps?" Amara asks, leaning forward on her elbows. "Do you mean refugee camps? Like where they used to hold climate change refugees while they processed their claims?"

"Used to?" Mick laughs bitterly. "Those were inhumane holding cells. Sometimes they'd keep people in there for nearly a decade. Babies grew to be children in those prisons, guilty of nothing other than being birthed in the wrong nation and having the wrong skin colour." He shakes his head. "These camps — the ones the government is running right now — they make those camps from before look like bleedin' Ibiza, they do." He stops speaking just long enough to light another cigarette. "Nothing gets processed in these new camps except death certificates. And it's not just refugees and the like ending up in them. Anyone speaking out against the government, against the chipping and the like — *gone*." Mick snaps his grime-covered thumb against his middle finger. "Faster than you can breathe one, two, three."

"How can you possibly know all of this?" Mr. Khan asks. "You'd have to have been in these camps, or else somehow have a way to glean intimate inside knowledge." He doesn't have to say what the rest of us are thinking: Mick doesn't look like someone who would be let in on sensitive government secrets.

Mick sits back and sucks deeply on his cigarette. "I know a lot more than you'd imagine," he says. His words are deliberate and slow, and he's looking at us like a snake might look at three baby mice. Something in his gaze is cold and calculating. "There might be time for me to share some of my secrets with you," he says, sending a winding trail of smoke into the air above his head. "But we'll have to see what you can give me in exchange for my secrets. Because the way I see it, the three of you just might be my way out of this place."

JASMINE

A loud scream fills the air.

"Fahima!" Atika shouts, her eyes wild with fear. "She's still in the sitting room."

"C'mon, then," Sara says, grasping her pole tightly with her sausage-like fingers and swivelling on the ball of her right foot to run down the carpeted hall, back toward the living room. Atika and Susie follow closely behind her.

I run back into the bedroom and wrench the metal curtain rods off of the two windows, letting the dusty floral curtains slide to the floor in a heap. I toss one to Lily where she stands in the doorway watching me.

She catches it with the fluidity of a cat. "Is this because of us?" she asks, biting her bottom lip nervously. I can't help but notice again how tired and unwell she looks.

"I don't know. Maybe," I say, jumping off the bed. "Doesn't matter now. We just need to get in there to help." Banging sounds and the occasional shout reach us from the living room.

Kiki pokes her head out of one of the bedrooms as we run back into the hall. Her curly black hair frames her head like an angel's halo in a hurricane. "What's going on?" she asks, her eyes half-closed.

"We've had a break-in," I say, not wanting to go into detail about the guys standing outside, staring up at the flat just before all of this happened. "Grab Dani and your poles and make it quick. Everyone's in the living room, confronting them."

Kiki's dark eyes widen. "What? Intruders?" She swivels around. "Dani! Get your bottom out of bed. *Now*."

"You should get your poles," Lily adds.

"Are they demons?" Kiki asks.

"I haven't seen them," I answer. "But it sounds like they're putting up a pretty good fight against three Seers in there, so …"

"Go!" Kiki interrupts. "We'll be right behind you." She disappears back into the bedroom as Lily and I turn and run toward the chaotic noise coming from the living room.

As soon as I kick the door open, it's clear what we're dealing with. A decapitated head sits at our feet — its glassy eyes seem to stare directly up at us. The face looks completely human, but I know the drill. Demons on this plane inhabit the bodies of those who are vulnerable, such as drug addicts. I don't know why. I'm not even sure if the person is dead while they're possessed. One thing I do know for certain: we don't know how to kill the demon besides decapitating the body it's in. So even if the person is still alive when the demon enters them, they're for sure not going to be once a Seer gets done with them. Problematic, to say the least.

I quickly scan the room. There are four demons still alive, and the situation is critical. Susie and Sara seem to be holding their own, but Atika is unarmed and losing her battle against a male demon with spiky, bleached-white hair. It's got her pinned down, holding her wrists above her head, digging its knee into the soft spot at the base of her throat.

"Atika!" I shout, springing forward. Her eyes bulge out like hard-boiled eggs and her face begins to turn purple. She's suffocating.

"Get off her, you bastard," Lily says, coming up beside me. She lifts her pole above her head and brings it down squarely on top of the demon's head like a woodcutter chopping at the remains of a tree.

The demon lets out a howl as its skull splits from the crown of its head to the top of its nose. It swivels around to glare at Lily, blood seeping down its face. With one swift pull, she brings the pole back up and over her head before jumping away.

I take advantage of the fact that the demon's focus is off Atika and pull her toward me by the arm. She's as limp as a ragdoll. For most people, moving an unconscious body that weighs the same as them would be virtually impossible, but because I'm a Seer, it's an almost effortless task. There's a loud popping sound from her arm, and I realize I've likely caused a dislocation. More worrying, though, is the fact that Atika doesn't respond at all to the injury.

The demon lunges toward Lily, but the large crack in its skull seems to be impacting its balance; it misses her completely as she jumps backward again. As soon as her feet hit the carpet, she moves her right foot forward and draws the pole back like a pro baseball player about to hit a home run. There's a crunching sound and then the splattering of blood as the curtain rod tears through the demon's jugular vein and neck. Its head drops to the carpet with a thud.

Lily wipes bits of grey matter and blood off her face and looks around the room. I follow her gaze. Susie and Sara are standing over the decapitated corpses of three other demons. Sweat rolls down their reddened faces.

"We need to get out of here," Sara says, wiping away her damp hair. She looks at Atika. "Is she still alive?"

I crouch down beside Atika. Her injured arm juts out from the shoulder joint at an uncomfortable-looking angle. Her face is pale. Taking a deep breath, I carefully place the index and middle fingers of my right hand against the side of her throat.

There's a pulse. It's faint and seems a bit irregular, but it's there.

"She's pretty badly injured, but she's still alive," I say, standing up. "Where's Fahima?"

Susie shrugs, her face concerned. "We don't know. She wasn't here when we entered the room."

"Bloody hell," Kiki says from behind us. "I guess Vashti was right. We *have* been found out."

"Okay, we've got to go," I say. "Sara, can you help me take Atika?"

Sara nods. "She's going to need a doctor, yeah?"

"Yeah," I reply. "Vashti can help us with that once we get to the new safe house, right?"

We kneel down on either side of Atika and quickly hoist her up, sharing the weight between us. I'm on her injured side, and try to be as careful as possible.

"Vashti will help us for sure," Susie answers. "Are you two going to be all right getting her down the stairs?"

Sara and I nod. I'm glad now that Sara is built like a bull, because the narrow staircase will be tricky to navigate down while carrying the dead weight of Atika. She still hasn't stirred at all, and that's starting to really worry me.

"We'll go ahead," Dani says, as she and Kiki step in front of us, holding their poles up, ready to attack.

Moments after we step outside the flat, the light in the hallway flickers like a firefly before going out completely.

"Bugger," Kiki says. "Looks like the rolling black-outs have started. Brilliant timing." She and Dani turn on their video watch flashlights and train them on the staircase.

The shadowy figure standing on the landing shocks all of us. Sara and I nearly drop Atika, we're so startled. As Seers, we should've been much more careful leaving the flat.

"Follow me, and keep your profile as low as possible. We can't have you noticed as we leave. They're onto all of you, and we still don't have the safe zone secured," Raphael says.

JADE

"I'm not sure what you're getting at," Mr. Khan says, keeping his voice level and his face neutral. He stares at Mick. Hard.

"You got here because of some sort of virtual reality game, yeah?" Mick says, sarcasm coating his voice. It's clear he doesn't believe us.

"Yep," Amara says, leaning her elbows on the table, mirroring Mick's aggressive stance. "What about it?"

Mick raises an eyebrow at her. "You're a real live wire, aren't you?"

"Would you say that to me I were a boy? If I were white?" Amara snaps, her dark eyes flashing angrily. "Doubt it. So, what exactly do you want from us?"

I know Amara's read his mind. And now she's on him like a pitbull on a dog abuser.

Mick's laughter punctures the air. "I want you to figure out how we can get back to where you came from. Canada. The United States. Where-bloody-ever other than here. That virtual reality device must be around somewhere, if you came here with it. It must be near where you landed, yeah?"

I stare at him. Everything about Mick is kind of ashy: his skin, his breath, the colour of his hair.

"I guess we can go back out on the platform to look for it," I say, trying to ignore Amara and Mr. Khan's raised eyebrows and concerned glances. "If you think it's secure down here, we can split up to look." I pause. "But what if we don't find it? I mean, our transition here was pretty bumpy. You saw how far apart from each other we landed."

"You saying you don't think this virtual reality contraption is 'ere with you?" Mick says, eyeing me suspiciously. "Where'd it go, then?"

I shrug. "I'm not saying that it's for sure not down here," I reply, taking my time and weighing my answer carefully. This conversation makes me feel like a bleeding seal in a shark tank. One wrong move, and I'm a goner. "It's just that we can't know for sure. Not until we look for it, anyhow."

Mick raises an eyebrow at me. I don't need to reach into his thoughts to know that he is doubting us — in a huge way. But I enter his thoughts anyway.

And I'm immediately glad I did, because Mick is not going to let us out of here alive if we don't help him leave. And that's because Mick is one of the most wanted persons in the UK. I mean, he's wanted big time. He knows what happens in the camps because he was once a parliamentary minister. Nearly impossible to believe, listening to and looking at him now. His accent and his story are fictional, a way for him to connect with the band of marginalized kids he's got down here with him — his own little army of troubled, angry South and East London youth.

Mick assassinated the minister of foreign affairs, who, along with the prime minister, was the mastermind of the new camps when the government started to hide these plans from the public. Mick had hoped it might stop the nightmarish camps from being created — it was a long shot. The high-profile assassination was pinned on a climate change refugee who'd come to the UK from Syria a few years previously, before the borders were closed. Still, Mick went underground, knowing that Her Majesty's secret service would be gunning to make him the victim of a quiet "accident." And he's highly aware that if he ever emerges from his underground sanctuary, he'll be apprehended immediately. He has no identification chip, but his identity is well-known, nonetheless.

I look over at Mr. Khan and Amara. Obviously, since there is no virtual reality machine, we need to think fast. Mick doesn't actually believe our story, and he's a lot smarter than we first thought. I'm not sure if he's just playing a game with us now, or what. The thing is, I highly doubt he'll give the three of us a moment alone to talk, so we won't get the chance to make a plan.

Amara raises an eyebrow at me and nods. She's read his thoughts as well. It's clear that at least one of us has to get out of here alive, even if that means the other — along with Mr. Khan — is left behind to face the consequences.

Amara's thoughts come to me. She wants me to make it out since Jasmine is still alive, even though part of her will never forgive me for taking the ring and, in her mind, causing Vivienne's death. She knows that two twin Seers together are much stronger than one whose twin has passed and who is, therefore, missing half her soul.

I shake my head quickly at her. I'm not going to willingly save myself and sacrifice her. Ideally, we'll find some way to get all three of us out of here. I feel my pocket for the ring. If something happens to me, Amara and Mr. Khan will need it. We can't chance its falling into the wrong hands.

"All right," Mick says, drawing each word out slowly. "I'll get one of mine to go with each of you." He stands up. "I'm only giving you twenty minutes, and then I want us all back here. If you haven't located it by then, we'll need to have a right chinwag."

We follow Mick back out to the platform. He sticks two fingers between his lips (which makes me want to vomit due to the dirt that's deeply embedded under his nails) and lets out three loud, fast whistles.

The guys and girls that were standing around Amara earlier assemble in front of us within two minutes. They emerge from various places in the station above us and farther down the tunnel.

"Simon, you go with the man," Mick says, nodding toward a red-headed guy who is built like the front of a train. I stare at him. He's got to be at least six four, his face is marked with freckles, and a long, thin scar runs the length of the left side of his face. The scar is raised

154

and the tissue is light pink, making it look a lot like one of the worms that used to crawl out onto the sidewalks when there was rain. It's been a long time since I've seen that happen, though. Those memories are amongst my earliest, from long before the droughts.

"Jerome, you're with the live wire here," Mick says, nodding toward Amara. She's humming softly again, and it takes a moment for Mick's words to register. As soon as they do, Amara narrows her eyes at him, but says nothing.

"I guess he's keeping us black folk together," she says to Jerome as he walks over to her. She gets no reply. Mick seems to have his group tightly controlled.

Martha's assigned to me. I should maybe be insulted. Mick seems to have gone by my small size and quiet nature. His mistake. For once, I'm glad that I'm short and skinny. I could take Martha down with my pinkie finger. We're not supposed to use our Seer force on ordinary humans, but this is no ordinary situation. Amara could easily take on Jerome, but she'd have to be a lot more aggressive, which would increase the chance of seriously injuring him. And that's something we're strictly forbidden from doing on purpose.

"All of you, meet me back in my office within twenty minutes," Mick says, scanning us. "And you'd best hope you have that machine with you."

JASMINE

"What the hell?" I say, making sure to keep Atika's weight steady on my shoulder. "How did you get away from the police?"

"That's not for you to worry about right now, Jazz," Raphael answers, his voice low. "You're all in extreme danger. Between the legion of demons heading here right now and the lost souls that are trying to merge with this world by inhabiting corpses in various states of decay, the situation is critical. A state of emergency is bound to be called. There are two cars waiting around the corner on the high street. We need to leave here immediately."

"But we don't know where Fahima is," Susie interjects, as Kiki and Dani follow Raphael down the stairs. "We can't just leave. What if she's still somewhere in the flat?"

Raphael pauses. He briefly glances back at Susie, his face grim. "She's definitely not in the flat," he says.

It doesn't take long for us to find out how Raphael knows this. As soon as we step outside the front door of the building, we discover the reason for her disappearance.

Her crumpled body is lying almost directly under the living room window. In the shadowy dawn light, I can just make out the shape of her body, her long dark hair spilling out over the sidewalk like water, the strange ninety-degree angle of her obviously broken neck. I'm glad Atika can't witness this. A halo of dark blood has spread out from Fahima's head. Thankfully, she's face down against the sidewalk.

Did she jump? Or did one of the demonic creatures toss her out like a rag doll?

I look away, tears filling my eyes. No one should have to die like this. And certainly no Seer.

I can't help feeling like this is somehow my fault. Just like I feel the deaths of Vivienne and Penelope (the little girl in the climate change refugee camp) were also preventable. And I have no idea if Cassandra is even alive right now. It brings back the intense guilt I felt for all those years after Jade was abducted and believed to be dead.

"Bloody hell," Kiki says softly, putting a hand over her mouth. Her dark eyes are wide with shock and sorrow.

"Jesus, poor Fahima," Susie says, tears rolling down her cheeks. "We should've gotten to her sooner … as soon as the knocking started. We should've been more defensive — the way we're trained to be."

She's right.

I also can't help but think that if I'm the Chosen One, and I'm here now in London, why don't *they* — that is, whoever is behind all of this, whoever is planning this Final Battle, this Darkness dude or whatever — why doesn't he or it just show up? I mean, why leave such a heartbreaking trail of bodies before this confrontation actually happens?

"Where are you taking us?" I snap at Raphael, trying not to make eye contact with him. I don't want to get those butterfly feelings. I'm the Chosen One, and it's about time I begin to step up. And that means not wasting time worrying about some crush. Especially some weirdo angel crush. I mean, that isn't even normal. "Are you planning on sticking around this time? Or are you just going to leave when we need you the most? Because as a guardian angel, you are a massive fail."

"Brilliant," Sara mutters over Atika's body. "You're a nutter on top of it all."

I glare back at her.

"This is not the time, Jazz," Raphael replies. "Your emotions are going to draw the demons here like moths to a flame. But you know that already, don't you?" He pauses. "Let me tell you, there's a lot more to this than you could ever imagine. There are people close to you, closer than you could fathom, who have the power to destroy you. To destroy everything."

"Thanks for vomiting your sunshine and positivity all around here," I reply, not meeting his gaze.

"I really think we have more important things to do at the moment than listen to you two row," Susie breaks in, her voice ripe with irritation. She looks at Raphael. "I don't know you, but I'm going trust you, only because

Vashti and Clarence sent you around with the cars. And I trust them with my life. Now let's get out of here." She takes one last, lingering look at Fahima's crumpled body. "We're sure she's dead?"

Raphael nods. "I checked before going in." He glances toward me. "It was too late for me to help her."

"Oh, okay," I answer, trying to keep my voice as emotionless as possible. I'm pretty embarrassed about Susie having to take charge, and I vow to keep my mouth shut a lot more around Raphael. The last thing I needed to do was ask him out loud why he didn't heal Fahima. At least he's saved me from looking completely crazy in front of our newfound Seer friends.

Soft fingers of pink light reach across the partially clouded sky. The temperature is already warm and humid. Very different than the damp, rainy climate we've experienced in the Place-in-Between.

Thought it's getting lighter, shadows still linger inside the park across the street. We're trying to walk as fast as we can. The light will make the demons less likely to attack us, but it will also make us a lot more vulnerable to being spotted by police and drone patrols as the city slowly comes to life. We'll be sticking out like a sore thumb already with Atika's unconscious body draped between Sara and me.

"There will likely be a few people out and about on the high street," Raphael says, stopping near the doorway of an expensive-looking clothing store. "Wanting to get their errands done as soon as curfew breaks and before it gets too hot."

Due to regulations, stores in Toronto carry mainly recycled clothes, but there's still a pretty big divide between those that carry regular clothing and the ones with designer stuff. I assume it's the same in London. If so, this store definitely looks like it's got the designer goods market covered.

"I think Sara and Jazz — I mean, Jasmine — should stay here with Atika whilst we get to the cars. Then I can reroute us over here to pick you up. We just can't go out there with Atika and expect not to be spotted." Worry crosses his face. "In fact, because of all the cameras in this city, we've likely already set off a cascade of security alerts."

"Not exactly a plan I love," Sara says. "But I get where you're coming from. Just hurry, though, yeah?"

Susie rushes over and gives her sister a huge kiss on one of her pimple-covered cheeks. "Stay safe. We'll be back super fast," she says as she turns to follow Raphael and the others around the corner.

An uncomfortable silence descends between Sara and me. Atika is beginning to feel like a gigantic sack of potatoes. My shoulder is aching from her weight.

"Can we put her down for a few seconds?" I ask Sara. "My arm and shoulder are killing me."

"Fine by me," Sara says. "Though I reckon they won't be long."

We gently place Atika onto the sidewalk. Sara straightens up and stares hard at the corner the others disappeared around. She looks worried.

Despite it being early in the morning, the air is already warm and humid enough that sweat breaks out on my forehead and trickles down my back. I squat down beside Atika and hold three fingers gently against the side of her throat. There is still a pulse, but it's very weak and fluttery. I press my lips together and join Sara in watching the high street.

"Is she alive?" Sara asks. For the first time since meeting her, I hear some softness, a tenderness creeping into her voice.

"Barely," I answer. Tears well up in my eyes. Maybe it's better if Atika doesn't wake up. That way she won't feel the pain of losing Fahima. That way they can be together, and their soul won't be fractured. I stand up and clear my throat. "I'm no doctor, but I don't think she's going to be with us much longer if we don't get her to a hospital or someone who can help."

"Balls," Sara says, turning away from me. She's silent for a few moments, but I can see her discreetly wiping the tears that've trickled from her eyes before facing me again. "So you know that bloke that's showed up? If he's from here, how do you know each other? You were taking the piss when he said he was an angel, yeah?" She tries to reach into my thoughts during this mini interrogation. Doing this, Seer-to-Seer, without permission is a bit like going through someone's things when you've been invited to stay at their house overnight. Not cool.

"Don't do that," I warn. "It's a long story. If I promise to tell you when the time is right, will you leave it alone for now? I mean, we have much bigger things to worry about."

"Like how no one's come back to get us?" Sara asks.

JADE

Martha and I walk into the tunnel, away from the others. We're using the flashlight of her video watch on full, which helps illuminate our way.

"How do you recharge your watch?" I ask. "I mean, how do you do it, if you're in here, underground all the time?" Video watches are solar-powered.

Martha glances sideways at me. Her skin is so pale it's almost translucent. For some reason, she reminds me of a fish. Maybe it's the googly, perpetually surprised look in her bulgy eyes. She raises an eyebrow at me as she brushes a dusty-looking dread away from her cheek.

"How do I know I can trust you?" she says, her blue eyes narrowing. "How do I know you're not here to spy on us?"

"Come on," I say. "Do you really think a big British spy agency is going to have a short, skinny little thing like me working for them? Do I look even remotely dangerous?" I flash her a self-deprecating smile. Of course,

I could snap Martha's neck like a dried wishbone faster than she can blink, but she doesn't need to know that. At least not yet.

She continues to watch me. I reach into her thoughts. I've convinced her that I'm not a spy of any sort, but am a bit surprised by the negative energy that comes at me next.

How can she not be chipped? Her family have likely been on the dole forever. Bloody Pikey. Shite fake accent as well.

It's hard, but I keep my face as neutral as possible and wait for Martha to answer my question.

"We're not down here all the time," she says. "We have shifts."

She pauses, afraid that she's revealed too much. She's deathly afraid of Mick.

"Shifts?" I ask, trying to sound as genuine as possible.

Martha raises an eyebrow at me. "We go above ground, usually at night, in shifts. Mick's done a schedule for all of us. There's this abandoned hotel above us. As long as we're careful and don't get caught up in the police sweeps for squatters or in any security alerts, we can recharge batteries, gather food and water supplies and anything else we need. We might stay up half a day, give or take. And as long as we're careful and only interact with trusted allies, it's okay by Mick. He knows loads of people. People with connections that can get us stuff."

We're deep into the tunnel now. Darkness closes in around us like a fist. My stomach is doing its nauseating dance again. Good to know about the hotel.

"I don't know if we'll find the machine here," I say. It's actually getting a bit damp this far into the tunnel, which reminds me of the Place-in-Between. Anxiety grips my chest and a sudden, powerful wave of dizziness hits me so hard, I almost have to sit down.

Martha turns to me. "You all right?" she asks.

For a second I fall for the fake concern in her voice and drop my guard. It's only for a moment, but that's long enough for Martha to wrap her arm around my neck with the ferocity of a boa constrictor. With her free hand, she slips the cold blade of a knife under my chin.

"One move and I'll slice you like an apple," she hisses, her breath hard against my ear.

"What the hell?" I ask. "Why are you doing this?"

But I really don't need to ask, because her thoughts rush at me. She wants out of here. She hates Mick and the others, and she really believes in this machine and my ability to find it. And when I do, she wants to be the one — the only one — who uses it to get her skinny ass to Toronto. Both her extreme hatred and her unstable mindset are crystal clear to me. Her thoughts pulsate with a manic, dark energy. They feel like bony spiders scrabbling around the inside of my skull. Martha is one sick puppy.

So now I have a couple of choices to make. I can try to get the knife away from her without getting my jugular severed in the process (seems unlikely), I can go along with her plan until she either realizes the story about the machine is completely fictional or gets so impatient that she tries to kill me and I have to take her out for self-defence, or I can kill her right now with one or two strong donkey kicks to her pelvic area and abdomen.

As Seers, we're never supposed to kill other human beings, not even in self-defence, unless there's absolutely no way to immobilize them. If I'm fast enough, I might be able to snap Martha's wrist in two before she can slit my throat. If —

Martha's arm suddenly loosens from around my neck, and the knife drops from her hand, grazing the sensitive skin of my neck as it falls. Her body drops onto the concrete behind me with a thud.

I twist around, fists up in front of my face, ready to defend myself.

"It's okay, Jade. It's me."

My hands slowly slip to my sides. It's hard to believe it's really him, but that flaming shock of red hair, the bridge of freckles across his nose and cheeks, and that all-knowing, hypnotic gaze could belong to only one person: Seth.

I open my mouth to speak, then immediately close it again.

Seth steps toward me. "Jade," he whispers.

I glance down at Martha. It's difficult to see her body clearly, but Seth's video watch throws enough light for me to at least see what's happened. Her right temple is caved in like a month-old jack-o'-lantern. Her eyes bulge from the delicate skin around their sockets, and her mouth is frozen open, as if she's still in the middle of a silent scream.

Dead. Clearly, her death was instantaneous.

I raise an eyebrow at Seth. "Bit extreme, don't you think?" I murmur. Somewhere in the back of my mind is this faint feeling that I should be upset — outraged, really — by the fact that Martha's been murdered in such a cold-blooded way. And yet, I feel numb. Her corpse means little more to me than a crumpled paper bag.

After all, Martha was holding a knife to my neck. With the intent to kill me ...

"She was going to kill you, Jade," Seth answers, as though reading my mind. "But you knew that. Didn't you?" He takes a step forward. Every cell in my body is drawn toward him. His scent is all around — it is the smell of cloves, of frankincense, of ancient pharaohs' tombs ...

My stomach lurches violently. It sounds crazy, but it almost feels like something is in there ... something that does not belong to me. Not fully, anyhow.

"I couldn't let anything happen to you, Jade," Seth says. He's closer now, so close I can feel the warmth of his breath on my skin. "And it was so justified."

Every cell in my body wants to connect with him, despite my memory of what happened the day of our picnic in Corktown Common. I've never felt so out of control in my life.

Except maybe during my time in the Place-in-Between ...

"We need you, Jade. You're the one who holds the fate of the human race ... of the entire planet, in fact." He glances down at Martha's body. If he feels anything about her death or about killing her, it definitely doesn't

show in his face. "She was going to kill you. We couldn't
— I couldn't possibly let that happen to you."

Each freckle on his face dances out at me. His eyes
lock on mine.

"How can I save the planet?" I whisper. "We've passed
the tipping point with climate change, and the barrier
between here and the Place-in-Between has collapsed. I
don't see what I could possibly do to reverse all of that."

Seth smiles. His teeth, impossibly straight and im-
peccably white, shine out at me. For a moment, I nearly
ask him how he got here — meaning both London and
the Place-in-Between, during our last visit. I open my
mouth, but Seth interjects before I can get a word out.

"Jade, you have no idea of the power you carry inside
you."

"As a Seer?" I ask, raising an eyebrow at him. "They
teach us all about it at Beaconsfield, actually."

"Yes, there are your powers as a Seer, but there's so
much more. More than you could ever imagine." He
stops speaking and glances down the tunnel, his ginger
brows drawing together in an expression of concern.
"The others will be heading back soon. Mick will lose
his already fragile hold on sanity when he discovers
there is no virtual reality machine that will allow him to
escape London."

"What can we do? Short of slaughtering the entire
group of them completely, how do we get out of here?"

A slow smile spreads across Seth's face at my suggestion. To my surprise, a jolt of excitement jars
my stomach. I recoil, more disturbed by the fact that

my body has reacted positively to the suggestion of such crazy violence than anything else.

"I wasn't being serious. You know that, right?" I say, my voice shaking.

"Of course," Seth answers, taking another step forward. We're now just centimetres apart, so close that I'm sure he can hear my heartbeat. Somehow, I'm certain he knows that the thought of murdering everyone momentarily excited me.

"And there's Mr. Khan and Amara to think about," I say. My voice is now barely a whisper. "I can't possibly leave without them. Mick will kill them."

Seth smiles again. It's really more of a smirk than a smile. The corners of his mouth tug upward, and his eyes sparkle with a gleeful cruelty.

"Oh, Jade," he says. "I think you know you can leave without them ... and that you will."

JASMINE

Atika's dead. One more name to add to the growing list of casualties in this war. Sara gently places the index and middle fingers of her right hand over Atika's pale lips.

"Rest in peace, mate," Sara says, her voice wavering. She straightens up and squints into the sunlight, eyes narrowed. "At least they're together. And hopefully at peace."

I nod. "It's like you read my thoughts," I reply, crouching down beside Atika's body. "Inshallah, fellow warrior."

"She should be buried within twenty-four hours," Sara says. "If the world was at all normal and not the effed-up piece of shite it actually is, we'd be able to get that done for her." She turns to me. "I'm gonna be straight-up with you — I still don't trust you, mate. But it seems I'm stuck with you. For now."

Before I have a chance to reply, a door swings open a few houses down, and a middle-aged woman with a rat's nest of curly orange hair steps onto the sidewalk. Despite the early hour, she's already got an anti-pollution mask over her mouth and nose. Her doughy, alabaster skin crinkles like tissue paper at the mask's edge, where her cheeks and the fabric meet.

I sit down beside Atika and quickly prop her into a sitting position against the brick wall behind us. Her mouth drops open at an awkward angle, making her look like she's had a stroke or something.

The woman turns to us. "You all right?" she asks, her voice muffled.

No, no, we're not okay. For starters, I'm sitting beside a dead girl, and not just an ordinary dead girl, but a Seer who had special powers. And I'm one, too. We can fight and kill demons, but it's a two-way street; they can destroy us, too. And that's why I'm sitting with a corpse.

"Too much to drink," I say with what I hope is a casual shrug and a wry smile. I'm glad that Atika didn't have time to put on her hijab before the demons attacked. Otherwise, my drunken stupor story might have fallen flat. I feel bad about it, knowing how disrespectful it is to Atika's religious beliefs, but I don't know of anything else that might make this woman leave us alone. If I say Atika's fainted or is really ill, the woman might insist on calling an ambulance and staying with us. I'm hoping this way, she might not be as eager to get involved.

"She threw up a bunch of times and then passed out," I say, wrinkling my nose and sticking out my tongue to express just how gross Atika's fictional vomiting was.

"So now we're getting her home before her mother kills her — and us — for being out all night."

Sara's head swivels toward me at the same time that the woman's eyebrows shoot up in surprise.

"*All night?* You mean you missed curfew?" the woman asks.

Damn. What was I thinking? Of course London has a curfew. Every major city does.

I open my mouth to speak, but the woman is already talking into her video watch. "Yes, I'd like the hotline for anti-social behaviour."

"You bleeding rat," Sara hisses. She turns and runs at the woman, giving her a violent two-handed shove to the chest.

A high-pitched, pig-like squeal of surprise and indignation escapes from the woman as she tumbles backward, arms spinning like a wind turbine.

"Run!" Sara says, grabbing my hand and yanking me to my feet.

I pause for a moment, looking down at the sidewalk. A fat, greenish-black fly buzzes around Atika's cheek before landing on and crawling along her blue-tinged lips.

"She's dead, Jasmine. There's nothing we can do. But you'll be joining her if you don't move yer arse and come with me right now," Sara says. She turns on her heel and breaks into a run in the direction that Raphael and the others went.

For a moment, I feel frozen. This is too much. Too much death. It all started with Dad, and now there's a pile of corpses … and it's all my fault. I don't even know if Mom is alive. Tears well up in my eyes.

The sound of screaming from somewhere ahead of us cuts through the already smoggy morning air. Sara's running toward the sound.

"Wait!" I yell at her, though I know she won't. She's worried Susie and the others might be in danger.

"You little bitch," the woman says from where she's fallen on her bum, legs splayed, on the sidewalk. She spits each word at me. Her mask hangs sideways, revealing thin lips coated in crimson lipstick. Two streams of sweat trickle down her face from each temple, and an audible crackling sound emanates from her chest every time she takes a breath. She stares up at me, her eyes bulging like two overboiled eggs. "You think I don't recognize you from the news clips? You're one of the terrorists. One of those climate change terrorists from Toronto. You think I'm going to let you poison us? Poison brave Londoners who —"

I cover my ears to block out the woman's words and run after Sara.

We see them as soon as we turn onto the high street.

Zombies.

Lost souls.

Whatever they are, they're the same sort of creature that attacked Cassandra. Same vacant stare, same low moaning and grunting sounds. And right now, directly in front of us and in the middle of a busy London street, about five of them are feasting in the bright morning sunshine.

"What the bloody hell?" Sara says, her voice low as she watches one of the zombies, a blood-splattered anti-pollution mask hanging askew from its mouth, pull a handful of flesh from the abdomen of a dead police officer. It begins methodically chewing on the flesh. A taser lies just out of reach of the dead officer's stiffening fingers. "Those aren't demons. Are they?" Her eyes widen as the zombie pulls a loop of steaming intestine out of the officer's shattered abdomen as though it were spaghetti. "I think I'm going to puke."

I grab her and pull her into the closest doorway. We press ourselves up against the door, trying to keep out of sight.

"Those definitely aren't demons," I say in quiet agreement. "Vashti said they were zombies. Apparently they're lost souls that are now here because of our world colliding with the Place-in-Between. They're taking over the bodies of the dead. Like demons, except they're only interested in one thing, and it's not hunting Seers."

"And that would be?" Sara asks, peering out at the demon that is still munching on the officer's guts like it's working through a bowl of popcorn.

"Eating the flesh of the living," I reply.

JADE

Thanks to Seth, everything's clear now. As I step quietly around the body of an elderly man who's sleeping on the ground, mouth open, a shiny line of spittle leaking from one corner of his thin, cracked lips, I pause to check a map of London on the video watch he gave me.

The man gasps for air for a moment, his chest collapsing like a century-old accordion. I freeze and wait to see if he'll wake up.

His breathing returns to a shallow snore, and I breathe out slowly with relief. He's not waking up. That's a very good thing, because I would've had to kill him otherwise.

Not that I'd want to, of course.

Or at least, I don't think I'd want to …

Gritting my teeth, I turn a corner from the hall and move stealthily along the wall of the hotel foyer, toward one of the front windows. The space is large and full of inky shadows that are hard to decipher. There's an empty reception desk to the left of me. The darkness is broken only by faint beams of early morning sun peeking through the gaps between the heavy curtains on the bay windows and coming through a skylight in the middle of the foyer.

With Seth's guidance, I made it out of the abandoned Tube station through an exit that Mick's crew apparently uses to come above ground, and from there, I entered this hotel (also abandoned, aside from a handful of squatters) to survey the outside surroundings before heading to my destination.

Keeping an eye on the shadows to ensure that none of them move, I slide up to the window and carefully pull back the heavy velvet curtain just enough to peek out.

Patting my pocket, I look outside. The ring is still there, digging ever so slightly into the flesh of my hip.

There's a road in front of the hotel that's dotted by the occasional vehicle, and beyond that, a park. Likely once lush and green, the park is now a yellowing mass of high grasses, spindly trees, and brush. At this early hour, and from this distance, it doesn't look like there are many people in it. In fact, I spot only one person walking a dog. From the way the man or woman — it's impossible to identify their gender from this far away — is stumbling slowly along, I take a guess that it's an elderly person.

A hazy film is already unfolding along the skyline behind the park. It's hard to believe, but it looks denser and dirtier than Toronto's smog. And our air pollution kills dozens, sometimes hundreds of people a day. I long for a blue sky rather than the yellow brown that is the norm.

The curtain I'm holding on to is dusty. I sneeze explosively. At the same time, there's a loud bang, like the sound a heavy box dropped from chest height might make.

I freeze and listen for any further noise. Complete silence. But I know I heard it. The sound came from somewhere behind me, near where the sleeping man is. Or was.

Time to get going. I'm not thrilled about travelling around the city in broad daylight; I'll try to make as much of the journey as I can by foot, as Seth told me that's the best way to avoid random microchip scans, since they are routinely done by the London Transport Police. Once I'm with Jasmine and the others, things will get more dangerous, of course. At least the ring will give us some semblance of safety.

A series of snapping sounds, followed by a gurgling not unlike the noise of a plunger violently sucking at a clogged sink, echoes from behind me. Cold fingers of dread reach into my bladder. These new sounds are coming from the same place the loud bang sounded a few moments ago.

Though I'd like to bolt out of the hotel, I need to investigate. Better to battle something in here than out on the street, where I'd draw attention to myself. And better to know sooner if I've been detected or am being followed. At best, it's nothing more than a fox or some other large animal scavenging. At worst, it's one of Mick's crew or a demon. A demon would actually be better, as I'm still able to control them with the ring. Anyone from Mick's crew? Well, I'd have to kill them.

I creep back toward the spot where I left the elderly man sleeping. Even before I get to the corner to turn in to the hall, I can hear it: the crunch of large twigs under heavy boots accompanied by the guttural, wet sound of someone slurping a bowl of noodles. And then the pungent, coppery smell of fresh blood mixed with rotting garbage hits me like a slap. I reel backward, covering my mouth and nose to keep from vomiting. It's got to be a demon or demons … but these must be the loudest, most foul-smelling demons ever. I move forward a step or two and peer around the corner.

A creature is gnawing at the old man's bony upper arm like it's at an all-you-can-eat feast. I'm pretty sure that it's not entirely demonic. At least, it's not the type of demon I've encountered here and in the Place-in-Between. Demons generally wound to kill — at least that's what they do to Seers — or they drink blood and inhabit bodies. As far as I know, human bodies aren't as tasty as fried chicken to them. I look over at the creature again. It's so busy tearing and gulping down bloody clumps of geriatric flesh, it doesn't even notice me.

Well, whatever it is, I'm going to make sure I'm not its dessert.

I begin to slowly walk backward. I don't want to take my eyes off of it, but I can't bear to continue watching the grisly feast. My stomach is taking that all-too-familiar rollercoaster ride again, and I can feel vomit — hot and acidic — making its way up my throat.

The back of my heel hits down against something that skitters away across the tiled floor, causing me to lose my balance. It might've been a pen or some other fairly small, hard object, but whatever it was, it sends me pinwheeling into the wall with a thump.

I steady myself, hold my breath, and listen.

Silence. The creature has stopped chewing the old man's body. Is that because it heard me? I've got no pole, and nothing close by that I can use as a substitute.

I turn my head. One of the curtain rods hanging over the large bay windows at the far end of the foyer might work. If the rod is really heavy, fighting the creature off will be more cumbersome, but still, not impossible.

The smell of blood sweeps over me like a veil. I swivel my head back around. The creature is now standing less than an arm's length away from me, its vacant, cataract-covered eyes staring right into mine.

JASMINE

"Jesus," Sara says, shaking her head. Strands of hair stick to the sweat on her cheeks, which she absently wipes away as she speaks. "You're not taking the piss, are you? This just keeps getting better and better. Where the feck are the others?" She presses her lips together, her eyes darkening at the cannibalism unfolding in front of us. "You don't think the zombies got them, do you?"

I shake my head. "The good thing — if there can possibly be a good thing about any of this — is that these zombies seem much easier to kill. They don't have the speed or the strength of demons," I say. "And I really don't think the zombies —"

Before I can finish my thought, two white cars come tearing around the corner from behind us. The passenger window of the first car slides down. Lily sticks her head out, her black hair gleaming in the sun.

"Get in!" she shouts, her eyes wild as she glances over at two of the zombies that have gotten to their feet and are awkwardly shuffling toward the car.

The back door closest to us slides open, and Sara and I dash for it. I leap in first, sliding across the cool interior like a baseball player heading for home plate and nearly slamming my head into the door on the opposite side. Sara jumps in behind me, and the door slides shut behind us without a sound.

"Seventy-nine Elgin Crescent," Vashti says. She's sitting in the driver's seat. I can't see her face, but recognize her no-nonsense voice and neatly arranged bun. "Do not stop for moving obstacles," she commands, her voice ripe with urgency.

As soon as I look out the windshield, I understand. The two zombies are now standing directly in front of the car; one of them is climbing unsteadily onto the front bumper.

The car starts rolling forward as the zombie gets onto the hood and begins to claw its way toward the windshield, its mouth hanging askew, its lips dripping with blood and bits of tissue. There's a thud and then a series of bumps as the car rolls swiftly over the other zombie. As we pick up speed, the first one continues clinging to the hood like a spider caught in a windstorm.

"Tenacious bugger," Vashti says under her breath. "Speed up," she commands.

The car accelerates, causing the zombie's loose skin to blow back in the wind like a rubber Halloween mask. Its mouth opens wide in what appears to be a scream, but all we hear is a low, loud moan, kind of like the sound a cow might make if you kicked it. Not that I support kicking cows. Or any farm animal, for that matter.

"Blimey," Sara says. "That's one stubborn creature."

"Faster," Vashti urges, gritting her teeth as the zombie bangs its fist on the windshield. The skin along the outer side of its hand splits open, leaving a smear of blood on the glass.

The car accelerates with a squealing of tires, and the zombie slides down the hood for a moment before regaining its grip and crawling slowly back to hammer at the glass once more. Lily starts and shouts out, panicked, as a bloodied spiderweb of cracks appears across the glass in front of her face.

The zombie raises its fist again above the damaged glass.

"That glass isn't going to hold," Lily cries. Her voice is climbing, approaching hysteria.

"Reverse," Vashti says, her voice as calm as glass. "Immediately."

The car doesn't even come to a stop before it reverses direction and accelerates again. My head snaps back like a rag doll's. For some reason, I think about what we learned in science class last year: for every action, there is an equal and opposite reaction.

It only takes a second or two before the zombie, who is as surprised as the rest of us by the car's sudden movements, flies off the hood.

"Yes!" Sara says, pumping a fist in the air. "Take that, you rotting hulk of shite."

"Forward again," Vashti says. She turns her head and gives Sara a quick smile. "This isn't a Millwall match," she says, her dark eyes dancing. "Mind your language, please."

"I support Crystal Palace, anyhow," Sara shoots back, a smile spreading across her face. I can't help but notice how stubby and grey her teeth are. They look like baby teeth that've been dipped in diluted grape juice.

"I'm a Chelsea supporter myself, and I know damn well you don't," Vashti murmurs as the car's tires bounce violently over the zombie. "On to the destination," she instructs the car as we turn a corner.

"What the hell is wrong with you people?" Lily cries out. I can see tears streaming down the left side of her cheek, and she sniffles wetly before continuing to speak. "My sister is struggling to stay alive because of one of these bastard monsters and you two are joking around as though we've just run over a squirrel."

Vashti reaches over and gently touches Lily's shoulder. "Cassandra's going to pull through just fine," she says. Her tone is kind but firm. It's pretty clear she doesn't tolerate drama. "Just a wee bit of gallows humour, lovely. That's all. Often the best way to cope with these types of situations."

"Well, I think it's insensitive," Lily says, sliding closer to the door until she's just out of reach of Vashti's hand. She sounds a little bit childish and pouty, but I get it. If Jade were the one messed up, and people were kind of joking about the thing that caused her injury, I'd be pretty pissed, too.

"And I think you'd best control your emotions much better than you did back there," Vashti snaps. "Or you'll make us all a flashing bullseye for demons."

I glance out the side window. We're passing by row after row of large townhouses that look as though they might've been white once upon a time, but are now smeared a dirty grey by air pollution. If I had to guess, I'd say we're in a pretty wealthy area, or at least one that used to be.

"Is the other car still with us? Are they okay?" I ask.

Vashti turns in her seat to look at me and then taps her video watch. "Yes, they took another route whilst we dealt with the tenacious zombie. They'll meet us at the flat. Assuming we make it there ourselves, that is."

JADE

Fresh blood drips slowly from the cracked skin at either corner of the creature's slightly grey lips.

It's definitely not a demon. Not only are its eyes not that familiar, all-consuming black, it doesn't seem as aware as the demons, either. In the five seconds or so that the two of us have been staring at each other, a demon would already have attached itself to my body with a frenzied violence.

Instead, it opens its mouth as if to yawn and lets out a low moan, as though someone just hauled off and kicked it in the shin. A grotesquely swollen, slug-like tongue sneaks out of its mouth and slowly slides around the perimeter of the thing's lips.

Instinctively, I raise my leg and kick toward its left quadriceps. My foot connects, then sinks into what I quickly realize is rotten flesh. A stench like death fills the air around us. The creature lets out a howl, more of surprise than of pain, and stumbles backward while

I wrench my foot out if its body. My foot makes a squelching sound as it's freed from the thing's leg. It's revolting, and I nearly gag, but there's no time for me to feel queasy. I need to destroy it.

Turning slightly sideways so I can keep an eye on the creature, I run to the curtains, leap onto the windowsill, and pull down the heavy metal rod and fabric with one swift movement. A tsunami of dust floats into the air around me, making me wonder just how long this place has been abandoned. After the borders closed, I imagine tourism took a massive hit.

The thing is lumbering after me like a toddler learning to walk. Its stink is absolutely everywhere. I quickly slide the curtains off the rod and turn toward it, ready to fight.

"Die!" I yell as I swing. It stumbles sideways so that the rod misses its head completely, but still lands with considerable force on one of its shoulders. For a moment, the creature teeters in mid-air as if drunk, and then spins to the ground.

Without missing a beat, I bring the rod down, over and over, onto its skull, its midsection — anywhere a fatal blow might be made. The smell of death and rotting flesh explodes from each wound to hang about me like a cloud.

Eventually, the creature's moans and twitching subside and then stop completely. Sweat is dripping down my forehead, and my arms ache. I drop the rod to the floor. Carrying it outside wouldn't be wise, since I'm trying to fly under the radar of the police and authorities. I look down at my right leg. The putrid-smelling, blackish-red goop that's coating my shoe and the lower part of my jeans is not exactly going to help me blend in, either.

There's a dining room on the other side of the lobby. I figure the probability of the water still being on in this place is slim. After all, water's a pretty hot commodity, so keeping it on in an abandoned building would be crazy…. Still, if people are squatting here, there has to be a water source somewhere close.

The shadows almost seem to follow me across the lobby, and I pause, looking back over my shoulder at the corpse of the thing I've just killed. My imagination is getting the better of me. I shake my head. It's dead. And was dead even before I mashed it. I laugh, but it's a manic sound that echoes through the empty lobby. At least I hope it's empty.

Unlike my imagination, my conscience appears to have abandoned me. Somewhere down deep in the very pit of my being, there's a tiny glimmer of guilt about leaving Mr. Khan and Amara behind. But I have absolutely no regret about it. Believe me, I'm aware of the fact that I should be feeling something more — a lot more — about the situation and the extreme danger I've left them in. But a larger part of me just, well … doesn't care. At all. The best way to describe it is that my emotions have been flattened; they're as dull as the tip of a well-used pencil.

My gaze wanders back to the curtain rod. Maybe I should keep it with me after all. Or keep it at least until I get out of here, in case that thing has family or friends lurking. As I turn to go back for it, my stomach does a sudden somersault, and I bend over to vomit all over the dusty wooden floor.

Straightening, I wipe my mouth with the back of my hand and move more quickly into the dining area. Weaving between the dusty, discarded tables and chairs, some still sporting vases with petrified flowers in them as centrepieces, I eventually reach my destination — the kitchen.

When I turn it on, the tap makes a spluttering noise before shooting out a rusty stream of water that eventually becomes clear after about a minute. I place my mouth directly under it and slurp greedily, allowing the liquid to wash away the sour aftertaste of puke. Hopefully the water is safe, though I'm so dehydrated, I don't care. After a few minutes, I peel off my jeans and my shoe and soak them in the water with a bit of cleaning solution I found under the sink. I know this means I'm going to be uncomfortable for a few hours, but it's better than smelling like a pile of horseshit.

There's a door at the back of the kitchen marked with a large unlit exit sign. For sure using this is a better idea than leaving by the front door onto a main street.

After wringing the jeans out and then managing to pull the wet denim up over my legs, I secure the ring back into the front pocket. Taking a deep breath, I ready myself. It's time to get on with things.

I crack open the door and peer out. There's a quiet street that's so narrow, it would be considered an alleyway in Toronto, and beyond that, the red-brick wall of another building.

I step out and take a deep breath, hoping to leave behind both the musty smell of the hotel and the stink of the creature I just killed. The heat hits me like a slap, as does the thick pollution that hangs in the air and sends me into a coughing fit.

Tears sting my eyes as I clear my throat and look out at the busy street ahead of me.

I check the notes Seth left for me on the video watch. *79 Elgin Crescent, Notting Hill, W11 2JD.*

According to the estimate on video watch, it's a forty-five-minute walk. I peer into the smoggy sky. Time to get going. Time to make sure the truth about everything that's happening in our world is exposed to the Seers.

I reach into my pocket and pull out the ring.

"And you need to go back to where you came from," I say.

I place it back in my pocket, take a deep breath, and walk out from the side street onto the sidewalk that runs alongside the busier road.

An elderly gentleman, his back so stooped it looks like he's permanently searching for something dropped on the floor, is coming down the sidewalk toward me. He's wearing a cheap cloth anti-pollution mask and, despite his wide-brimmed sun hat, his skin is a maze of spider veins and brown age spots.

"G'day," he says, his voice weak and muffled. He begins coughing hoarsely as soon as the words escape his lips.

"Oh, it's going to be a very good day, indeed," I say, plastering a wide smile across my face as he shuffles past.

JASMINE

The car slows in front of a row of large white town-houses. I glance out the window. If we're just going to hop out here and walk into one of these places, I'll feel a little exposed.

Vashti swivels around. "We need to be quick about this and as discreet as possible. The more of you there are, the more likely we are to be detected. I'm —"

Her words are cut short as the screams of sirens fill the air around us.

Vashti's eyes grow large. "Did anyone see the two of you?" she asks Sara and me.

The woman. The one on the sidewalk. Not only did she recognize us, we left her with Atika's corpse and her video watch. We should've killed that woman.

"Um, no, we should not 'ave," Sara snaps at me. "That's against the Seer code. We don't kill humans."

"What are you talking about?" Vashti asks, her eyes darkening with concern. The sirens are growing louder.

"This woman ... she saw us," I say. "She recognized me and said she was going to alert the authorities. And she saw Atika's body.... We actually had to leave Atika there."

There's a sharp intake of breath from Lily.

"There was no other choice," I say.

"Bloody hell," Vashti whispers. She rubs her temples with her fingers, deep in thought, then turns to me and hands me two fobs. "The silver is for the front door. The black is for the door to the flat. Flat 5. Top floor. And Jasmine?"

"Yeah?" I reply, taking the fobs from her. It's only then I notice her hand is shaking.

"Next time, kill her," Vashti says, her voice as hard as ice. "We're at war, and extraordinary times call for extraordinary measures to stay safe. That said, get out, get inside, and stay there until Clarence gives you further direction. No matter what, do not go outside or even look outside unless Clarence instructs you to."

"What about you?" I ask. "Aren't you coming in with us?"

I know the answer even as I ask it. Vashti's thoughts spill out to me.

"No!" I cry out. "You can't! We can't lose you."

"Get out, Jasmine," Vashti says. Her voice is almost a growl, her face a mask of fury and determination. "I may be old, but if you push me, I will kill all of you. Get out. *Now*."

Sara and Lily open their doors and quickly slide out of the car to stand on the sidewalk.

I stare at Vashti, tears sliding down my face. I can't lose anybody else. I'm frozen. Maybe if I don't move, Vashti won't, either.

"This isn't about you, Jasmine … and yet, it is," Vashti says, her voice devoid of emotion. "At least it's not about you in the self-centred, selfish way that you think it is. If you don't get out of this bloody car this moment with the fobs, those young women out there on the pavement will be killed. And that will be completely, totally, and utterly your fault, because I will be compelled to drive away to save you." She looks at me, her eyes softening just slightly over the noise of the sirens. The police must be just around the corner. "I've led a good life, Jasmine. I need you to remember that. I have no regrets. And my job as a Protector is over. My Seers are dead. The least I can do is save others. Now, get out before you no longer have the choice."

I nod, unable to meet her gaze as I slide out of the car. Lily and Sara are at the front door, their eyes wild with fear.

"Hurry the eff up!" Sara yells.

I race up the short walkway and wave the fob over the sensor beside the front door, just as a convoy of at least five Metropolitan Police cars and vans tear around the far corner.

The door to the house swings open automatically, the ancient brass knocker in the centre of it glinting in a stray beam of sunlight. Sara pushes Lily and I through the opening before jumping into the foyer after us. She kicks the door shut just as Vashti's car speeds away from the curb outside, its tires squealing against the soft asphalt of the road.

"Do you think they noticed us?" Lily asks, breathless. Her cheeks are flushed. "The police, I mean?"

"I guess we'll find out, won't we?" Sara says, looking at me, her eyes narrowed. "Nice one, you. Bit of a stupid move just sitting there, innit?"

I wipe at the remnants of the tears on my cheeks, not wanting her to notice. I feel it would be a really bad move to let Sara see any sign of weakness in me.

The blare of the sirens is fading now as the police pursue Vashti.

"You know what she's doing, right?" I say, trying to keep the defensiveness of out my voice.

"She's leading the police away from us and from here," Lily interjects. "She's keeping us safe."

"But you realize it's suicide, right?" I say, my voice rising like hot lava. "After she contacts the police to tell them we — you and I — are with her," I say, nodding toward Sara, "she's going to drive herself into the Thames. And then she's going to put down the window as the car sinks, so the authorities will think our bodies washed away and that we drowned trying to escape. They'll only search the river for so long before giving up and assuming we're dead. I wanted to stop her … to save her. That's why I hesitated."

"That's rubbish," Sara snaps. "How do you know she's going to do all that?"

I raise an eyebrow at her. "She let me in. She wanted me to know. And she doesn't want us to feel bad because

she's lived a good life and because Protectors are supposed to do whatever it takes to keep us Seers safe."

"I don't know," Sara says, cocking her head sideways
at me. She looks me up and down as though I'm some
sort of slightly disgusting science experiment. "Again,
we're supposed to just believe you? Because I'm starting to think it's a little strange how death follows you.
Her sister," she says, with a head nod toward Lily. "Then
Fahima, Atika, and now Vashti?"

There's nothing I can say. She's right, and she doesn't
even know the half of it. Eva and Moore's executions are
happening tonight in Toronto.

"Jasmine's trustworthy, if that's what you're wondering," Lily says, her voice quiet but firm. "We should
probably just get upstairs to the flat to see if the others
made it," she adds.

As we walk up the thickly carpeted stairs to the flat, I
keep replaying what Sara just said in my mind. And, as
grateful as I am to Lily for defending me, I couldn't help
but notice that she didn't look me in the eye the entire
time she did so.

J A D E

79 Elgin Crescent.

That's where Jasmine should be. I know she's okay because I would've felt it if anything really traumatic had
happened to her. We'll be reunited, which will make us
stronger. The strange thing is, I don't really feel anything
about seeing her again. No real happiness. Just a flat
nothingness.

As I walk along various side streets to stay as far
under the radar as possible, I'm shocked by just how
brown and dry everything is here in London. Maybe
I shouldn't be all that surprised, seeing as the whole
world is basically drying up. Even when torrential
storms occur, all the water just floods and causes land-
slides and stuff like that, because the ground is too dry
to properly absorb the heavy rains. But before I disappeared, England had still been a pretty green country, just like most of Canada was. In fact, I think they
only started to experience bad droughts after we did.

I'd have to ask Jasmine to be sure, because I was in the Place-in-Between when climate change really sped up.

A frantic buzzing reaches my ears. I look across the street. There's a drone moving up and down like crazy in front of the upstairs window of a red-brick house. Obviously something interesting is happening up there, but I can't risk looking overtly curious or staring long enough to find out what.

Instead, I begin to walk faster and turn my head in the opposite direction, hoping that the drone is solo. The last thing I need is to do battle with some robotic insect that could put my life in danger by identifying me to the police.

Two identical gunmetal-grey vans with metals bars as thick as a bodybuilder's arms over the windows slide around the corner a few blocks ahead of me. My heart jumps into my throat. They definitely look official: these are police vans or some sort of military van.

Either way, the threat to me just skyrocketed. I jump behind a low brick fence that separates the sidewalk from the garden of the house behind it just as two police cars roll up behind the vans. None of the vehicles have their flashing lights on, nor are they using their sirens. But they are travelling fast.

My heart thrums violently in my chest, making me feel somewhat lightheaded and dizzy. I press myself as close to the fence as I can and then slowly peek around the corner at the break where a metal gate is set in the fence.

Police officers in riot gear, shields over their faces and military-style weapons in hand, climb out of the vehicles with the quiet stealth of jungle cats stalking their prey. Something's definitely up. They seem to know exactly who or what they're looking for, which is good, because that means it's not me.

They're heading toward the house where I saw the hovering drone. It's gone now. The officers pour through the front gate and up the front garden, half of them moving toward the back of the house while the rest stay at the front, weapons drawn and ready.

Who or what is behind that window?

I wish I could get a clear look at what's happening, but I'll need to settle for this small sliver of a view if I want to keep safe and as out of sight as possible.

There's a loud bang as the front door is kicked open. All the officers except for two that continue to stand guard at the door disappear inside, their loud, adrenaline-fuelled shouts filling the air.

Sweat rolls down my forehead and into my eyes, making them sting. I wipe at them with the back of my hand. A wasp buzzes uncomfortably close to my face. It's annoying, but I can't take the chance of trying to shoo it away. That much movement might alert any drones in the vicinity. I'm pretty surprised to even see a wasp, because there aren't many insects around anymore other than flies and cockroaches. The decline in insects began before I was abducted; I remember doing a project on an endangered insect of our choice. I chose the monarch butterfly. My first summer back from the Place-in-Between, Jasmine told me they were now completely extinct.

More shouts. The officers are emerging from the house again. It's clear that the ones at the front of the pack are shielding the others from sight. And it doesn't take long to see why.

There are two girls in total. Each one is being restrained by at least two officers. They're handcuffed, but still struggling wildly. One of the officers follows behind, clutching a crimson-stained cloth against his injured skull.

I hold my breath, trying to get a better look. It takes a second, due to the girls' thrashing, but my hunch is right. Identical twins that can barely be restrained by armed police officers — officers who are likely part of an anti-terrorism squad.

They're Seers.

And, for some reason, they are also very much wanted by the UK police.

JASMINE

I swipe the fob over the sensor beside the front door of the flat. As soon as the green light flashes, Sara twists the knob and hurries inside.

"Susie?" she cries out, walking through the hall toward the flight of stairs in front of us. "Susie? Are you here?" Anxiety is ripe in her voice. I've never seen Sara so unsure and scared.

Lily and I climb the stairs behind her. On the second floor of the flat, the space opens into a kitchen with a living room area attached. From two sofas in the living area, several people turn in unison to greet us as we walk in.

Susie leaps up from the sofa, runs toward Sara, and throws her arms around her sister's thick neck.

"Thank bloody god," she says, a wide smile of relief spreading across her face. "We were so worried about all of you when we saw those creatures climbing onto the car."

"Zombies," I mutter. "They were zombies." I'm not even sure why I've said the word. It's not really the time or place.

"Yeah, so I was told," says a weak voice from the sofa. "One nearly had me for dinner."

"Cassandra!" Lily cries out as she rushes over to her sister.

I follow behind her. Cassandra's lying across half of one of the sofas, her head propped up on a fuzzy, faux-fur pillow, her ebony hair fanned out around her like a halo. She's pale and hooked up to a machine that's monitoring her and feeding fluids into her arm via a tube. A slim older woman whose face is deeply lined sits beside her. The blanket covering Cassandra's lower half shifts as she hugs Lily, and the woman gently re-drapes it over Cassandra's legs.

"Careful," she says as Lily sits down on the edge of the sofa, clasping her sister's hand. I think back to the moment Jade and I were reunited in the Place-in-Between. I know all too well that feeling of not wanting to let go. The woman smiles at me. "I'm Sadie, Cassandra's nurse."

"Hey," I say, plastering a smile across my face, not wanting to let on how concerned I am about Cassandra's injuries. I turn my attention to Cassandra. "How are you?"

She arches an eyebrow at me. The dark circles around her eyes are so deep, it looks as though her eyes could sink to the very back of her skull. "Girl, I was gnawed on like a chicken leg by that thing. How do you think I am? I've had a chunk of stem cells and extracellular matrix put into my right upper arm and I'm stitched up like Frankenstein." She rolls her eyes and purses her lips in a pouty smile. "But other than that, I'm spectacular." She glances at Sadie. "I have been told I'm healing fairly fast, so glass half-full, right?"

I laugh. "Jesus, I guess you're competing for my smartass title. It is so good to see you. I was really worried." Leaning over, I give her a quick hug, which ends up being awkward with Lily in the way. All three of us end up giggling uncontrollably — not only with relief, but also exhaustion.

"We may have only a night here, if that, so don't get too comfortable," says a raspy, but deeply melodic voice from behind us. It sounds like a bass guitar that's seen one too many gigs in a smoky bar. I swivel around. "And your sister isn't staying long. Sadie needs to take her to a safer spot, if there is such a thing. She's stubborn, though, and insisted on seeing you, Lily."

Cassandra shoots Clarence a quick thumbs-up as he stops talking and turns to face us. He's standing at the bottom of a staircase at the other end of the living room. His chocolate-brown eyes are dark with worry. "There are raids taking place all over the city right now. And Vashti's car was stopped before she made it to the Thames."

There's an audible intake of breath from everyone in the room. "They'll torture her," Dani says, her voice breaking. "What if she cracks and ends up telling them about us? About where we are?"

Clarence shakes his head. "No, they won't, she won't, and you need to keep your emotions down. All of you need to do that," he says, wagging a finger that's been distorted by arthritis as his gaze sweeps across the room. His eyes, which are more yellow than white, with whispery threads of red capillaries throughout, make me wonder just how old he actually is. "Strong emotions will lure the demons to us."

"Come on, mate," Kiki says. "We've all heard the horror stories about the anti-terrorism squads and what they do to prisoners ... especially prisoners of colour, yeah?"

"Precisely," Clarence says, clearing his throat. "Which is why Vashti was not unprepared."

"What does that mean?" Susie asks.

"Cyanide," he replies, his voice devoid of emotion. I can feel his sadness, though. It comes at me in waves. He was in love with Vashti. "One tablet under the tongue as soon as she knew there was no other choice."

"Eff me," Sara says, her voice barely a whisper. "This is getting to be a bit too much."

Clarence shuffles over closer to us and slowly lowers himself into a worn leather chair, his body shaking like an earthquake. He definitely seems a lot older than when we first met him at the Trafalgar. I guess I wasn't being very observant at that time — I need to watch out for that. It's dangerous not to be attentive to small details.

He folds his hands together, knuckles up, and rests his chin on them. I notice he shakes almost constantly, though the movement is less noticeable than when he was trying to sit.

"Things are not going to get any bloody better, and you must get used to that fact. We're heading to battle. I don't know quite as much about it as my younger brother does, but I do know that this is just the tip of the iceberg. Because tonight we must watch the terrible events that are taking place in Toronto."

"Are you sure it's happening?" Lily asks. "Eva wasn't even given a fair trial."

Clarence shakes his head, his eyes full of sorrow. He looks a lot like one of those bloodhound dogs, the ones that look eternally sad with their big, droopy, red-ringed eyes.

"When I said things are not going to get better, I wasn't messing about," he says, sighing deeply. "As Vashti told you, Beaconsfield was raided. And I haven't heard from my brother in the past few days, as he had to go into hiding and cease all communication. All of that aside, nearly every country has done away with the right to a fair trial — or any trial, for that matter — when it comes to matters of national security or terrorism. Thus it was highly unlikely Eva would get a trial at all, and even if she did, I guarantee you it wouldn't have been fair. That's why climate change refugees can be imprisoned indefinitely just for trying to escape countries that are imploding. Human rights are a farce in our contemporary world." He pauses for a moment. "After the water was poisoned in Toronto, we knew things would worsen, that the government there would want to make an example of anyone they could pin some blame on. Just like the American government did after the Los Angeles fires. Eva is the only one of you they've got. And, as such, they will use her to send a very clear message to all of you, to all of us defending the right of human beings to have access to adequate resources, to anyone questioning the moral legitimacy of borders and these leaders' absolute power."

"Can't anyone stop it? The execution, I mean? Can't the CCT create a diversion to buy Eva time?" My words tumble out so quickly they nearly fall over each other. We can't have anyone else die.

Clarence shakes his head. "There are so many things we can't control, Jasmine. For decades the CCT tried to influence environmental policy, to prevent politicians and the elite — which are often one and the same — from taking us over the tipping point with climate change. That didn't work. We can't change the destruction that is already wrought. Sometimes we have to accept the unacceptable."

I watch his hands tremble as he speaks. And all I can think about is how Raphael isn't here. The fact that he leaves every time things get bad makes me wonder if he's actually on our side at all. Maybe, like Jade said, he's one of the people I shouldn't fully trust.

JADE

After the close call with the drone and the London anti-terrorism squad, I'm even more cautious. This means it takes me nearly twice the estimated time to reach the safe house. I sit for a moment across the street behind a large tree and watch the house. It's large and imposing. According to Seth, Jasmine and the others are in the top flat, and they're with some people I need to keep my guard up around.

My stomach does another of its high-diving somersault motions, and I double over and dry heave onto the dusty grass beneath me. I've gone so long with no food and such little water, nothing comes up. My throat burns as though acid's been poured down it.

Taking a deep breath, I stand up and get ready to go in. I feel like shit; I'm dehydrated and exhausted, not to mention the fact that the smell of the creature I killed still lingers on my shoe and my jeans. Not the best first impression to make with the new Seers, or anyone else.

I look both ways along the street and then up in the sky for possible drones before dashing across and quickly ringing the bell.

No answer. I ring again, leaving my finger on the bell pad a few moments longer than necessary. Beads of sweat begin to trickle down the back of my neck. The street is still empty, but I know it won't remain that way for long.

I should've been prepared for this. No one in that apartment is going to answer unless they're expecting someone. That would be far too dangerous.

Panic begins to rise in me. What now? Why didn't Seth think of this?

And that's when my stomach begins to turn. This time it's different, though. The movement feels completely independent of me. It's slower. There's no nausea. Instead, a surge of energy rushes through me. I feel stronger, composed, and extremely sure of myself. Well, not of myself, exactly. More of something within me. If that makes sense at all.

Which it really doesn't, not even to me.

I turn my gaze on the door sensor and stare hard at it. This strange, slow burn starts to fill my abdomen, and suddenly the ring in my pocket shudders like it's hypothermic.

My eyes are no longer mine … someone or something else has stepped behind them. I'm looking from far away even though I'm in my own head.

The sensor begins to waver beneath my gaze like water. My gaze? Our gaze? Its gaze?

Images come tumbling forward at me: skeletal children dying in the rubble of bombed-out buildings while warplanes scream above; pedestrians being mown down like bowling pins by massive transport trucks and vans; and groups of scared men, women, and children piling into rickety rafts and sailing out into shark-infested oceans in the middle of the night.

I've seen this before. I saw these images when Seth touched me at Corktown Common ...

The sensor keeps morphing and changing. It's got a mouth now. I think it's a mouth. And it's laughing. And it's expanding. Toward me. And there are teeth. Large, carnivorous teeth. Screams fill my head, so loud, I feel like my skull might shatter.

I fall to the ground, my head hitting the concrete like a ripe melon.

Darkness consumes me.

JASMINE

"Jasmine?"

I bolt upright, sweat rolling down my face, my shirt drenched.

Though it's hot in the flat, that's not the main reason for my perspiration. I've just been awoken from a horrible nightmare about Jade ... but every second I'm awake, the memory of the dream slides away from me with the speed of a snake on steroids.

Lily is standing at the side of the bed.

"How long have I been asleep?" I ask, stifling a yawn. My mouth is sticky from dehydration. After our talk, Clarence made us all get some sleep. He wants us to be well-rested so we can better endure watching the execution and any news out of Toronto that may accompany it. As well, he wants us to be ready — physically and mentally — if we need to make a quick escape from here, a possibility he believes to be highly likely.

"Two hours or so," Lily answers, her face scrunching up with concern. "Jasmine … Jade's here. She's downstairs with Clarence and Cassandra."

My heart skips beat. "What?" I ask, jumping out of the bed and grabbing my clothes off the floor. If this is a dream, I don't want it to end. Jade's here. We'll be safer together.

I look over at Lily. She seems troubled.

"I stayed downstairs to be with Cassandra. I was sleeping on the couch when Jade came in, and …" Lily pauses, biting nervously at her bottom lip.

"And what?" I ask, pulling on my jeans and twisting my hair into a loose ponytail. The under layer of my hair is heavy with moisture. It feels good to have air on my neck.

"That's just it. She just … came in," Lily says, moving closer to me. She's whispering now. "The bell rang once or twice, but of course we didn't answer it or ask who it was over the intercom. I think Clarence was hoping it was just someone buzzing the wrong apartment number." She pauses again and looks over her shoulder toward the door, as though she's afraid Jade might be standing there.

"What do you mean she just came in? C'mon, that's impossible. She'd have to get through the front door, and then also into the flat."

Lily nods. "That's what I'm talking about. She said both were just open, or unlocked. Something like that."

My blood runs cold. "No, they weren't," I say. Now I'm also whispering. "You know they weren't. And I was the last one to enter the flat. I closed the door behind us. It locked automatically."

"I think we should get back down there," Lily says. She thinks that Jade might harm Cassandra.

"Why? Are you worried about leaving Cassandra alone with Jade?" I say, narrowing my eyes at her. "What the hell, Lily? I agree we need to find out what the story is, but she's my twin, not a threat. Worry about demons and police and corrupt politicians. Not my sister." I begin to walk toward the door.

"You're not supposed to just do that," Lily replies softly. "And you'll see why I feel that way when you get down there."

"What do you mean?" I ask, stopping and turning back to her. The coldness is back, invading every cell in my body.

"There's something not right about her. I can't tell you what exactly, because I can't put my finger on it. Sort of like it's Jade, but not Jade. It's hard to explain."

I pause, trying to push down the defensiveness bubbling up in me like hot lava. "She's been through a lot more than you, me, or any of the other Seers." *Except maybe Eva*, I think. Seeing your sister raped, mutilated, and then murdered pretty much tops everything. She and Jade might be tied for trauma. "I mean, we don't even know how Jade got here, or what's happened to her and Amara since we got split up coming back from the Place-in-Between."

Lily throws her hands up in surrender. "Okay, okay. I get it. Just come down and judge for yourself before you start hating on me, all right?"

Jade turns around before Lily and I even reach the bottom of the staircase, which is weird because our socked feet didn't make a sound, not even the creak of a floorboard, as we were walking down. It's like she sensed us before seeing us. I read once that cockroaches can do that: they can sense the smallest changes in the air around them.

A wide smile spreads across Jade's face as she leaps toward me, throwing her arms around my neck.

"Jasmine!" she says, her breath hot against my neck. "Thank god you're okay. I was so worried."

I nod into her hair as tears blur my vision. "Where were you?" I ask as soon as we release our hold on each other. "And where's Amara? Do you know how Mom is? Mr. Khan?" I'm trembling with happiness, but also with anticipation, in case any of Jade's answers are not good. The fact that I have to ask her these things at all, the fact that I can't connect to her thoughts and feelings, doesn't escape me.

Jade shrugs her shoulders. "I don't know where Amara is. We transitioned here so I could return the ring, but she didn't transition with me. Something strange happened. I hit my head when we transitioned here — on the sidewalk, I think. When I came to, Amara was gone." She pauses, looking thoughtful. "Maybe she took off."

"Amara wouldn't do that," Lily says, her voice quiet. "It's a pretty serious thing to suggest, even. And first, you said she didn't transition with you. Then you immediately contradicted yourself and said she did. Which is it?"

Jade either doesn't hear Lily or chooses to ignore her, because she just keeps on talking without even looking her way. "As for Mom and Mr. Khan, we spoke to Mr.

Jakande while we were in Toronto. He said they were okay, but I don't know if I believe him …"

"My colleague wouldn't tell a lie," Clarence injects, his voice shaky with anger. "I don't know who you think you are, but you can't just come in here and make these sorts of comments about your fellow Seers and one of my CCT family."

Jade turns to him. "I'm so sorry," she says, her voice as sweet as honey. "That was just my feeling when I read his thoughts."

Behind the syrupy sweetness, there's this weird flatness in her voice. And though I can't read her thoughts, it doesn't take a brain surgeon to realize she's not sorry. Not at all. Lily's right, something is really off with Jade. It's like she's on automatic pilot or something. She's talking like a bad actor reading a script. I mean, things were already weird before we left for the Place-in-Between to return the ring, but this is a whole new level of strange.

Clarence continues to glare at Jade for a moment before his face softens. "I'm sorry," he says. "I think we're all on edge today. We've lost someone dear to us, and there are things happening in this city — and in yours — that put us in more danger than ever before." He sighs heavily. "If that's even possible."

"I'm worried about Amara," Cassandra says from the couch. "If she was gone when you came to, maybe something happened to her during or right after transitioning. She might be hurt or in danger. Which I'd say is way more likely than her taking off on you, Jade. Lily's right, Amara's not like that. None of us are."

Jade nods in agreement, but her gaze lands on Cassandra as coolly as a winter breeze. "Oh, I'm certainly not saying she'd leave me on purpose. Maybe it was in self-defence. I just know she was really upset with me about Vivienne ... and rightly so." She fishes the ring out of her pocket. "But that's why we were transitioning here. To reunite with all of you, but also for me to make things right by returning the ring."

Cassandra arches an eyebrow at her. "Where did the two of you land when you transitioned? And how did you know we'd be here, in this specific flat?"

Good questions, and I feel like a fool for not thinking of them myself. I guess my joy at seeing Jade made me overlook things.

"Mr. Jakande told me that you'd be here," Jade says, flashing Clarence a wide smile. "I don't know exactly where we landed. Near a park. It wasn't far from here."

"Did you speak to him after transitioning?" Clarence asks. The question comes out of him in a deep rumble full of suspicion.

"No, of course not," Jade says, with a wave of her hand. "That would've put both of us at such risk. Mr. Jakande told me where you'd be today when I contacted him in Toronto, so I just used the GPS on my video watch to track my location and give me a route here. It took a couple of hours of walking, though, so I'm completely dehydrated. What's the water situation like here in London?"

"Better than in Toronto, thankfully," Clarence says. "There are rolling stoppages, and bottled water is given out in priority areas, which means to the wealthy, mainly. But there's still water for the masses, and it has, thus far, avoided *contamination*." He dances around that word like it's explosive, which makes me wonder if he has any doubts about our innocence. Or maybe, with everything that's been happening, I'm becoming super paranoid.

"We've got some in the fridge," he adds.

"I'll get it for you," I say to Jade.

This time I'm staying attentive, and I won't forget the way Jade detoured the conversation in order to avoid giving us a clear answer as to how she knew exactly where we'd be.

With a heavy heart, I walk over to the fridge. The last person in the world I want to be suspicious of is my sister.

JADE

Water …
  So thirsty …
  Body no longer mine.
I scream the words, but nothing comes out of my mouth.

Jasmine walks over to the fridge, takes out a jug, and fills a clean glass with water. Sunlight glints off it as she holds it out to me. To *us …*

I'm able to still read her thoughts, though they come to me now as if through a mist.

She wants to believe me, but knows something's wrong. The concern in her eyes is evident. My thoughts are not accessible to her. And that's because my body is now shared. It's not me who's blocking her. I'm inhabiting only a small, dark corner of this body, of this mind — I've been colonized, and I fear that even this tiny space I still occupy will be consumed soon. When that happens, will I disappear completely from existence?

JASMINE

Clarence made us go back upstairs to try and nap for another few hours. He expects we'll have to vacate this flat during the early hours of the morning, if not sooner. But there's no way, even in this darkened bedroom, that I can close my eyes for more than a few seconds.

I'm far too worried.

Lily was right. Something is seriously wrong with Jade. I mean, it's hard to know if she's just really exhausted or is maybe suffering some sort of PTSD from everything that's happened in the last seven years or so, but even the way she speaks is different.

I stare up at the ceiling, unable to see anything in the inky blackness. Down deep, I know it's something more serious than any of that, though. More serious and a lot stranger. If I think about it, the strangeness started just before we headed back to the Place-in-Between. If it had started during or after our time there, I'd have said that returning there brought back Jade's trauma from before.

But things were off before that. And then there was that guy she seemed to know.

' Maybe he has absolutely nothing to do with any of this, but something tells me he does. The way he looked at Jade, and she at him. The fact that she pulled the stunt she did by taking the ring without even telling me. My face still gets hot with anger at the thought of that. And she was nowhere to be found when we needed everyone to help battle the demons and save Vivienne.

Jade said she wants to try to return the ring tomorrow. Clarence told us that it would be virtually impossible to get to Spitalfields and the right place at the Roman wall without putting ourselves in a lot of danger — too much danger. Apparently, we're on the other side of London from there. That means we'd have to take public transport, which is incredibly risky in terms of being identified. We'd be taking a huge chance. But then, Clarence also reiterated what we've heard so many times before: if we are to have any protection, the ring needs to be in its rightful place before the Final Battle begins.

The door slides open, sending a large sliver of light into the room. Dani stands in the opening. She looks angelic with the light framing her curls.

"Clarence wants everyone downstairs. He's got the news on. The live stream of the execution is about to start," she says, turning on her heel to go. The flatness in her voice tells me she's trying to normalize this, or maybe she already has. It's really the only way any of us can still function, the only way we can keep moving forward.

Susie, Sara, and Lily are in the room with me. We all get up and silently make our way downstairs. A heavy blanket of dread and anticipation hangs around us. It was hard to convince Lily to leave Cassandra for even an hour in Clarence's very capable hands and take a nap, but seconds after hitting the bed, she was sleeping like a rock. Jade opted to stay downstairs and rest on the sofa across from Cassandra. I suspect Clarence was watching her like a hawk. At least, I hope he was.

We get downstairs to find the holographic newscast already streaming from a three-dimensional screen at the end of the room.

"This is crazy," Cassandra says. She's propped up on pillows to a near-sitting position, and though she looks surprisingly better, her face still pinches with pain when she moves.

Lily sits cross-legged on the floor in front of her sister. The rest of us gather on the sofas, ottomans, and floor.

Jade comes over, perches beside me on the sofa, grabs my hand, and squeezes it. I look over at her and smile, though I'm sure it must look as fake as cardboard. Hand-holding is something Jade and I have never done, and it feels completely unnatural.

I turn my attention to the news.

A group of three or four journalists are sitting at a large round table. "We're here at the BBC newsroom, reporting live about the CCT executions taking place tonight in Toronto," says a young, very thin male reporter with hair so blond that it's practically translucent. A silver ring with a single bead on it glints from his septum.

"Whilst raids of suspected CCT strongholds took place today across the capital, in Toronto, Mayor Sandra Smith is assuring citizens of her city that their safety and survival are her top priorities by coming down hard on CCT terrorists and sympathizers. We take you to Toronto, Canada, right now."

The scene cuts to an image of Beaconsfield surrounded by police tape, officers, and military vehicles. Several heavily armed officers flank a nervous-looking, middle-aged reporter.

"This is what Toronto's deputy police chief, Nigmendra Pratap, had to say when we spoke to him earlier today," the reporter says.

One of the officers steps forward. His dark eyes are deeply serious.

"After days of high-level surveillance, we've taken the necessary steps to secure and lock down the suspected CCT training camp you see behind me. According to our sources, terrorists were using this secondary school as a front to conduct training exercises — often radicalizing young female students with the aim of turning them into foot soldiers and suicide bombers."

I stare at the image of the reporter in disbelief. "What the hell?" I shout. "Is he serious? Where's Mr. Khan? Ms. Samson? What have they done with everybody? How can they lie like this?" Panic surges through my body.

"You know the answer to that better than almost anyone in this room, Jasmine," Clarence replies quietly. "You know precisely how these lies are constructed."

Of course he's right. I saw Smith's propaganda machine first-hand. Corrupt governments, especially hers, will do anything to protect their power. Anything. Even if it means sticking innocent children in dilapidated camps and bleeding them to feed the demons. That much and more I witnessed with my own eyes.

"We now go live to downtown Toronto, where the executions are scheduled to begin at half seven, our time," one of the female reporters states.

The scene changes again. This time, Toronto City Hall, with its two tall, curving buildings, springs into three-dimensional being. Sandra Smith is standing on a stage set up in front and to the side of the buildings, in Nathan Phillips Square. The camera pans 360 degrees, showing us another stage, this one much higher, set up just behind the multicoloured letters of the *TORONTO* sign.

The camera swivels around to capture the audience. It's hard to tell from the brief glimpse, but I estimate there are at least ten thousand people there, maybe more, on the streets and sidewalks adjacent to the square. Many of them are chanting, "Hang the terrorists! Hang the terrorists!" More than a few violently punch at the air with their fists on each word. People are waving flags — mainly of Toronto and Canada — and more than a few hold signs showing support for Smith and calling for the torture and eradication of the CCT.

At least two dozen drones are flitting around in the sky above the audience and around the entrances to City Hall. Security is at an all-time high for this event.

"Tell me this isn't really happening," Lily says, closing her eyes and leaning her head back for a moment. "My mom told me that Toronto was once the most progressive city in the world. Now look at it."

"She was right," Clarence says, resting his chin on his folded hands. He looks like he might start to pray. "Bloody barbaric, this is. Just shows how fast things can change with the wrong people in power."

Sandra Smith's back. Her spiky hair is a greyish silver with a slight blue tinge at the tips. She raises a fist gloved in black leather into the air. It's at least thirty degrees in Toronto, but that doesn't matter — everything has been carefully contrived by Smith and her cronies for maximum drama and perceived strength. And the image of leather covering fragile human skin achieves this aim quite well.

A thunderous round of applause, with more shouts of "Hang them now!" punctuates the air.

Smith allows the noise to continue unabated for about a minute as she surveys the crowd. Her face is a mask of solemnity, but there's an undeniable glint in her eye that tells me she's loving every second of this adulation.

Arching an eyebrow, she brings an index finger to her lips like some sort of deranged primary school teacher. It takes a minute or so, but the crowd eventually falls silent.

"This afternoon, the world is watching. Watching our city, Toronto, stand as a model for the rest of the world. We are showing them that we're putting our citizens first and that we will stop at nothing to ensure the security of our city and the rest of the province. In a moment, two CCT terrorists will be brought out to face their fellow Torontonians ... and to face *justice*." The word *justice* comes out like the hiss of an angry cat. The crowd erupts with screams and shouts of approval once more.

Loud, thumping drums and bass music fill the air. People throw their hands in the air. The whole vibe is suddenly more like a club dance floor than an old-school execution.

The camera pans over to the stage set up behind the glowing *TORONTO* sign. Two silver posts shaped like upside-down L's emerge from the stage, springing toward the sky like stainless steel stems.

Except these stems will not bring life. They'll bring death, and that fact is quickly reinforced as nooses drop from the arms of the posts as soon as they've reached their full height of about ten feet.

"What the bloody hell? They're actually hanging them?" Susie says, breaking the silence in the room. "And I thought you Canadians were supposed to be the peacekeepers of the world or something like that. This is positively medieval."

The camera pans back to Sandra Smith, who holds her hand up for quiet. The crowd falls silent like obedient dogs.

"The CCT is a scourge on modern society. Not only are we and all the remaining countries and city states trying to survive climate change and find ways to mitigate the suffering of our citizens as we do so, we now also have to spend money, time, and resources fighting terrorists bent on destroying humanity. The last bombing on the TTC, perpetrated by Taylor Moore, killed thirty-eight people and left several others maimed. Eva Gonzales, a young woman who illegally entered our country from Cuba and was detained, continued her criminal activity by escaping from custody, then aided and abetted the CCT in pulling off the most heinous mass murder in Canadian history ... the poisoning of the water supplies being given out to Toronto's most vulnerable. Toronto was only weeks away from running out of water, but I managed to secure hundreds of millions of bottles for us. Enough to see us through until Ottawa can sort out a plan for our city." She pauses, shaking her head, as a collective rumble of anger, replete with snake-like hissing, ripples through the crowd. As one, they surge forward toward the stage where the executions are set to happen.

"Hang the bitch!" someone screams out. The shout is so guttural, so full of hate, that it sends a shiver up my spine. I look over at Jade and my heart stops. Hopefully I'm wrong or just misinterpreting things, but I swear the beginning of a smile is tugging at the corners of her lips.

"Unfortunately, it gets worse," Smith says, closing her eyes for a moment, in a massively overdramatic gesture. "As Toronto's finest closed in on the group of highly trained teenaged girls that perpetrated this crime, Gonzales attacked them brutally, rabidly, snapping their necks and kicking them with such hate that internal bleeding caused by blunt force trauma was also listed as a cause of death. Bradley Browning, twenty-nine-year-old father of two, died on the scene. He'd been with the force for only six months. He leaves behind his wife, Jennie, who is seven months pregnant." Tears glint in Smith's eyes. I know they are crocodile tears, but I've got to give her credit: she knows what this audience wants and is stirring their collective fear into a frenzy of rage.

Cue a petite, heavily pregnant woman being helped up the stairs to the stage. She waddles, cupping the bottom of her baby bump protectively with the palm of one hand, to stand beside Smith. Her tears are definitely genuine and flow freely down both her flushed cheeks.

Mayor Smith puts an arm around the woman's shoulder and draws her in close. "Jennie Browning will now have to explain to her unborn child why his or her father was cruelly and senselessly torn away while trying to defend our great city." She turns to Jennie. "Is there anything you'd like to say?"

Officer Browning's wife nods and sniffles loudly. She takes the mike and stares out at the crowd, her long lashes blinking away tears.

The crowd is completely silent. It's as if everyone is holding their breath.

"Kill the bitch," she replies, her blue eyes narrowing.

JADE

Jasmine knows something is wrong with me. So do the others. I wish there were some way to send out an SOS or some other kind of alert to them. Instead, I try hard to move my hands and feet, to do anything that might signal to them that I'm in here, deep inside, fighting for my life.

But I can't.

It's as though I'm encased in wet cement that's setting fast. I'm unable to move even my pinkie finger. The world outside is hazy. I'm like a fish stuck at the bottom of a murky tank, trying to look up and out at what's beyond me.

In fact, this thing controlling me has already reached out and contacted several people. Important people. It's let them know where we are. I'm like a walking microchip. The others are in so much danger.

And there's nothing I can do.

I've never been so frightened. I can't remember much about being taken to the Place-in-Between when I was young, but I'm certain this is far worse.

The thing that's taken over my body wants blood. And chaos. Destruction and death.

Whatever this giant, pulsating force is, it's much greater than anything I have ever imagined. I know now it was the source of the screams I heard when Seth touched me. It's of this Earth, but also of the universe and beyond. And it's ancient, as old as the moon and the stars and the seas.

Most of all, it's been awoken from a long, deep slumber. And it's *hungry*.

JASMINE

I hold my breath as the camera swivels around 360 degrees again to reveal a cluster of heavily armed guards. They're escorting two hooded figures up the steps of the stage to the gallows.

"They're really going to do this, aren't they?" Lily says to no one in particular. Cassandra takes her hand and gives it a little squeeze.

I don't want to watch, but it's a bit like a car accident. I'm torn as to why we're watching this. I know we need to be informed, but do we have to watch the actual demise of one of our friends, one of our fellow Seers? Not to mention an innocent man alongside her?

And that's when I notice: the smaller figure, the one who is likely female, is too small to be Eva. Too thin. Not only that, but she's walking as though in pain and with a slight stoop. Though I haven't known Eva that long, I would have bet my life she would walk up to those gallows with her head held high.

A noose is carefully placed over each of the prisoners' heads by an armed guard. A tsunami of cheers rises up from the crowd. The guards turn toward Smith. They're waiting for her next command.

And that's when I realize Smith never needed Solomon's Ring — clearly, there are already enough people willing to do her bidding, thinking they're keeping themselves and their loved ones safe from some enemy that doesn't really exist, an enemy that Smith and her administration have fabricated to keep control over Torontonians. The demons she controlled were basically just a more violent addition to her loyal fan club.

"Let's go live now to Trafalgar Square to witness the crowd that has gathered there to watch the live stream from Toronto," one of the female broadcasters says. The scene splits in half, allowing us to simultaneously watch the events in Toronto and the enormous crowd of people gathered in central London. Thousands of people, probably hundreds of thousands, are there. Some are sitting on and hanging off of two large, black metal lions under a tall, thin column, while others are seated along the rim of an unused fountain — all of them are watching several massive screens displaying the execution. Like in Toronto, the mood seems almost celebratory. There are occasional outbursts of cheers, as well. They're more like spectators at a soccer game than at an execution of fellow human beings.

"Despite the raids taking place across the capital today, it looks as though a sizable crowd has come out to witness the events across the pond, in Canada. We take you back there right now, as we've just gotten word that Mayor Smith is about to start the proceedings."

The screen shifts back completely to the scene in Toronto. Smith silently nods at the guards. Apparently, that's their cue, because one of them speaks into his video watch, and suddenly the nooses tighten as the silver ropes begin to quickly disappear up into the arms of the poles, hoisting the two figures off their feet and into the air. Their bodies jerk and twist violently for a few moments before becoming perfectly still.

As quickly as the execution began, it's over.

There are shouts of joy as people in the audience hug and high-five each other.

"I think I'm going to be sick," Dani says, covering her mouth and leaping to her feet. She races over to the kitchen sink and leans over it, retching loudly.

"Jasmine! Look!" Lily says. She and Cassandra are staring in open-mouthed horror at the images playing out on the screen.

I turn back to see the picture zoom in on the faces of the dead, their bulging eyes, protruding tongues.

The crowd's cheers and whistles of approval reach thunderous proportions.

I stare at the image, unable to believe what I'm seeing. Because I was right.

It wasn't Eva being executed.

It was Ms. Samson.

All of us in the room sit in stunned silence as the drones continue to swoop back and forth, filming close-up shots of Taylor Moore and Ms. Samson's lifeless bodies as they gently sway above the cheering crowd. Ms. Samson looks so thin and fragile, almost childlike. Tears roll down my cheeks. I don't even want to save humanity if this is what we're like. The world would be better off without our species.

Cassandra is the first to break the silence.

"If Ms. Samson is dead," she says, her voice slow and deliberate, "then where's Eva? Does this mean she's safe?" She wipes at the tears that are trickling down her cheeks.

Clarence shakes his head. "That we can't be sure of. However, just as we have contingency plans here in London for any situation in which the authorities capture our members, or in which Seers such as yourselves are in grave danger, I'm sure they had the same at Beaconsfield."

I slide a sideways glance at Jade to observe her reaction to it all. Pretending to be preoccupied by brushing away my own tears, I stare at her. Her face is emotionless. She's showing about as much feeling as a brick wall.

"How come people aren't freaking out about the fact that the wrong person's been executed?" Lily asks.

"People who cheer on this kind of thing don't care much about all of that. They're not thinking clearly. That's why the followers of these corrupt governments are more dangerous than the leaders themselves," Sadie answers, her eyes darkening. "And, just you watch, a story will be spun over the next few hours to explain it all. Fake news that these same people will lap up like honey."

Clarence's video watch buzzes. He glances down at it, his bushy eyebrows drawing together in a gesture of deep concern as he reads the message.

"We've got to go," he says sharply, as he taps his watch and looks up at us. "Our location is on the raid list for tonight."

Sadie stands up. "We'll need a medical van to take Cassandra in," she says, worry lining her voice. "I want to reduce the chances of being stopped and questioned."

Clarence nods. "I'm not a hundred percent sure that will guarantee you security today, Sadie, but it's worth the chance. I'll call for one now. We'll shut everything down, and you can meet them in the back garden. Be sure to take her down only when you get the message with the safe word." He reaches into the pocket of his worn corduroy blazer and pulls out a little bronze tin.

"I know you have these for you," Clarence says. "But you'll need some for Cassandra as well. We can take no chances, especially now."

Sadie nods as she takes the tin from his shaking hand.

Lily's eyes grow wide. "What are those?" she cries, jumping up and rushing toward the nurse. "Is it poison? It's the same poison as Vashti took today, isn't it? You're not going to poison my sister!"

Sadie quickly puts the tin into her pocket as Lily tries to snatch it from her hands.

"Sit down, Lily," Cassandra says through gritted teeth. "You've saved my life enough times. The first time when I was tried as a witch in the Place-in-Between, and countless others. This is bigger than us. Clarence is right."

I stare at Cassandra. She's let me in. She means most of what she's saying to Lily, except for the very last part. And that's because she's pretty certain she's dying. The surgery on her arm was successful, but an infection is setting in.

In 2032, even a serious infection is easily treatable, of course, but given our situation, there's no guarantee that the nurse can obtain the necessary intravenous antibiotics or find a safe place to administer them. Both Cassandra and I realize this. It's not like they can just wheel her into a hospital. And this is why there is a good chance she will become a casualty of war.

Tears sting my eyes. Though I'll admit that I haven't always felt all warm and fuzzy about Cassandra, in the end, we're more similar than we are different. We're both first-borns and fiercely loyal to our sisters and fellow Seers, and we're both more than a little impulsive.

I look over at her. She shakes her head at me, then shoots me this sad little smile. She doesn't want Lily to know what's happening, even though she realizes that once the infection takes hold and her pain worsens, her twin will figure it out. But by that time, we'll be on our way to our next destination. Hopefully one that will bring us closer to Spitalfields and the Roman wall, so we can deposit the ring back in its rightful place.

"Dani, look out the window," Clarence says. "But be discreet. The cars should be here. One silver, one black. They'll be across the street."

Dani gets up and slides over to the window, her long legs carrying her across the room in just a few steps. She brushes the edge of the drapes aside and looks out. "They're out there," she confirms somewhat breathlessly as she turns back to us. "Are you sure it's safe?" she asks Clarence.

He shakes his head as he slowly and shakily pulls himself up out of the chair he's been sitting in.

"Safe is a concept, a state of being, that no longer exists," he says. "The faster you realize this, the better off we will all be."

He nods at me. "Grab the brown leather satchel sitting on the dining table for me. We must go."

JASMINE

It tears my heart apart watching Lily hug Cassandra goodbye. She clings to her sister until the last possible moment. When I first saw Jade again in the Place-in-Between after spending five years apart, I didn't want to let go of her, either, because I was afraid she'd somehow slip away and I'd never see her again. I know how much this is hurting both of them.

"Everyone's waiting for us downstairs," I say from behind them. I try to keep my voice from being too sharp, but it's difficult, knowing that each second we spend here increases the risk of our being caught in the raids.

"I love you," Lily sobs, clutching Cassandra's wrists. "And I'll see you soon, okay? As soon as all of this is over. Then you'll be better."

Cassandra nods, tears sliding down her cheeks. She's shaky on her feet. The nurse watches, concern etched across her face.

"I love you. Be safe. Now go," Cassandra whispers, her voice hoarse. I can tell from the look in her eyes that each word is difficult to get out. The pain must be getting worse.

Lily turns and holds her head up, though her shoulders heave from sobbing. I slide an arm around her shoulder as we head out the front door of the flat. But I don't turn around to say goodbye to Cassandra. I can't bear to. Because I know seeing her again would be nothing short of a miracle. The chances are practically non-existent, and I don't want to remember this fragile, shaking version of Cassandra, with her jet-black hair hanging lifelessly over her shoulders and tears streaking her pale cheeks. I want to hold onto the pain-in-my-ass, sarcastic, beautiful version of her. The one I'll admit I was sometimes intensely jealous of and may have disliked, but now realize I also loved. That's the memory I want to carry out of here.

The others are in the foyer, all standing along the wall. There's only the dimmest light coming from a single bulb hanging above us, and there's no guarantee that it won't go out at any moment.

"You will need to put the ring back in the wall as early as possible tomorrow," Clarence says. "The cars will take you to a flat very close to Aldgate Station. Only when the ring is back in its proper place will you have a modicum of safety. But again, you mustn't count on safety. You cannot let your guard down. Things will likely move more quickly now, and you'll need to be ready for battle. Everything you need to know is in there." He nods at the satchel around my shoulder. "Guard it with your lives until you reach the Aldgate flat, where you can read it. And guard that ring in the same manner until you are able to place it in the wall."

"What? You're not coming with us?" Susie asks, her eyebrows drawing into a frown. "You're just leaving us on our own? That's rubbish. You're our Protector." She nods toward Sara.

"It's true. How can you not come with us if things are as bad as you say?" Sara says.

Clarence places a hand on each of their shoulders. I hold my breath, part of me wondering if Susie will haul off and punch him. "I fully intend to meet up with all of you, but I can't leave quite yet. There are a few things I need to take care of here. But enough talking. You all need to go."

"Not before I have the ring," I say, turning to Jade. "I'd like to keep it in here." I pat the smooth leather of the satchel. "It makes no sense to have each of us carrying such critical items."

Jade looks at me. Her eyes narrow a bit just for a second, as though she's trying to figure me out. It's a strange gesture, almost like that of someone sussing out a complete stranger. Then her eyes widen with surprise and she laughs. "Don't you trust your twin?" she asks.

I try to reach into her thoughts once more, hoping that maybe it will work this time, that our connection will have somehow, miraculously, restored itself. Nothing. I feel like I'm reaching my fingers out and hitting a brick wall. It's as frustrating and discouraging as screaming into the wind.

"Give her the ring, Jade," Lily snaps. "We don't have time for this bullshit. I don't know about Jasmine, but I personally don't trust you. Why would I? You took the ring out of the wall without bothering to tell any of us in the first place."

Jade's eyes widen again, but I'm certain I detect a feigned surprise, a mocking condescension, as she turns toward Lily.

"Okay, I hear you," she says. She reaches into the pocket of her jeans, fishes out the ring, and hands it to me.

Almost as soon as the ring hits the palm of my hand, it begins to warm up and vibrate. I close my fingers around it for just a moment and feel a surge of energy course through my body, making me feel stronger and more assured about what lies ahead.

Clarence cracks the front door open and peers out. "It's clear," he says. "Remember, curfew has started. You need to get into the flat as quickly as possible. The lack of people is even more dangerous than a crowd is. You'll stand out like sore thumbs."

We dash out the door. The headlights of the cars flash on as we approach, and the engines purr to life. Without a word, we split into two groups, each one dashing into its respective car.

Jade gets into the car beside me and sits silently, staring out the window as we slide along the streets of London. In Toronto, some people are exempt from curfew, such as office cleaners, first responders, and subway repair engineers, but there are checks in place during curfew. I'd bet my left arm that it's the same here, which makes me wonder how we're going to make it to our destination without, at the very least, being stopped and asked for identification.

I look over at Jade. She's still staring out the window, angled away from me, so I can see only her silhouette against the window. Not only does she have this blank expression, but every few seconds, the corners of her mouth and eye twitch as though she's got some weird tic or her face is moving independently of her or something. After watching for about a minute, I'm so disturbed, I turn away. The distance I feel from Jade causes me to think about Mom and wonder if she's okay. She must be worried sick about us, which hurts my heart. Though I try not to think about it, I realize there's a good chance I'll never see her again.

Dani clears her throat nervously. She's sitting on the other side of me, her hands folded tightly in her lap, her dark eyes staring out toward the windshield.

"Aren't there checkpoints in London?" I ask.

She nods, pressing her full lips tightly together. "Always. Yes. All over the city. I'm not sure why we haven't come across one yet."

I follow her gaze out the window. Rows of large white houses give way to shops, cafes, and restaurants. All are closed now due to the curfew. Some are even boarded up.

"It seems so empty," Lily says from the front seat. "Not just of people — so much of it is closed down. Stores and stuff."

Dani shrugs. "Yeah, a lot of places closed down forever coz there's no tourism anymore. Loads of the shops and restaurants around here closed up over the last five or so years. We're near Oxford Circus and Piccadilly now. You know, where Madame Tussauds was and stuff. Not that our family ever came here much. We stayed pretty much in and around Hackney. You had to have serious pounds to come here to do anything. Things must be the same in Toronto, yeah?"

There's no time to even respond to Dani, because our car is suddenly bathed in blood-red light. Lily sucks in her breath sharply. I glance around to see what's going on.

There are two heavily armed police officers waving our cars to the side of the road. Several cruisers, their lights flashing, block us from continuing any further. I hold my breath, my heart beating double time. Surely Clarence and the other Protectors anticipated that something like this might happen to us and had a plan.

As we slow to a halt, Lily turns from her seat at the front of the car.

"What do we say?" she asks, her eyes wide with fear.

I feel cold from my toes to the top of my head, and I clutch the satchel closer to my side.

"I have no idea," I answer as the first police officer raps on the car window with the butt of his automatic rifle.

JASMINE

The automatic window slides down and the officer peers in. His face clouds with concern as soon as he sees us.

"What are you young ladies doing out after curfew on your own?" he asks, flashing his light at each of our faces and then throughout the interior of the car. I notice how his other hand slides down to the handle of his gun as he does so, and my heart leaps into my mouth.

None of us makes a sound. I'm holding my breath.

"I asked you a question," he says. This time his voice is harder, even a bit menacing. He turns his head toward his partner, a petite female who is checking the other car. "Sam, I'm going to need the chip reader for this lot. Apparently, they don't know you can't plead the Fifth in England. Or they're foreigners."

Lily turns to me, her eyes wide. We're thinking the same thing: we don't have microchips.

"Let us go," Jade says suddenly. "We're fine. Don't worry."

The officer frowns, his bushy brows furrowing as though he's concentrating deeply.

"You need to let us go," Jade repeats, her voice low. There's a roughness to her voice that makes the command sound like a growl.

On impulse, I move a bit closer to Dani, away from Jade. There's something else in her voice that's making my skin crawl.

The female officer approaches our car, stands beside her partner, and peers in at us. "Bloody hell, they're just kids in this car as well. What are all of you doing out here after curfew?"

Before any of us can answer, both of the officers' radios burst to life with a fury of loud beeps and flashing yellow lights.

"This is a Code Severe. Repeat, Code Severe throughout the Greater Metropolitan London area. All officers on duty must return to headquarters for further instructions. All off-duty officers will be called in as well."

"Balls," the male officer says with a grimace. "Only two hours left in our shift …"

The female officer's video watch buzzes loudly. She glances down at it. "Well, you can kiss getting off anytime soon goodbye," she says. "You won't believe this. It's the Thames reservoirs. They've been compromised. The BBC is reporting on it already. And calling it terrorism. What are they thinking?" Her face contorts in frustration, her thin lips drawing downward.

The male officer's eyes shift to us and then back to his partner. I read his thoughts. He figures since everything is already being splashed across the news, he doesn't need to be too careful around a bunch of teenaged girls. If only he knew.

"Well, they're likely right. About it being a CCT attack. Has all the hallmarks of the other water attacks, like Toronto," he says.

My heart leaps into my throat again. For sure one of them is going to be triggered by this and recognize us. And then we'll end up like Ms. Samson. Or worse. I think about what Vashti told us concerning that woman on the high street who saw Atika's body and recognized me. *We're at war.* If it comes to it, we have to take down these two officers to get away.

The thing is, the male officer is not even paying attention to us anymore. He's checking his own video watch now.

"Christ. They've even told the public that the North London Aquifer is nearly dried out due to drought." He shakes his head. "Well done, Beebs. We're going to have bloody chaos on the streets in a few hours; it'll look like a civil war out here."

"Let us go," Jade says to him. She's narrowed her eyes so much that they're practically just dark slits in her face. She's shooting the officer a super-venomous look, but he seems oblivious. And she's completely ignoring Lily, Dani, and me.

The male officer suddenly looks up from his watch and back at us, then slaps the top of the car twice in a gesture that comes across as almost jovial. "Girls, you need to get to where you're going straight away. This is not the time to be out; the city is going to be on lock-down soon. Do me and all first responders a favour: get indoors and stay there unless you hear otherwise." He flashes us a smile. "And fill up as many containers and bottles you can find with water as soon as you get in. We're in for a bit of a difficult time where London's water supply is concerned."

The window slides up and our car begins moving again. I look over at Jade. She's smiling, staring straight ahead.

"What happened there?" I ask her, trying to keep my voice steady though every cell in my body is on high alert.

Jade turns to me, her smile widening. "What do you mean?" she asks.

"With the police back there," Dani says, turning toward Jade. "How did you do that? It's like you were using mind control or something." She stops speaking for a moment. "Correct me if I'm wrong, but as far as I know, that's not a Seer thing."

"I have no idea what you're talking about," Jade insists, flashing Dani a smile so sweet, it might as well be honey-infused. "I just gave him a suggestion to help us out. You're joking about mind control, right?"

Dani throws a quick glance in my direction. "I guess it was just coincidence," she says, her voice ripe with uncertainty.

Jade throws her head back and laughs, teeth gleaming. For some reason, this gesture strikes me as almost shark-like. I shake my head. I need to stop. This is my sister. I'm letting my imagination get the better of me. Maybe because of the tension I've felt between Jade and me recently, along with the fact that our connection has seemed to be severed.

"Of course it's a coincidence," she says.

But as hard as I try, I just don't believe her.

JASMINE

We arrive at the flat about fifteen minutes later. Luckily, the car was programmed to take a route using less-travelled roads, allowing us to avoid any more police checkpoints as well as the rioting crowds that we glimpse once or twice when crossing main roads. Some of the streets are already filling with people, the growing crowds illuminated by intermittent fires set in the scattered trash, recycling, and compost bins.

"Your destination will be on the right in approximately five hundred metres," the smooth female voice of the car's AI informs us. I look ahead to where we're going. It's pretty clear right away that this area isn't nearly as nice as the last one. The street is narrow and dimly lit by only one or two sodium streetlights. Graffiti-covered, metal-shuttered doors are the norm for at least half of the houses that stretch along it. Several skeletal dogs run past us as the car begins to slow. Though less foot traffic here means less attention drawn to us, I'm still nervous.

This is the kind of place we were always taught to avoid when we were younger. I instinctively clutch the leather satchel tightly to me, reminding myself that the ring is in there. For now it guarantees us safety — if demons are involved.

Dani's video watch beeps. She taps it. "It's Kiki. They're right behind us. Clarence just sent her the security codes for the building keypad and for the flat." She bites at her bottom lip as she finishes reading. "That's weird," she says. "No Protector is meeting us here. Apparently, it's too dangerous to try to reach us. Clarence says there're already reports of rioting and looting south of the river."

"Because of the water situation?" Lily says, turning in her seat.

Dani nods. "Yeah, but ..."

"But what?" I ask. Jade is staring out her window again, the back of her head facing me. How can she not be concerned about this?

Dani glances up at us, her dark eyes fearful. "Apparently, there's been some sort of massive cyber attack as well in the last hour or so. At least that's what the news is saying."

There's a sudden knock on the driver's side door that is so loud, it makes my heart leap into my throat and Lily give a startled yelp.

"Hurry up," Sara says, cupping her meaty hands around her eyes and peering in at us. "Get out so we can get inside."

We rush out and over to one of the buildings. A misty drizzle is beginning to fall. Ordinarily, this would be a time to celebrate. Any kind of precipitation is such a rare event. But considering what's happening right now, it feels more like a dark omen.

The front door is still intact, though it's in desperate need of a paint job. Yellow spray paint scrawled across the pollution-darkened brick beside the door reads, *The Haram Gang was here.*

"Let's hope they're not here anymore," Kiki says, eyeing the graffiti as she steps up to the security keypad. She puts her left arm around her sister's waist. "Together. You and me. No matter what happens from here on in, I'm not leaving your side. We'll be each other's Protector."

Dani rests her head briefly on Kiki's shoulder, her dark curls gleaming with drops of misty rain. "You better believe it," she replies.

As Kiki begins tapping the code into the keypad, I look over at Jade, my heart heavy. She's watching Kiki intently and either doesn't notice my gaze or is pretending not to. I desperately miss Mom and Mr. Khan and wish there were some way I could contact them, some means of finding out if they're okay. And I wish I had Jade the way Kiki and Dani have each other. Even before our connection was severed, there was tension between us, a sort of resentment that seemed to stem from Jade.

The keypad flashes green and Kiki pushes the door. It doesn't open easily. We find out why as soon as we step into the foyer: it's packed with boxes of discarded clothing, toys, and small household items. I wrinkle my nose at an overpowering stench of mildew mixed with at least a few rodents that have died and rotted in this space.

"Bloody hell," Sara says, covering her mouth. "What a shithole."

The stairwell leading to the flat isn't much better. It's poorly lit, and the carpet covering the steps is full of holes and dark, blotchy stains. I'm kind of glad for the dim lighting, as I don't want to know what those stains are from.

Fingers of dread creep along the inside of my abdomen as Kiki opens the door to the flat. We're on the top floor of the house. None of the flats we've passed on the way to this one betrayed any signs of life behind their doors — no voices, no music, no footsteps, no dogs barking. Only silence.

A ripple of relief moves through us as soon as we step inside the flat. I make sure I'm last so I can take one final glance behind us. The shadowy stairwell is making me nervous for some reason. Maybe it's just the eerie silence, or the way the dim light seems to play tricks on my eyes. I'm also beyond exhausted and know that must be playing a part in the jittery feelings I'm having. In the distance, I can hear sirens. Things are likely getting really bad out there, if the reports Clarence gave Kiki are true.

"Well, at least this place isn't as gross as I thought it would be," Lily murmurs as I close the door behind me.

She's right. If ever there were a lesson on not judging a book by its cover, this is it. A large living room with a gas fireplace that's already burning greets us. The wooden floor gleams up at us, its pale surface broken up by several colourful carpets.

Wait.

The fireplace is burning.

I grab Lily by the elbow. "Did Kiki turn on the lights? Did anyone else? How did the fireplace get turned on?" I ask her.

Lily shrugs. "I don't know." She opens her mouth to say something else, but her words are cut short.

"Hey, Jazz," says a familiar voice from the kitchen area. "I was told you'd be here."

My heart stops. For a moment, I wonder if I'm hallucinating after so much loss, so much uncertainty … after the horrible execution of Ms. Samson.

"*Chica!* Come on. I'm not a ghost," Eva says, reading my thoughts, though the shock on my face would likely be enough to discern my feelings. She smiles widely as she walks over, throws her arms around me, and kisses me on both cheeks. A brightly coloured head wrap covers the zigzagging map of scars on the side of her head — remnants of her battle with the men who killed her sister. New burn scars, courtesy of the Toronto Police, run the length of the left side of her face. "Turns out I can transition on my own, you know? Not as easy with three fingers missing and no other Seers, but I managed."

"Who told you we'd be here? How long have you been in London?" I ask, hugging her back. I'm so happy to see someone from home, from Toronto. It gives me hope that more of my loved ones will survive.

A wave of dizziness washes over me as I pull away from Eva. It's a feeling I've unfortunately become familiar with. Dehydration. My mouth is so dry that my tongue sticks to the roof of my mouth as I speak. "Is there still water?" I ask.

Eva nods. "Kind of. I filled up as many containers as I could find when I first got here, so we've got some stored for sure. Nothing but a trickle is coming out of the taps now, though. Conservation will be key." She gives Lily and Jade quick hugs, then waves at everyone else. "I'm Eva."

After quick introductions, we each pour ourselves half a glass of water. Though I know it's not enough to sustain the eight of us for long, Eva's managed to fill an upright water cooler that she discovered in the kitchen. Impressive.

Once we're settled in the living room, taking small sips of water to make it last longer, Eva tells us what happened: Ms. Samson arranged through Clarence's brother, Frederick, to visit Eva in custody. Of course, she didn't visit under her own identity, but rather, as Eva's grandmother. Frederick gave Eva the message that she was to transition with Ms. Samson's help during the visit; she was needed for the Final Battle. Ms. Samson would be left behind in the cell.

Knowing what she does about the Seers, Smith has been fully aware of Ms. Samson's importance to us. After all, she was the world's oldest living Protector. So Smith's anger over Eva's disappearance was tempered by her opportunity to execute Ms. Samson.

An elaborate story was broadcast to the media by Smith's government: Eva was the one behind the switch, having forced her grandmother at knifepoint, to trade places with Eva in order for her to escape. It made the narrative of Eva's being a cold-blooded terrorist and murderer even more chilling in the eyes of the public. Not only had she killed police officers with her bare hands, she also effectively murdered her own granny to obtain freedom.

A heavy blanket of silence fills the room for a few moments. We all take a moment to remember Ms. Samson. The collective sadness is obvious.

"That's a story filled with plot holes, if I've ever heard one," Lily says. "Smith's followers will believe anything, won't they?"

Eva nods. "Yeah, they will. But because everyone in Toronto is terrified due to the water attack, it doesn't take much at this point to sway even those who hated Smith before. For instance, she kept reminding everyone I was an illegal from Cuba to scare people about CCT refugees, and at the same time she was claiming my *abuelita* was Ms. Samson. A Jamaican woman." She rolls her eyes. "Of course, it goes against all common sense, but water is our life force. When that's threatened, people get desperate. Common sense: gone." She snaps her fingers above her head to emphasize her point.

"And now it's happening here as well. A water crisis in a city of ten million plus," I say with a nod toward the window. I notice it's covered by a thick black opaque blind — the type that doesn't allow any light in or out. Whoever designed these Seer safe houses thought them out well.

"Clarence said there were raids throughout London today and Seers were getting arrested, yeah?" Susie says.

"I wonder if we're being scapegoated for the reservoirs being contaminated."

My fingers touch the soft leather of the satchel. I wonder if the ring is pulsating away in the pocket I zipped it into. Just the thought makes me shudder. There's something about its power, about its energy, that makes me realize how possessing this ring can corrupt a person. Just like it did to Solomon. Though I am not looking forward to touching it again, I am eager to get it back into the wall.

"Clarence wanted us to read what's in here." I say, placing my glass on the coffee table across from me so I can open the satchel. "He said it was important information. About the Final Battle, I'm guessing."

The inside of the leather bag smells old. Ancient. There are two yellowed documents that aren't made of paper, but something thicker, like skin. It's hard to tell, though, as they are encased in plastic sleeves.

"I reckon those are so old, they'd turn into a heap of dust like a vampire if we took them out of those plastic sleeves," Susie says.

I nod and look the first one over. It's a map — a really old one — with a large, slightly wonky star drawn overtop of it. The star was clearly drawn in old school ink, and is pretty sloppy, as the star's arms aren't even at all.

"That's London. I mean, centuries-ago London, but a lot of what's on there is still around today," Dani says, pointing a red-tipped fingernail at the map. "But why the pentagram on top of it?"

"Pentagram?" Eva asks. "What's that?"

"The star symbol. It's gotten a bad rap over time, but its meaning, as I've been taught and believe, is deeply magical. It's a protective symbol, like the Earth, and closely related to her." Dani traces a finger lightly along the surface of the plastic. "See how it has no beginning and no ending? This shows the interrelatedness of all creation. Infinity and eternity. And it offers protection to those who believe."

"How do you know all of this?" Lily asks, leaning over my shoulder to get a better view.

"Dani and I are Wiccan," Kiki says. "Brought up as witches. Seers. With a strong belief that our power is a gift from Mother Earth. This symbol is a good thing."

"Thank god for something feel-good in all of this," Jade says, though there's little expression in her voice. She's standing just to the side of Dani. The way she's speaking, you'd think she was reading from a script.

I turn the map over. There's something written on the other side, in the same sort of ink. It reads, *This mappe sheweth the protection from the demonic pow'rs and all evil f'r all London'rs as did marke by the churches of Hawksmo'r.*

"What do you think that means?" I ask Kiki and Dani. "It has to do with the pentagram, right?"

"Turn it over again," Kiki says. She sits beside me on the couch and examines the map closely. The spicy odour of her body fills my nostrils. We're all likely smelling pretty ripe by now.

"Each point on the pentagram is a church," she continues. "I'd guess they're all designed by this Hawksmoor bloke. For sure, no woman would've been allowed to be an architect in those days."

"What do they mean about protection? And isn't that the church we were at in Greenwich?" I ask Lily, pointing at one of the only churches south of the river. "That one. St Alfege. When we transitioned back from the Place-in-Between for the first time."

"That's it for sure," Jade answers. "I'll never forget how terrifying our experience there was."

She's been so silent up until now that I'm shaken by her interjection. No one else reacts, but I can't help feeling she's playing a role. There's such a fake undertone to her words.

But maybe our connection isn't as broken as I've believed it to be. I look over at her again.

"I was terrified as well," I say. "Terrified I would lose you again. I love you so much, Jade."

My gaze remains level on her face, her eyes, as I speak. And there it is, only for a moment; it's a quick flash, but Jade is suddenly there behind those eyes. Just like the time Jamie Linnekar was suddenly present despite the demon occupying his body. Jade is still conscious in there somewhere. But who or what is possessing her? Whatever it is, it certainly isn't demonic, or, at least, it's not any type of demon we've encountered before.

"The area within the pentagram is supposed to be a haven from demons, evil spirits, and negative energy," Kiki replies. "I reckon that blurb means that the parts of London within the pentagon formed by those churches are safe. What else did Clarence put in there for us?"

I reach in and pull out a piece of paper that's been folded several times into a neat square. I unfold it.

There's shaky handwriting scrawled in blue ink. It's immediately clear that it's from Clarence. I clear my throat and begin to read.

My Dearest Seers,

If you are reading this, you have at least made it to the flat. The time, according to the Lost Scrolls, has come when the human race and, indeed, the world in which it resides are at risk of extinction. This risk is due partially to our decline into war and greed and our destruction of the planet and her resources. Many of the world's water reserves have been poisoned over the last few days and hours. This is the fulfillment of a prophecy that states, "Only when the last tree is cut down, the last fish eaten, and the last stream poisoned, will you realize you cannot eat money." The other part of what is happening is explained in the Lost Scrolls, which tell of the return of the Darkness, the primordial force that split the worlds and that will bring them back together upon its return. That time is now. The amount of consumable water left on this Earth will not sustain most of the population for more than a few months. This crisis is what the Indigenous Water Defenders and the CCT have been trying to prevent for decades, but those in power, those who control the majority of the world's riches, have won.

The Scrolls describe seven female warriors, twin Seers descended from Lilith, that will battle the seven Archons with help from the seven Archangels at the Final Battle. There is one female Seer who will be tasked with destroying the Darkness. She is chosen. If the battle is successful, the Darkness will be destroyed. The powers of Light shall triumph, and then the era of Shambhala will begin: a time when all those left on Earth will labour for the good of humanity and all the planet's creatures. But if the Darkness reigns, humanity will be immediately exterminated, and the Earth will become a wasteland, a desert where little life survives and where demonic entities reign free amongst the lost souls, whom they will mercilessly and eternally torture. It will be known as the Netherworld, and the Earth and all her bounty will cease to exist.

Your poles are waiting for you in the first bedroom of this flat. Tonight, you must sleep. By tomorrow, the streets will be awash with blood, as the war has begun. You will need to get to Greenwich. This is a place of great power. It is where you shall battle. Remember that St Alfege's and the area directly north of it, as well as southwest and northeast, will provide sanctuary. But only if the ring has been put back. And you mustn't hide in safe spaces. The lack of water will soon cause the greatest suffering that any of the Earth's creatures, including humans, have

ever known. Defeating the Darkness will bring
about peace and a cleansing rejuvenation of the
Earth. A boat will take you from St Katharine
Docks to Greenwich. You must be at the dock by
5:00 a.m. From there, it is a short journey to the
Royal Observatory in Greenwich Park.

Perhaps, if all goes well, there is a chance
we will be reunited. However, the violence
and bloodshed that are about to take place in
London and, indeed, throughout the world
make it hard for an old man in my poor state
of health to survive — even for a day or two.
As such, I will bid you farewell. May you stay
strong in the face of evil.

In solidarity and with love,

Clarence Thompson

I finish reading. We're all quiet for a few moments.

"Well, there are seven of us," Susie finally says, lifting
the heavy blanket of silence.

"Whether any of this is true or not," Lily says, "staying
cooped up in here would mean running out of water in
just a few days, if that. Clarence is right. The chaos outside
these four walls is only going to get worse — much worse."

There's a murmur of agreement.

"Yep," Eva says. "If we stay here, we eventually die.
And I didn't escape the gallows to die of dehydration.

If this battle is real, we have a chance not only to save ourselves, but to save the planet. After all, this is what we've been training for, right? It's a no-brainer, and so, I'm heading to bed. I have a feeling I'm going to need all the sleep I can get."

"I'm going to get my pole and sleep out here on the sofa, if that's okay," I say, getting up. "I just feel like someone should be on guard. You know, considering what's going on outside — with regards to both demons and humans."

I figure everyone will be asleep within the hour, and then I'll safely be able to leave.

JASMINE

As soon as I open the front door of the flat, I can smell it. The air is heavy with smoke, the acrid smell of burning tires, trash, and other toxic materials, and this stench hits me like a slap. I double over coughing, my eyes filling with tears.

Turning on my heel, I walk back into the foyer of the house and rummage through one of the partially opened boxes of clothes, praying that no rat or spider nests are disturbed by my movements. My fingers come across a cotton T-shirt. I pluck it out of the bin and tie it around my nose and mouth securely enough that it will help filter out some of the smoke, but not so tight that my breathing is impeded. I realize wetting the cloth would make this a much more efficient filter, but even if I were lucky enough to find some H_2O, there's no way I'd use it for that. Not unless it was water straight out of the river. Eventually, I might get desperate enough to drink that, too, even if it makes me sick. I suspect many

Londoners will do the same. If the Final Battle is as near as Clarence says it is, I guess Londoners dipping into the Thames for drinking water isn't such a big concern. But if this battle isn't happening in the very near future, then I predict some pretty serious water-borne diseases will be spreading through the city in the next week or so — if everyone doesn't kill each other first.

I asked Dani if I could borrow her video watch just before we all headed to sleep, saying I'd use it to alert the others if I heard anything kicking off outside the flat or on the street directly below us. At the moment, I'm not as worried about using it as I might've been otherwise. The police are likely up to their ears in emergency calls, what with the riots, so I doubt they have too many officers tracking calls tonight. My guess is the military will be on the streets by morning to try to restore the peace. Maybe even sooner. But hopefully not before we get to Greenwich.

I've got my route to the wall mapped out and the satchel secured around my shoulders. It's bulky and a bit awkward, but I don't want to risk just holding it. If I run into trouble, I need to be able to use my pole without worrying about the satchel. Unfortunately, considering the screams and shouts I'm hearing in the near distance, I might have to use my pole against normal human beings tonight. I hope not.

It's well after midnight, so I've got a few hours before everyone back at the safe house wakes up to get ready to walk to the boat. I'm going to stick to the side streets to avoid the main roads, though that's no guarantee that

I won't still run into things kicking off. The walk to the Roman wall near Tower Hill shouldn't take much more than fifteen or twenty minutes, according to the video watch, so if all goes according to plan, I'll be back in the apartment in time to get an hour or two of shut-eye.

I'm heading toward Vine Street, trying to stay as close as possible to the buildings. Though I don't let my guard down, this street is completely empty, from what I can tell. It also helps that I seem to be walking along the backs of most of the buildings. I guess most of them face outward onto parallel streets.

As I round the corner to Cooper's Row, a street that should take me right down to Tower Hill and the Roman wall, a group of about eight people charges up the middle of the street in my direction. Some have their hoods up, others have masks covering their faces, and they carry lit tiki torches.

The blood freezes in my veins. I'm fully exposed. Putting my head down, I continue to walk, making sure to stay as far to the right side of them as I can.

"Hey, little sister," one of them shouts as they get nearer. It's hard to see his face, but he's tall and built like a weightlifting steroid junkie.

I stand straighter, refusing to be intimidated, even though he's at least a foot taller than me. "Hey," I say, throwing my shoulders back and making sure to meet his gaze.

"Want to join us to find more water? We're going to hit up some high street shops." He nods toward a shopping cart that an incredibly skinny girl is pushing. She's near the back of the group. I stare at her legs: they're so twig-like, I wonder how she finds the strength to push the cart, which is filled with at least three cases of bottled water. And … a kitten? I shake my head before taking a second look. The kitten is such a tiny smudge of grey sitting on the top of the water bottles that, for a moment, I mistake it for a glove or some small article of clothing. Then it looks up at me with these powder-blue eyes that are so full of terror, my heart feels like it's shattering into a million pieces in my chest. Maybe it's all the loss that I've experienced or a just case of massive sympathy for this kitten, but something won't let me just pass her by.

"Whose kitten is that? Is it yours?" I ask the skeletal girl.

She stops for a moment and tilts her head sideways at me, an amused little half smile tugging at her lips. Deep hollows frame her eyes. "Nah, it ain't mine. We just picked it up from a rubbish bin. It's a good luck charm, innit?" She picks the kitten up by the scruff of the neck, causing it to wail with fear.

"Can I take her?" I ask. I'm not sure what exactly I'm going to do with this kitten, but I am now certain at least part of this group is high on something pretty potent. When I reach into their thoughts, I can feel it. Sort of like grabbing a live electrical wire with your bare hands.

"Sure," the girl replies with a shrug. "I can't feed her and I ain't giving up any of our water for her, anyhow." She picks up the kitten, who gives a loud mew in protest at being lifted off the safety of the water bottles again, and hands her to me.

The group moves on, chanting loudly about storming a street called Downing or something like that as though the encounter with me never happened. I stare down at the warm, shivering smudge of fur in my hand.

She looks up at me with sad, soulful eyes and emits another pitiful mewl. "I'm going to name you *Mithra*," I say, gently running my fingers over her head. She stops shaking and looks up at me. It's clear that she not only wants to live, but also wants to trust me.

"I'll keep you as safe as I can," I whisper, bending close and burying my face in her soft fur. Her chest begins to rumble, low and steady. I straighten up, glance around, and slip her into the leather satchel. "You'll be okay, Mithra. I promise," I say as I continue to walk south toward Tower Hill and the Roman wall. Really, I have no way to ensure she won't get harmed. I can't even keep safe the people I care most about in this whole world. I just hope I'm reducing some risk to them by returning the ring by myself to the wall tonight.

The rest of my walk is uneventful. Though the smell of smoke still hangs heavy in the air around me and the screams of sirens punctuate the night air, I don't run into any other people. But I'm not really surprised; this area doesn't seem super residential.

The segment of wall near the Tower Hill Tube station is pretty substantial. Warm, moist air envelops me; clearly I'm pretty close to the river. I look around. It's so quiet here, it's almost unnerving.

I open the satchel, unzip the pocket, and reach inside for the ring. Every cell in my body screams at me not to. As soon as the little metal circle is in my hand, it begins to warm and vibrate. Mithra pushes her forehead against my hand and gives a little cry.

"You've gotta stay in here," I whisper. "Once this ring is back, I'm going to have to be ready for anything … including demons." I lift Mithra up and plant a gentle kiss on her head. For a fleeting moment, being here, feeling Mithra's purr — so powerful for such a tiny creature — makes me feel safe. Safety — Clarence warned us not to fall prey to believing that it exists anymore.

I place Mithra carefully back into the leather bag and turn back to face the wall. It's massive and built of a grey, brick-like stone. As I run my fingers along it, searching for a crevice that runs deeply into the structure's core, I can't help but wonder if the Romans that built this wall could've possibly predicted their world would eventually be destroyed. The ring is starting to vibrate even more for some reason, and I can feel its power coursing through every cell in my body. I feel like a junkie that's just gotten a hit; this ring is strong and the temptation to keep it and the power it wields is so dizzying now.

My fingers move along a large crack in the wall, and I reach in up to my wrist. My forearm is too wide, so I can't fit my hand in any farther. Nevertheless, this crevice clearly extends quite far into the stones. Good enough. I want to get rid of the ring as soon as possible. I pluck it from the palm of my right hand and toss it into the crevice as far in as I can, waiting for the tinkling of the metal as it lands, but no sound reaches my ears.

It's gone.

And gone along with it is protection from any demons I might encounter on my journey back to the Aldgate apartment.

JASMINE

I haven't gone more than a block when something slams into me sideways. As my body tumbles into a wall, my shoulder hits the brick with such force that pain sends a shower of stars dancing before my eyes.

Mithra. I twist, trying to keep the rest of my body, satchel included, from striking the hard surface. That could kill Mithra. I'm going to keep my word to this little furball. No harm will come to her while I'm alive.

I spin around, my mind reeling. How did someone manage to sneak up on me like this and catch me so off guard?

Clutching my pole in front of my body in warrior stance, I look up, ready to face my opponent.

A tall man with a body like a brick is standing in front of me. I catch his eyes. He's not a demon. He's some sort of goon, the kind of guy you see standing out in front of clubs.

"What the hell?" I say, lowering my pole. I'm super aware of the fact that I'm wanted as a terrorist, so if I can get out of this situation with minimal conflict and attention drawn to me, all the better. "Why did you do that?" I ask him. No one should be able to sneak up on me like that and push me with such strength, not when I was already on high alert. My face burns with both annoyance and embarrassment.

"Sorry, Jasmine," a voice says from behind the goon.

My blood turns to ice. I know that voice. In fact, I know it well. Too well.

Sandra Smith steps out from behind the man. She's slender and petite enough that his body provided her with full coverage.

"I know you've been taught to notice any moment of weakness, any chink in an opponent's armour. It was fleeting, but for a moment you weren't fully present. You were lost in your thoughts. Not the best move," she says with a smirk.

I open my mouth and promptly close it again. Raphael. That's what, or more precisely, *who* I was thinking about. I was wondering where he was and if I'd ever see him again. And, if I'm truthful, I do want to see him. I was imagining it — only for a few seconds, but that was enough time for Smith's goon to attack me.

"How are you even here?" I ask, glancing around. Out of the corner of my eye, something darts from the railway tracks at the end of street. My shoulders tense. It's likely just a stray dog or fox, something like that. But it could be a demon. They must know I'm here. "And how did you know where to find me?"

"Why are *you* out here?" Smith asks, throwing my question back at me. "And of course I've kept track of you. After all, you're my special helper. How did I do it? Sadly, Jasmine, more than one person whom you've trusted is willing to betray you when the price and/or conditions are right."

I know she wants to get a reaction from me. But even if what she's saying is true, and someone close to me has given away my whereabouts, I'm not about to give Smith the satisfaction of upsetting me. I glance at the goon. He's watching me intently, his face devoid of emotion. My eyes slide to his waist. Beneath the thin blazer he's wearing, I detect the outline of a gun. This is serious. I'm going to have to be cautious. Smith is like a wild animal, ready to strike. I know her well enough to realize I'm in huge danger.

"You see, things aren't quite as we've been made to believe," Smith says.

"What do you mean, made to believe?" I ask, gripping my pole tighter.

"Listen, I'll make this quick. The world simply can't heal with so many people using her resources. There's not nearly enough to go around. Overpopulation got us human beings into this mess in the first place."

"Well, I'd say human greed and the desire for power had a lot do with it, too," I say. "You're an environmental scientist. You know that." It's a dig. She's the most power-hungry person I know.

"But all of this is really quite meaningless now, isn't it?" Smith asks. "And I'd hazard to say that at this point in my life, I'm more of a politician, a strategist, than a scientist."

I frown. Where is she going with this? "Besides," I say, "billions of people have died in the last few years because of climate change, and now with the water poisonings, there will be many more. The population is actually declining. Rapidly."

"And that's really not a bad thing," Smith interjects, "it's too little, too late, but …"

"What the hell?" I snap. "Have you lost your mind? What do you mean it's not a bad thing? You're talking about the deaths of millions — if not billions."

The goon uncrosses his arms, and I notice one of his shovel-like hands sliding slowly toward his waist. I need to tone it down.

Smith springs forward and grabs me by the elbow. Hard. "Hear me out. We want what's best for the human race and for our planet. With a greatly reduced population, the world will heal. The type of poison being used is quick and painless — people are not suffering. Think it about it, Jasmine. With the technologies that are out there shared between just a million people at most — the best and the brightest — and an emphasis on improving AI and carefully planned future procreation, suffering will be drastically reduced, if not eliminated."

I pull away from her as much as I can without risking the goon taking me out. "What you're suggesting is mass murder. On a crazy scale." I stop. "You're behind the water poisonings in Toronto, aren't you?"

Smith nods. "But you knew that already, didn't you? Of course, I didn't act alone. It's well-coordinated, Jasmine. Do you think what's happening here in the UK, and with the rest of the world's water supply, is just a coincidence? More cities and countries will follow in close succession. Within days and weeks. And who do you think hacked all the banking, transit, and security systems? A select group have held the world's resources and power for quite some time now. I mean, think about it: air space is closed, yet I was able to fly here in my private jet. You could have the same privileges."

Adrenaline and anger surge through my body with the intensity of an electrical charge. I need to get a hold of my emotions. I've got to be drawing any demons throughout the city toward me like moths to a flame right now. "This 'plan' is evil. Those who will survive aren't the 'best and brightest.' It's just those who control the power and wealth in the world. Like you. It's the same bullshit that's always existed."

"None of us — not one human — is going to survive if something drastic is not done, because the Earth won't survive unless extreme measures are taken immediately. This should've been done years and years ago. You may not remember when Pakistan became uninhabitable, but I do. It was 2020, too hot to even step outside for weeks on end. Even the camels couldn't survive. Basically, they were slowly baked alive. You're right that most of those who are in on this are a part of the elites. But you're not part of the privileged class in any way, are you? And neither is your mother or your sister.

I think you're just being too stubborn and narrow-minded about the benefits of this plan. About what you and your family could gain. Privilege. Power." She stops speaking and cocks her head at me, her metallic silver hair glinting out at me. This is a well-orchestrated game she's playing. "By the way, how is your mother, Jasmine? Do you have any idea if she's okay?"

Her words cut at my heart like a knife. I grasp my pole so hard, it feels like my knuckles might burst out from my skin. She's baiting me and I'm not going to fall for it.

"No," I reply through gritted teeth. "But you knew that."

"There's a car waiting for us near St Paul's Cathedral," Smith says matter-of-factly, ignoring my reply. "We will be taken to safety to wait this all out. But we need to go now."

"No," I say through gritted teeth. "It's wrong. It's a sick plan."

Smith shrugs and pretends to examine one of her perfectly manicured nails. "I was hoping you'd see it my way, as your mother is with us in Toronto and really needs you to agree to all of this. Otherwise, I can't guarantee her safety. And as for you ... now you know way too much, Jasmine. Just like Ms. Samson ..."

"It was Ms. Samson you wanted all along, wasn't it?" I ask, spitting the words out like venom. "You weren't really after Eva at all."

Smith laughs. "Yes, that woman was powerful. She was full of such light and such good. A talisman, actually.

The Darkness couldn't fully emerge while she was alive. The little Cuban mutt? It would've been a bonus if I'd been able to put her down, but it was easy to give her up in exchange for Samson."

"Well, this Cuban *perra* is an ancestral daughter of Che and Marti and the great-great-granddaughter of Antonio Maceo. She's a poet, a revolutionary, a liberator ... and yes, a righteous killer." Eva's voice, deep and guttural and full of both pride and rage, shatters the night air. In her words, there's a ferocity I've never heard from her before.

I swivel my head around at the same time Smith and her goon do. Eva is standing, pole ready, on top of two large garbage receptacles, one foot on each. She raises her chin defiantly at Smith, the soft light from a streetlamp catching her scars. I'm struck by her beauty. "You thought you could bury us, but you didn't realize we were seeds," she exclaims, punching the air with her pole.

Smith laughs. "Jasmine, this girl is mad. She's right about one thing and only one thing: she's a bona fide killer. She didn't seem to care when she transitioned out of that cell that she was knowingly condemning your precious Ms. Samson to a terrible fate. Come with us. We need people like you to help rebuild our world. There's a car waiting for us a few streets over. Everything is arranged. And you need to think of your mother. Like I said, she's with us in Toronto. We've put her up in a hotel where she has everything she needs, including a reliable water supply, and she is safe. What security does she have if you continue to align yourself with this band of misfits? The world is about to descend into chaos. We have bunkers ready to see this out."

I shake my head. "No. What you're doing is wrong. Beyond wrong. Worse than Hitler wrong."

Smith shakes her head sadly. "Your resistance defies logic, Jasmine. A population of only a few hundred thousand will ensure that the Earth's remaining resources are protected. Think of the animals, the birds, the insects that will be saved by our reducing the destruction that overpopulation has wrought. We'll be able to fully implement environmental technologies to support the regeneration of our planet."

"She doesn't have your mom, Jazz. Don't believe her," Eva interjects. "And it's mass murder. No one who wants to be on the right side of history would consider your *loco* plan, lady."

Smith's head snaps up to stare at Eva.

"Who really killed your sister, Eva? Who took the last breath from her lips?" Smith asks, hands on her hips, a sly smile dancing across her face.

For a moment, Eva visibly wavers from her position on the garbage bins and comes dangerously close to losing her balance. Smith's obviously hit a nerve.

"I suppose there's no harm in letting you both in on my little secret," Smith says, turning her attention back to me for a moment. "And I'm sure you're wondering how I know you decapitated your own sister," she says, her eyes glued on Eva again with hawk-like intensity.

"She was suffering," Eva interjects. It's evident she's trying to keep it together as much as possible, but her voice is beginning to waver. Badly. "Those *singaos* left her severely wounded. She'd lost so much blood. I had no access to medical attention, to painkillers.... She asked me to do it. I couldn't just let her suffer so much."

"But it was you who decided her fate, wasn't it? You've always wondered if she might have lived, if you'd just tried. It took me, a former Seer, to read your mind and know this, to know about your murderous past. Your sister, a young father doing his job serving and protecting, the list goes on.... But where will it end?"

My blood runs cold. *Smith, a Seer?*

"I thought Seers lost their powers once they became adults," I interrupt, trying to maintain my composure. I don't want her to see my surprise.

"There are always outliers, Jasmine. Outliers like me," Smith says. "My power is quite weak compared to yours, but Eva's thoughts about her sister are so powerful, so dark ... it's virtually impossible not to hear them. She's practically certifiable." Smith looks at Eva again. "Aren't you, darling?"

Before I can blink, Eva lunges at Smith. A moment later, her pole slams down onto Smith's shoulder.

"Eva! No!" I shout as Smith's goon reaches under his jacket. His thick fingers are on the trigger before she even has time to turn.

The shot slices through Eva's free hand like it's butter. She screams, but manages to hold on to her pole with her good hand. In a moment, and before he can fire another round, she's on him like a wild animal. She hacks at his thick neck; his bones crunch under the force of her blows. Sweat rolls down the side of her face, mixing with the tears that are spilling from her eyes, both causing wet strands of her hair to stick to her skin. She's thinking of her sister, and the pain is tearing her soul apart.

Through my shock, Vashti's words flood my mind. War. This is war. Though I'm not even sure what the sides are any longer, especially after finding out Smith is one of us — or was one of us. She doesn't seem to be anyone's Protector, though. One thing I know for certain is that if I don't act fast, I'm about to die. So is Eva. There's no way Smith will let us out of here alive after telling us everything she did.

The goon falls to the ground with a sickening thud and Eva turns back toward Smith, who is slouched over, clutching her injured shoulder.

"Go, Jazz!" Eva shouts at me as she strides toward Smith, her face a mask of determination. "Get back to the house and get the other Seers out of there!"

For a moment I'm frozen, feeling the damp night air pressing against my skin as I watch Eva raise her pole to shoulder height, ready to strike Smith again.

"Move your ass, *chica*!" Eva screams at me. "I don't want you to see this."

As her pole connects with the side of Smith's head, a shot rings out. Eva stumbles backward, arms outstretched and eyes wide with surprise. Her mouth opens and closes silently as a red stain blossoms across her chest.

I jerk my head around. Two men are emerging from a side street adjacent to us. Their guns are drawn and they look a lot like Smith's other goon. We should've known more of her entourage would come looking for her after a set amount of time.

A second shot shatters the night air, and that's when I turn and run in the opposite direction, away from Eva and toward the train tracks, my heart pounding like a jackhammer in my chest.

I don't look back and I don't stop running for at least fifteen minutes. A part of me imagines I can outrun the image of Eva being shot, of the pain on her face and the expression that told me she knew she'd been mortally wounded. Eventually, I begin coughing uncontrollably and slow down to a walk. The smoke from the fires around the city is making it unbearable to breathe the already polluted London air. My lungs burn as though I've been drinking acid.

As I sit for a moment on a concrete barrier dividing the roadway from the sidewalk, a muffled cry reaches my ears. Mithra. I'd almost forgotten about her. My hands shake as I reach into the satchel.

She looks up at me, her blue eyes wide.

I reach in again and lightly stroke her head. "This is it, Mithra," I whisper. "The Final Battle is just beginning, and I've already lost one of my best friends. And she was the best Seer I've ever known. Eva should've been chosen, not me. She was a true warrior."

"Get up, Jazz."

My head snaps up, and I quickly return Mithra to the bag.

Raphael is standing over me, his black hair hanging in front of his face as he extends a hand to me. "You need to recover from this. There was nothing else you could've done. If you hadn't left Eva, Smith's men would've killed both of you. And Eva doesn't have her twin; she knew that would be an impediment during the Final Battle, so she made the ultimate sacrifice. Did she know Smith would be waiting for you tonight? No. But she followed you out this evening to keep you safe, to watch over you. We've kept a close eye on her ever since she killed those men on the ship. Seers who kill humans for vengeance tend to go mad. Rogue. Like Mr. Khan's sister. Like Smith. So, it was only natural that a Seer who'd had to watch her sister be tortured and then ..." He pauses, his dark eyes sad. "But we needn't have worried. Eva was more like Mina; she was able to overcome her sister's death and be completely selfless. In fact, after her sister's death, Eva seemed more committed than ever to saving others. Like those at the camp."

I take Raphael's hand and he pulls me to standing. My legs feel shaky, almost jelly-like, and my head spins.

"I can't do this anymore," I say. "It's too much. Both Mina and Eva gave up their lives for me. It's crazy. I don't want to be chosen or anything like that. Pick someone else. Eva should've been the Chosen One."

Raphael smiles. "Yeah, if I'd had a say in it, she'd likely have been my first choice as well."

Tears slip down my cheeks. I don't even know if it's because of Eva, or exhaustion, or just losing so many people in the last two years.

"Jazz, I was only kidding," he says, pulling me close to him.

My heart begins to beat loudly, so loudly I'm afraid he'll hear it.

"What you need to remember is that this is all just a game. There's an endpoint. Remember that. All you have to do is get to the finish line."

I breathe in deeply. That tingly electric feeling is back. He smells of the sea and saltwater. And home. Of our apartment at 1 Oak.

I need to get my head out of my bum. This is not the time to be daydreaming about a crush. What an idiot I am.

"How can you say this is a game? My friend was just murdered." I don't tell him that, for a brief moment, I actually contemplated joining Smith. The fear of Mom being hurt, but also, the temptation of guaranteed privilege, of guaranteed survival, almost trumped everything for me — including my morality.

Raphael releases me, turns me around so that I'm facing him, and then gently holds me by my upper arms. He gazes into my eyes. "I am telling you this because I fear for your sanity. Tomorrow you must remember what I just told you. It's a game, and you need to make your moves in a rational manner. Each move counts. In order to destroy the Darkness, you will need an angel's sword. That means that, no matter what, when the time is right, you must take the sword. The others will help fight both the demons and the Archons ... and any other obstacles that may stand in the way. But they can't do anything about the Darkness. If you keep your eye on what needs to be done — eliminating the

Darkness — then all will be well. You are the only one who can destroy the Darkness."

"What do you mean, Jade's gone?" I ask. "Where would she have gone to?" I'm standing in the middle of the apartment, the warmth of the fire at my back, staring at Lily and the others. We all clearly need more sleep, but don't have that luxury. At least we get to drink glass after glass of water, the whole store that Eva gathered. After all, we're not coming back here, and there's no telling whether there will be any consumable water once we hit Greenwich. And we need to leave. If Smith was telling the truth, then not only do her goons from Toronto know where we are — and, quite possibly, about our plans to head to South London — but also, the UK government will soon be sending some of their more corrupt officers our way.

"I hate to say it, Jasmine, but if you'd stayed here like you told us you were going to, Jade wouldn't have been able to leave undetected," Susie says.

I raise an eyebrow at her. "I was returning the ring to the wall, for your information," I say, trying to keep my voice as calm as possible. My face burns with annoyance.

"No one's blaming you," Lily insists. "It was a courageous thing to do ... and selfless. We recognize that you risked your personal safety so we wouldn't have to.

But Jade likely couldn't have left if you'd been here. It's just the truth."

"The *truth*?" I snort, dropping my pole to the floor. "There is no truth any longer. You know how Clarence told us to forget about the concept of being safe? Well, you can forget the concepts of truth and honesty, too. Because Eva's not here, either. Someone betrayed us to Smith."

"What do you mean, *Eva* betrayed you?" Kiki asks.

"No, not Eva. I don't know who. Someone who knew our plans. Smith was waiting for me when I started on my way back here. And Eva had followed me to the Roman wall. To keep me safe." I pause, not wanting to tell them how the situation ended. Not wanting to tell them that Eva is dead.

"Where is she now?" Sara asks, clenching her fists. "Coz if she's in danger, you shouldn't have left her."

"She's dead," I say, my voice barely a whisper. I look away from everyone's gaze and down at the floor as I take another gulp of water. Tears blur the wooden planks at my feet.

"But someone told Eva about this place. About a safe house, yeah?" Dani says. "We never asked her how she knew to come here out of all the flats in London. And we didn't ask if someone brought her here. Maybe that person is the one who betrayed you? Us? And Jade knew exactly where to find us as well. Kind of convenient how she's disappeared at this time, isn't it?"

I shrug. "Just like Clarence said, we can't believe that anywhere or anyone truly offers safety." *It doesn't matter, anyway*, I think. *Because Eva's dead, so we can't ask her.* "I don't even know how much we can believe in this safety zone — the pentagram or whatever — made up by those churches."

"Um, your bag is moving," Lily says, her eyes widening.

"Shit. Mithra." I open the bag and take her out. She looks up at me, her mouth opening in a silent meow. I scoop her up in my hands. "Can someone get me a bowl? I need to give her some water."

Dani strides over and strokes Mithra's head. "She's beautiful, Jasmine. But you're not seriously going to bring her with us, are you?"

"I can't leave her here," I say, taking the bowl that Lily's gotten from the kitchen and placing both it and Mithra on one of the carpets. I pour the remainder of my water into the bowl. Mithra gingerly touches the surface of the water with one paw and then licks the water off her fur before beginning to lap it up in earnest. "That's a death sentence. She was already being dragged around by a bunch of junkies out on a water hunt." Tears sting my eyes. "And there's been too much death. I'm not even sure if my mom and my Protector are alive. I know it makes no sense, but I've got to do this. I've got to keep this kitten safe."

"You bring her, you're responsible for 'er," Sara says flatly. "Any water she needs comes from you."

I want to punch her in the face. "I think you can see I'm already taking full responsibility for her," I say through gritted teeth.

"Okay, enough," Lily says. "We've got to go." She looks over at Kiki. "You said you've got the route on your watch?"

Kiki nods.

As we leave the apartment and head out into the smoky morning air, poles in hand, I can't keep one thought from running through my mind: with Eva and Jade both gone, there are now only six of us. According to what I've been told about the Final Battle, there are supposed to be seven Seers. Seven Seers. Seven Archangels. Seven Archons.

However, I'm not sure I can even believe that any longer …

JASMINE

The boat driver either works for the CCT or has been paid enough not to care about shepherding a group of unaccompanied teens, some of whom he likely recognizes from news alerts, down the Thames during a city-wide lockdown. I'm sure he must've been paid in advance and in cash. Cash currency is pretty rare these days. From what he's telling us about the entire banking system having been shut down by hackers, it's soon going to be beyond precious.

I glance out and across the Thames. We're heading out of the docks area and toward the river. A large building with the words *Butler's Wharf* on it stands like an imposing giant on the opposite bank. The sun is just rising; the words are barely visible in the early dawn light and through the yellow-grey veil of smoke. Shouting and the occasional loud bang, like that of a firecracker or a gunshot, can be heard in the distance. The city is filled with negative energy right now. Fear, anger, sadness … the dark forces must be loving this. And becoming so much stronger because of it.

"I'm keeping the motor down," he tells us, his voice low. He holds out his free hand to each of us in turn while his other hand holds up the corner of a large canvas tarp. We're going to be hiding under it for the duration of the ride. "The police are likely to have patrols out here on the river, though …" He trails off as he turns to look at the fires dotting the periphery of the river on both sides of us and deeper into the city. "They've got their hands full out there."

I'm the last one to get on the boat and duck under the tarp. We huddle together in silence as the boat slowly makes its way downriver. At one point I doze off, unable to keep my eyes open. The heat from our bodies and our breath makes the temperature under the tarp unbearably warm, and that, combined with the fact that I've had literally zero sleep, makes it impossible for me to stay awake, despite my fear of what could happen while I'm napping.

I've no idea how long we've been under the tarp when the boat bangs up against land. I hold my breath. Is this a planned landing? Clutching our poles tightly, we wait for a signal from the man. We don't dare say a word to each other until then.

After a few minutes, the man lifts up a corner of the tarp. Sunshine streams in at us.

"Deptford Wharf," he says, squinting at us. He's not nearly as young as I'd thought he was when we were getting into the boat in the hazy dawn. Or maybe he's just had a really hard life. Deep wrinkles are etched into the skin at the corners of his eyes and across his forehead, and his skin is an ashy grey colour.

"Thanks, mate," Sara says as we climb out.

"I was told to let you know you're needed at the observatory," he says, nodding at us. "As soon as possible."

"Who told you?" I ask. "We've had just about enough of being shuttled around and getting only half-truths."

He smiles at me and shoots me a wink. "Can't tell you that, now can I, Jasmine? But I suspect you already knew I couldn't — and wouldn't. What I can tell you is that you're all going to have to be careful with the looters and the desperate people out there. I feel bad for you lot. I'm heading out of London as fast as I can. At least I can hide out in the countryside. Planning to find me an abandoned stable somewhere with a well that might still be in use."

We climb out of the boat and onto shore, using the large rubber tires and chains that are fastened to the side of the wharf, and the boat continues down the river, toward the Thames Barrier.

"All right, we can do this by keeping close to the river and then heading up to the observatory once we're closer to the Old Naval College," Kiki says. "I think that would be best, as it keeps us from having to go deep into residential areas. And we can split up to be less conspicuous. I think that might be better."

"I don't know," I say. "There's strength in numbers. And we don't have the ring any longer, remember? That leaves us open to demonic attacks. Even if it is daytime."

Lily nods. "Jasmine's right. The collision of London and the Place-in-Between seems to have eroded all the rules."

We agree that sticking together is the best plan. As we move closer to the town centre, the blare of sirens fills the air. The smoke is thicker here. Shops are on fire along the road directly behind the Cutty Sark, and people are racing in and out of them, carrying all the bottles and food and goods they can manage. Police cars and vans drive toward the crowds, sirens and lights on full. A wall of shielded riot police marches toward the largest group. Some people leap out of the way, others pelt the officers with stones and other objects.

"Clear the high street and go home!" a loudspeaker blares. "You are breaking curfew and will be detained and charged by the authority of His Royal Highness, King George the Seventh."

This seems to incense the crowd even more.

"Jesus," Susie says. "It really does feel like the end of the world."

We pick up our pace to pass behind the Cutty Sark before moving through a small park, pausing behind a few trees as a series of loud explosions coming from the direction of the rioting shakes the air around us, causing a murder of crows on the grass in front of us to rise into the air in an angry symphony of caws.

"This is crazy. Why are we listening to some bloke that's just ferried us down to South London and into the middle of chaos?" Dani says, wiping away at beads of sweat that line her forehead. She turns to her sister.

"Can't you get ahold of Clarence and ask him what the bloody hell is going on?"

Kiki shakes her head. "I tried on the boat. His video watch is showing him as inactive." Her eyebrows draw together in a worried furrow. "It's not showing his beats per minute, either. That means he's either not wearing his watch, or ..." She trails off, her bottom lip shivering with emotion.

"We've got to get to the observatory either way," I say. "Someone or something wants us there. The only way we can find out anything is by going."

"The Trafalgar is near here," Dani says. "We could get into the flat upstairs and wait there. Vashti encoded my fingerprints on the pad. Wouldn't it be better if we hid until it's dark? Maybe someone there can help us find out what's happening with Clarence."

"Or we can stick close to the buildings in the Naval College, then cross Woolwich Road and enter Greenwich Park. Hopefully the park itself will be pretty empty. There's no reason for any protests to be happening there," Susie says.

I lean back against the tree and stare at the Thames. The water level seems incredibly high; it's almost level with the ground on either side of it, each wave threatening to spill over the river's edge and onto land.

"I'm not sure we should hide any longer," I say, "mainly because someone has been reporting our every move lately, and we don't know who that might be." A muffled explosion shatters the air from somewhere to the left of us, back in the vicinity of the Cutty

Sark. "But also, I think this is the time for us to find out exactly what's happening. And I have to find my sister and make sure she's okay."

"I agree that we should get to the observatory," Sara says. The warm morning air and bright sun has already caused streaks of red to bloom across her cheeks and nose. She looks uncomfortable.

Loud shouting and hoots of anger on the path nearby cut our conversation short. We all visibly tense up and hold our poles tight.

A group of about ten men and women are moving in our direction. They're carrying bottles of water and cans of cider. From the looks of things, the cider is already being consumed pretty quickly.

"Hello, girls!" one of the men says, raising an eyebrow flirtatiously at us. He's got bulldog jowls and a paunchy stomach. God, even with the world possibly ending, men are still not respecting boundaries. I wrinkle my nose at him. We are young enough to be his daughters.

"Leave them alone, Ritchie," another man says as he tips a cider can to his lips. He wipes his mouth with the back of his hand. "We need to get back to the house and hunker down until this insanity is over."

There's a low moan from just behind the little crowd of cider drinkers. Blood drains from my face.

I jump to my feet, along with Sara, Susie, and Lily. Dani and Kiki slowly stand.

Another moan is heard, but this time from the direction of the Thames. And this moan is bubbly, wet, and even more guttural.

No way.

The first zombie makes its presence known pretty fast. There's an ear-shattering screech from one of the women at the back of the group; the zombie is tearing out the side of the neck of the man she's standing beside.

A geyser of bright crimson blood sprays out, covering the woman's shirt and turning it into a monochromatic Pollock painting.

"Oh, my god. Oh, my god," she chants. It's clear she's going into shock. She's grabbing at the sides of her head, her eyes wide, and rocking her body forward and back.

Sara leaps forward and swings her pole into the base of the zombie's skull. Though it's too late for the man: his head is already flopping around like a rag doll's, and the vacant, glazed look in his eyes confirms he's passed. Hopefully his death was swift.

The zombie lets out a deep moan as Sara's pole becomes embedded in its skull. It loosens its hold on the dead man as Sara tries to wrench her pole out. It seems to be enmeshed in a tangle of ligaments and tendons.

"Holy shit," Lily says. Her eyes widen as she lifts her pole across her chest, taking a defensive stance.

I follow her gaze. There's a second zombie. And this one is hoisting itself out of the Thames. I blink hard, unable to believe what I'm seeing for a moment.

The Thames zombie is bloated and chalk grey. Its long, tangled brown hair is highlighted with swaths of blue-green algae. One eyeball bulges precariously out of its water-logged socket. It pulls itself to standing and begins lumbering toward the screaming woman, water dripping from its sodden, half-naked body. Each foot-step it takes makes a squelching sound.

I don't even want to think about how the original in-habitant of that body ended up in the river. She's now a vessel for a lost soul. Maybe she is a lost soul now. After all, unless she slipped and fell in by accident, she was likely feeling some pretty negative vibes at the time of her death. Or didn't even realize she died.

But now the creature is just hungry. These zombies seem to think that eating living flesh will stop their own degeneration. I'm not sure that theory makes a lot of sense, but I'm also not going to let this fishy monster stick around long enough to find out.

"Watch out!" I yell to the shocked woman, who is still staring at the body of the man lying at her feet. I'm not sure if he was more than a friend, but she's so out of it from her grief that she doesn't even notice the ap-proaching danger.

I spring forward at the same time as Lily. I'm going for the zombie, though, and Lily's read my mind. She throws herself at the woman, grabbing her around the waist and sending her flying to the ground like a profes-sional football player tackling an opponent.

Jumping over them, I bring my pole up in the air and cleanly slice the Thames zombie's skull in two.

"Holy shit," one of the men in the group says, his mouth hanging open in awe. "You're some kind of super-ninjas or something."

I straighten and brush my hair back off my face. "Get yourselves inside. Barricade your doors and windows, and don't come out until all of this is over," I say.

"What the bloody hell is going on?" the other woman in the group asks. "This is madness. How are we supposed to know when this hell is actually over?"

"That," I say, looking her straight in the eyes, "I honestly can't tell you."

JASMINE

The buildings of the Old Royal Naval Academy loom over us. They're impressive grey giants that've withstood at least five centuries. The last two have left them pitted and blackened, their outer walls eaten away at by acidic rains and pollution. The walkways along the buildings offer us some sanctuary with their intermittent stone pillars and dark recesses, though I feel more and more that hiding is not only useless, but also will put us at more risk. Every bone in my body urges me to get to the Royal Observatory as quickly as possible.

"There's the observatory," Dani says, crouching down and pointing up the large, sloping hill in front of us.

I follow her finger and see a large red-domed building at the top of the hill. It's not a short trek there, but the park looks completely empty, aside from a couple of hungry-looking stray dogs.

"And there's a path right behind that line of trees," Dani adds, pointing to the left. "We could stick to that and be a bit more concealed."

I pause, sitting back on my haunches. Unlike so many other times in my life, when I've acted on impulse, I want to think about this. If I truly am *elegido* or the Chosen One, as I've been told over and over, then whatever is up there is ultimately going to be coming after me. I'm the bait.

"All of you head toward the path," I say. "I'm going to go straight up the hill. If I'm attacked and things look manageable, join me. If we're crazy outnumbered, head back to St Alfege Church. To the protection of the pentagram."

"We'll never get through those police barricades," Kiki says, nodding her head toward them. "That's where all the action is happening — on the high street, right by the church."

"Besides, if there are demons or other dark forces waiting for us, what you're about to do would be suicide," Lily says. She stands up. "You're not going alone. I'm going up the hill with you."

The others murmur in agreement.

"Even though you're a massive pain in the arse," Sara says, a smile crossing her ruddy face, "you are one of us. And we Seers need to stick together."

Without another word, we pick up our poles and begin to walk toward the hill. We're still crossing the children's playground when the first demon jumps out at us from one of the trees, its clawed hands reaching for my hair and face. I barely have time to drop and roll out of the way when another one appears.

They're definitely targeting me …

Dani jumps in front of me to block the second demon and screams as it grabs her by the legs, causing her to lose both her balance and her pole. Kiki sprints forward, smashing her pole into the demon's back so that it momentarily releases her sister. A quick second strike decapitates the creature. Its head rolls like a bowling ball, striking Dani's feet as she leaps up.

Lily and Susie have taken on the first demon, neatly removing its head from its body with surgical precision. Lily wipes her pole on the grass to clean it off.

I survey the scene around me. About ten feet in front of us, standing in a horizontal line on the vivid green expanse, are at least a dozen demons. They stand straight and tall like some sort of netherworld army. Each holds a long metal pole with a sharpened end.

"And Jesus wept," Sara says, with a sharp intake of breath. "They've got spears. We're done."

Raphael's words come flooding back to me. *This is a game.*

I think I understand now. Or at least I hope I do. Otherwise, Sara will be right and we'll all be dead. I simply need to strategize each move. The demons are just the beginning. Like any game, there will be multiple challenges to overcome.

"We're okay," I say. "Remember, they feed off our fear. It makes them stronger."

"Maybe," Lily chimes in, "if our fear makes them stronger, our confidence may do the opposite. For every action, there is an equal and opposite reaction. Right, Jasmine?"

She's just read my mind and voiced my thought. I nod, giving her a knowing smile. "Absolutely. I mean, they're staring at two of their own who are headless thanks to us. We've got this."

We turn and fall into a horizontal line to face the demons. We're mirroring them, our poles held diagonally across our chests, our shoulders back and our chins high. There are four more of them than there are of us.

But that's okay.

Sara is the first one to move. She emits a guttural war cry that spurs both sides into action. I follow her lead, and soon every Seer is charging forward, screaming and shouting fiercely, ready to battle to the death. And, honestly, if someone were on the sidelines watching six teenaged girls run at a group of ten adult demons with spears, they wouldn't give us very good odds. Not at all.

Lily is sticking close to me even though I don't want anyone risking herself to protect me. I try to get a few feet away from her as we take on the demons, but she's having none of it. She's on me like a magnet.

"Give it up, Jasmine," she says with a rueful smile.

Two demons come charging straight at us, with a third leaping over Dani to circle back around and come up behind me.

"Blimey!" Dani exclaims, twisting in surprise as the demon jumps over her right shoulder and hits the ground running.

I watch her swing around, trying to catch the creature with her pole as my first blow against one of the demons is blocked by its spear. We're suddenly engaged in a fight that looks a lot like a combination of kendo and jousting. As I bring my pole up, the demon uses its spear to block me. Unlike the demons we've encountered previously, these ones appear to be strategizing. And these demons are faster and stronger than any that we've ever encountered — but so are we now. We've trained for more than a year and a half, and we are no longer novices when it comes to killing these types of creatures.

There's a loud yelp of pain from somewhere to my left. It's Kiki. I can't risk looking to see how badly she's been injured.

"Jasmine! Behind you!" shouts Dani.

I swing around and, thanks to the warning, am able to swing my body down and away from the spear that is about to smash the top of my head. Sweat trickles into my eyes and makes my sight blur. My eyes sting, but I don't have a spare moment to wipe the sweat away. Instead, I swing my pole at the first demon and connect with its upper arm, opening a deep split along its fleshy triceps area.

It turns to me with an angry roar of pain. My heart sinks. I was trying to hit its neck, not wound it so superficially.

I jump back as it jabs its metal spear toward my midsection. As I do so, a sharp, hot pain blossoms across my right ankle. I tumble onto the dried grass, throwing my hands downward to take the brunt of my weight as I land, rather than putting it on my right leg and ankle.

Within seconds, the demon is standing over me, a triumphant smile spreading across its face.

"Jasmine," it chortles, strands of greasy black hair falling like a curtain of spaghetti over one side of its face as it speaks. "Say goodbye ..."

The smile turns to a grimace and then a wide-mouthed shriek of surprise as flames lick the back of its head. It drops its spear onto the ground as an odious, sulphuric smell fills the air. In a matter of moments, the creature in front of me has become a demonic tiki torch. It slaps frantically at its head as the fire spreads.

I leap to my feet and swing. The burning head lands on the grass.

Cassandra comes over to stand beside me. "I'm feeling better, thanks," she says as she spins around, lifting up a hose with a metal gun-like thing on the end. She's got what looks like her oxygen tank strapped to her back. Aiming at one of the demons about to attack Lily, she presses the trigger. A long, angry burst of orange flame shoots out of the end of the gun and hits the target. The demon's face is engulfed in flames.

"Leave my sister alone, you bitch!" she cries, pumping her fist in the air as the demon's face begins to crumple in on itself like a barbequed jack-o'-lantern.

Lily blows Cassandra a kiss before taking a baseball stance and knocking off the demon's burning head in one swing.

There's no time to spare. Cassandra is off, moving from demon to demon, setting each of the remaining ones on fire, leaving them to be decapitated by the rest of us as the creatures howl and spin like whirling dervishes. Cassandra's flamethrower is impressive, spewing fire for more than twenty feet several times.

As the last demon falls, we stand, exhausted, and take in the scene. Sara is stomping on small patches of fire in the grass ignited by demons. The smell of burnt flesh hangs in the air.

Lily hugs and kisses Cassandra. "How did you get here? And how did you make that thing?" she asks, gesturing at the flamethrower.

"Those nurses taking care of me know a few things about stuff like this. After all, the CCT has been preparing for battle, too. All the nurses are a part of the CCT," Jasmine grins. "Pretty cool, huh? I didn't need my oxygen tank anymore after Raphael came by and healed me, so ..."

"You're the seventh," I interrupt with a wide smile. "You fulfilled the prophecy." I pause. "And you saved my life ... I'm glad to see you, my friend." And I mean it. There may have been a time when I felt Cassandra was my nemesis, but she's just proven to be my greatest ally.

"Where's Kiki?" Dani asks, frantically looking around. "Kiki!"

I'd forgotten about Kiki's cries during the conflict.

We scour the area, careful not to get too far away from each other. There's no sign of Kiki anywhere. Tears stream down Dani's cheeks.

"Bloody hell," Sara says. "What now?"

We all follow her gaze up the hill.

Several sword-carrying figures are descending the hill and coming toward us. Though they're still fairly far away, my heart freezes as soon as I recognize two of them: Mr. Jawad and that strange boy that Jade seemed to know. The patch over Mr. Jawad's eye confirms his identity. They're joined by five others: two men and three women.

Seven.

Something grabs my arm and I scream.

"Jazz, you can't freeze up like this." It's Raphael. "This is it. The Darkness will prey on your greatest weaknesses. It will try to break you." He turns to me. "No matter what happens, I'm not leaving you this time. I'll be with you. Always. You need to get past the Archons and nearer to the observatory."

I turn to look behind me and see that Gabriel, Uriel, Michael, and three others are here. The Archangels. They are all carrying swords, as is Raphael. And they're walking forward, their gazes firmly focused on the figures that are approaching.

There's a cry from beside me. A zombie has grabbed Susie's pole, pinned her to the ground, and pressed the pole against her neck so hard that Susie's face is slowly turning a deep purple. It's about to strangle her. I glance around. Zombies are emerging from behind us and from the line of trees to one side of us. There are so many. Too many. It's like an army of the undead.

It's a game, Jasmine. Strategize. I close my eyes and listen. The voices that Raphael told me to listen to are now audible. They are with me. And the most important voice of all: the energy of the Earth. She's wounded, but still alive. A warm light bathes me as she speaks: The Seers were created to keep balance for the Earth. A balance between the elements, and a balance between Darkness and Light. The Archons and the Archangels were part of that. But Darkness began to prevail and human greed, spurred on by the Archons' breaking ancient commandments, tipped the balance. The witch trials were the first attempt to rid the world of Seers and their powers. Then came the Industrial Revolution. And thus began a slow, agonizing death for the planet. And yet, we Seers can still balance things. We can bring the elements and the spirit of the Earth back into balance. The spirit of the Earth is Light; the Darkness is a primordial element that represents only death and destruction. It mustn't dominate. It mustn't win.

The pentagram. I snap back to the present. Without me and Kiki, there are only five Seers. But that's enough. Exactly enough. I run over to Lily.

"The pentagram," I say, breathlessly. "Use its protection. That's what Hawksmoor knew. All the elements of the Earth will be invoked. And the spirit. It will protect all of you from the zombies and from any of the dark forces. Get everyone together to create it now."

"Fine. But you get to the observatory!" Lily shouts over her shoulder at me as she dashes toward Susie and the others. "You heard Raphael. Leave us and go!"

I take one last look at my friends and then start to run, trying desperately to hold the satchel close to my side so that Mithra won't be jolted around and hurt. The

Archangels charge ahead of me as the Archons pick up speed and race down the hill, their swords held high above their heads. I zigzag to the right and away from both groups. The clanging of metal sings from behind me as I reach the middle of the hill. The Final Battle. So this is the way it all goes down.

Though my lungs are burning, I can't slow down. If destroying the Darkness will save not only the world, but also my friends and Raphael and his family, then I need to do it as fast as possible. Every cell in my body is begging me to turn and see if Raphael is okay, if the pentagram is protecting everyone, especially when I hear grunts and shouts of pain from behind me. But I don't. And, as I reach the peak of the hill and run into the main courtyard of the Royal Observatory, the scene unfolding there grabs my attention fully.

Jade is standing there, straddling a silver line set in the cobblestones, and also holding Amara in a choke-hold. In her free hand, she's positioned a knife against the delicate skin under Amara's chin. To one side of her lies the crumpled body of a middle-aged man who looks like he might've been sleeping rough for a while. A pool of bright crimson blood spreads out from underneath him across the cobblestones. If he's still alive, he's not going to be for long.

"Jade," I say, taking a step toward her, being careful to keep my pole at my side.

"Jasmine. Don't."

My head snaps toward the voice. It's Mr. Khan lying against a tree just behind a silver art installation of some sort with a hand across his abdomen. A dark-red stain blossoms across his shirt.

"Mr. Khan," I cry out, taking a few steps toward him.

"Don't, Jasmine. You heard the man. You were always such a rash girl. Always the cause of so much hurt."

I freeze, my bladder loosening. Turning my head, I stare at Jade, my mouth falling open in shock.

Amara is visibly shaking, tears spilling silently down her cheeks. She's humming softly.

It's my mother's voice I'm hearing. But somehow it's coming from Jade.

"*Mami*?" I say. My legs are trembling uncontrollably. I need to sit down.

"When you ran into the house that day, you knew it was a demon that you left your sister with. And yet you still ran away. Jade's disappearance broke my heart. Made me get sick. All your fault. I wish you'd been the one abducted. You were always the difficult one." The voice is changing again, getting lower.

"What have you done with *Mami*?" I shout at Jade. "How is this possible?"

"Jasmine, your emotions," Mr. Khan says. "You're making all the dark forces here stronger. And what is here with us now is already the ultimate force of Darkness."

I look over at him. His skin is ashy and dark circles ring his eyes. I can hear his breathing. Each time his chest rises and falls, a wheezing and crackling sound fills the air. He's dying.

"You were such a temperamental baby, Jasmine. All those late nights with you crying, staying up because of your colic and then having to work the next day. No wonder my body turned against me." It's my father's voice now. I watch as Jade's mouth twists and contorts like a circus freak's. Her lips are chapped. Flakes of dry skin hang off of them.

I take another step forward. "I'm sorry," I say. My pole falls from my hand and lands on the sidewalk. Whatever is happening to Jade, however these messages are reaching me, they're spot on. It's everything I've ever felt. All my insecurities. I can't do this.

I'm losing my mind again.

Someone grabs my arm and pulls me backward. Raphael holds me against his chest. "No, Jasmine," he says into my ear. "That's not Jade. And that's not your parents. It's a type of shape-shifting. The Darkness is manipulating you."

"The Darkness?" I say, staring at Jade. Her tongue darts out of her mouth and slowly licks the side of Amara's face. I want to scream, but jam my knuckles into my mouth to stop myself.

He turns me around. "The only way you can destroy it is to use an angel's sword and the power it holds."

I stare at the sword in his hand for a moment before reaching out.

Raphael snatches it away from my grasp. "No. You can't just touch it. Not yet. You won't be able to use the power inherent in it."

"Jasmine? You brought Eva to our school. To our circle. Back from the CCT stronghold. Look what that did to me. I was left hanging … swinging in the breeze just like so many of my people. Strange fruit," Ms. Samson's voice sings, ending with a cackle. Jade then takes the knife and begins to run the blade along one of Amara's cheeks, drawing beads of bright blood to the surface of her skin. Amara stops humming and begins to whimper.

I look back at Raphael.

"How can I get your sword's power?" I ask. "And then what do I do to make this stop?"

Raphael gazes at me, his eyes solemn. "You drive it through my heart to unite my power and yours. And then you strike the Darkness with it. Just the strike of an Archangel's sword will destroy it. But you are the one who must be wielding it. You are the Chosen."

"No," I say. "No way. I'd rather it be me, not you and Jade. How can you even think I'd do that?"

"Once you do, all of this will be over. The world will be saved and the kingdom of Shambhala will emerge. Balance will be restored and the Earth will regenerate. There is no choice. Otherwise, all is lost. This area of the universe will be only Darkness. Antimatter. Jasmine, you need to trust me."

I look up into his deep-brown eyes and can see centuries of human experience reflected back at me. The sadness, the joy, the loss. Layers of emotion and lives so richly lived.

Reaching out, I take the sword. It feels cold to the touch and heavy at first, but then it begins to vibrate and heat up, like the ring always did.

"I trust you. I love you," I say, as I lift it to the height of my shoulders.

"You don't love him," the Jade-like thing hisses from behind me. "You're just a little murdering bitch. Just like you killed me by leaving me with Smith and her goons, you're going to kill Raphael." Eva's voice. I close my eyes.

"I love you, too," Raphael whispers as I use all my strength to plunge the sword into his chest. A surge of energy rushes through my body as though I've just been shocked with some sort of crazy-strong electrical current. When I open my eyes, Raphael is gone. Tiny gold flecks are scattered on the ground in front of me.

I turn to face the Darkness. I'm no longer afraid. In my heart, I hold the secrets to a new world, a world where humanity works for the betterment of each other, of the Earth, and of all its creatures.

"Jasmine," it says, mimicking Jade. "What are you doing? We're sisters — twins. We share a soul. Killing me is like committing suicide."

"You're not my sister," I say through gritted teeth, stepping forward.

"Always so jealous," an unfamiliar voice says. This voice sends shivers through my marrow. It is guttural, rough, and full of ancient hate. "So petty, aren't we? Think of all the hours you spent allowing the jealousy you felt toward Cassandra to fester. How could someone like you think you'd be chosen by the forces of Light? Jade was the actual Chosen One. That's why we took her away. Why we kept her alive in the Place-in-Between. Oh, how she fought when we first entered her. How she tried to tell all of you that something was wrong. How she tried to prevent us from telling Smith and the others where you were. She even wanted to return the ring at one point. But now she's so much more powerful than you. She's immortal as a part of us. She was chosen by both the Archons and the Darkness. And we are the beginning and the end. Jade is now intertwined within us. You cannot defeat us, little girl. And if you try, you will only destroy your sister. Nothing more."

"Really?" I ask, raising my chin up. "You are only Darkness. And everyone knows Darkness cannot exist without Light. In fact, Light always drives away the Darkness. And that means you need to go back to hell or wherever you've come from. We are the Seers — the Daughters of Light. We are the guardians of this planet and all her bounty. And she, the Earth, *will live!*" I raise the sword high above my head, and with a scream that comes from the very core of my being, I bring the sword down on its right shoulder. There's a cracking sound and a spray of blood as the thing collapses onto the cobblestones.

JASMINE

I rush over to Jade. It's strange, but I know just what to do. Laying my hands on her shoulders, I close my eyes, feeling the surge of energy again. The gold flakes dance in my mind's eye. Warmth travels from my fingers through Jade's flesh. *Raphael.*

Jade's eyes flutter open. "Jasmine?" she says, her voice hoarse. "Where am I?"

I put a finger to her lips. "Rest for a minute," I say. "I'll be right back."

Though his eyes are closed and his breathing is shallow, Mr. Khan is still alive. His faint heartbeat makes me want to cry.

I lay my hands on his abdomen. His blood wets my palms. And I close my eyes. This time there's the gold, but there's also the sound of Raphael's laughter, and the feel of his heartbeat intertwined with mine.

Jasmine, Raphael's voice says from deep within me. *You did it. Go look out at London.*

I step forward and look down over the hill; it's slowly turning from a dried and dusty compilation of grasses into a vibrant emerald-green carpet. Lily and the others are walking up the hill toward me. As I look out at the white, majestic buildings of the Naval College and then at London beyond, a crazy thing starts to happen. Tendrils of greenery, and vines, and the arms of trees are growing up and over and around the buildings. Within minutes, much of London is consumed by nature. The Thames shines brightly and the sky above it fills with birds and insects of every colour and shape imaginable.

There's a faint mewl from the satchel. I open it and take Mithra out, placing her on the cobblestones.

"You're safe now, little one," I say, bending down and kissing her on the top of her head. "We all are."

EPILOGUE
JADE

Kiki and I take our time at breakfast today. As I sip my dandelion tea and stare out over the Thames from the balcony of our little flat, I can't help but think about how lucky we all are. After all, just a year ago, both me and Kiki were nearly dead, and the world was on the brink of descending into chaos and destruction.

"What are you thinking?" Kiki asks, reaching out and taking my free hand in hers. The sun lights her face. I watch as it dances in her curls and warms her skin.

"Mainly about us, about everything, really," I say. "About Mom's visit next month." Everyone in the world now gets one airline ticket a year. They can stay as long as they want wherever they go, and recycled fuel and cleaner, noise-efficient planes mean less impact on the environment. I'm hoping she'll want to stay in London, but it's her first time here, so it depends. I know she's been teaching dance in Toronto and might not want to leave her students. Still, video calls every day aren't the same as being able to hug and kiss her good night.

Kiki smiles at me. "I can't wait to meet her," she says. "I hope she decides to stay. And I hope she likes me," she says, nervously biting on her lower lip.

"She'll love you," I say, leaning over and giving her a quick kiss. Her lips are warm and taste like honey from the tea. "How could she not?"

That's the thing. Now, families never have to be apart, if they don't wish to be. In this new world, there are no borders, no citizenship. People can move freely and, no matter what employment they take on to contribute, they receive housing and income. I'm still going to school, and I hope to teach environmental science someday. Not all of the Earth has healed and regenerated yet, so many areas of the planet remain uninhabited. I want to study the regenerative process and help determine when and how those areas should be repopulated.

I think back to Jasmine saving Kiki on the day of the Final Battle. She'd been badly injured by a demon and, according to Jasmine, was bleeding out fast. Jasmine's careful with her powers these days and rarely uses them, but she does work at a London hospital, helping whenever it is not yet a person's time to move on. When she's not working, Jasmine spends a lot of time alone, writing. I think she's writing down our story as a warning to future generations, should greed and the desire for power rear their heads again. So many people died from the water poisonings that the first few months involved teams of people just burying bodies. Clarence was one of those who didn't make it. I think his heart was so broken, he likely didn't mind passing on after making sure we were safely on our way to Greenwich.

"Hello, girls," Mr. Khan says, appearing in the open doorway to the balcony. "Hope you don't mind. The door was open, and I tried to buzz you on your video watches repeatedly. You have training in less than thirty near Canary Wharf." His voice is tinged with exasperation, but he smiles when he sees our little table with its teapot and biscuits.

"We'll get there at the right time. The Docklands is running well today," I say, lifting the teapot. "Want a cuppa?"

Mr. Khan smiles. "Sure," he says in mock defeat. "I get that there's not as much urgency to train these days, but we still need Seers to be ready. In case." He takes a seat on the empty chair beside Kiki.

I nod at him. He's right. Though everything is working well right now, it would be super careless if we forgot about the past. Humans are still human. And there are far fewer Seers in the world now than ever before.

"We'll make it there on time," I assure him. "In case."

ACKNOWLEDGEMENTS

A huge thank you to everyone at Dundurn Press for helping not only with *Darkness Rising*, but with the entire Daughters of Light series. As always, I want to extend immense gratitude to my agent, Amy Tompkins, of the Transatlantic Agency, as well as my editor, Allister Thompson, for their support and guidance. Thank you to my partner, Robert Stewart, for supporting me and walking this journey with me.

Book Credits

Project Editor: Jenny McWha
Developmental Editor: Allister Thompson
Copy Editor: Catharine Chen
Proofreader: Shari Rutherford

Cover Designer: Laura Boyle
Interior Designer: Lorena Gonzalez Guillen

Publicist: Elham Ali

dundurn.com   dundurnpress
@dundurnpress   dundurnpress
dundurnpress   info@dundurn.com

FIND US ON NETGALLEY & GOODREADS TOO!

DUNDURN